T0274603

Without a Shadow

Without a Shadow

H. J. REYNOLDS

CamCat
Books

CamCat Publishing, LLC
Fort Collins, Colorado 80524
camcatpublishing.com

Hardcover ISBN 9780744308341
Paperback ISBN 9780744308365
Large-Print Paperback ISBN 9780744308389
eBook ISBN 9780744308372
Audiobook ISBN 9780744308396

Library of Congress Control Number: 2023944566

Book and cover design by Maryann Appel

Interior artwork by ArtVector, il67, marrishuanna, Pan-Pavel, sargotkitte

5   3   1   2   4

To my parents, for the stories.

1

Two a Dozen

IT WAS JUST A GAME at the start. Adlai learned the rules from her father; they would go out into the blazing sun, when the day was at its hottest with shadows burning black holes in the sand, and he would say, "Pick one, Little Drizzle," and she would slip her hand out from his to search the crowd.

Even back then the marketplace had the best crowds, and not just of people, but of things. Star charts were piled to the high heavens; telescopes winked a thousand suns at every turn; gems dripped on stringed necklaces; long, luscious silks slipped like water through her hands . . .

And then there was the smell: aromatic herbs smoking in pots, and the stench rising out from the herds of exotic beasts that were either caged or flying in chains high above the tents, their claws swiping at careless passersby.

When she looked at the people in the market and the baubles all around her, Adlai felt like the luckiest girl in the world. All she had to do was turn to her father and say, "There, over there," and he would play the game.

The Shadow Game, he called it. You could only teach your shadow one trick. So, while she distracted the vendor, her father would come near—not quite by the stall of her choice, but nearby. It was always difficult for her not to look back—he'd tell her off if she did—but she loved seeing it happen.

His shadow would move; it would shimmer like a haze and become longer as it reached for something—all the while his body staying stock still—and when it passed over the item, his shadow would become faint. Fainter and fainter until his shadow would be gone altogether—along with what she'd wanted.

That was when they would leave the crowd to go back home and her father would present her with whatever small thing had caught her eye. Sometimes he'd give Adlai an extra surprise. A little trinket or silk scarf. Always he picked something golden—the color of her hair, he'd say.

THERE WERE NO curtains in the attic room, just a collection of bright, colorful scarves draped haphazardly across the single window that glared down above Adlai's bed. Cold sunlight filtered in through the rainbow of fabric. A few of the scarves were starting to fade; reds turned to browns, blues to deathly gray. She would have to change those out. There was nothing more depressing than waking up to rags fluttering their last.

Her roommate, Penna, was already up and dressed. Her dark figure was quietly making her bed, and Adlai turned away with a sigh. Getting up was never easy. Adlai wanted nothing more than to sink back into her dream. It had felt so real: Her father had been right there in front of her, his shadow snaking over a stall as he played the Shadow Game one more time. She pulled out the drawer of her bedside table and looked down at the heap of trinkets inside. Some were worthless. A dented tin matchbox, earrings with a cluster of fake pearls, an aged book on a royal family that had long since died out.

Others, though, she thought might fetch a decent price if she tried to sell them. Her fingers brushed over a bangle that had a large fiery topaz embedded in the gold. Everything in her drawer was golden. Her father had picked each one for her, seemingly not based on its value but based on something else she couldn't quite understand as she stared down at the odd collection.

They shone. The worthless trinkets gleamed as much as the truly expensive ones, and perhaps that's all they ever were: pretty, shiny things to distract a child who asked too many questions and who didn't know how to listen.

She was about to close the drawer when she saw the bee pendant. She remembered him giving her that one. It was of a golden little honey bee with the tip of the wings grabbing on to the thin chain on either side of it. Adlai hadn't worn the pendant for a while, but it winked at her as she sat up, and the memory that came with it was a sweet one. Bittersweet, as it was one of the last things he'd given her. On impulse she reached out and fastened it around her neck.

"Did I wake you?" Penna called over in a soft voice. Adlai shook her head. Now she was up, she wondered how it was possible she'd been deeply asleep only moments ago. A baby was crying on the floor directly below them, and if she strained her ears further, she could pick up a thousand other noises. Much like a dripping tap, once heard they were impossible to unhear.

Living in an orphanage with twenty other kids of varying ages wasn't the best environment for peaceful sleep. But Penna and Adlai were fortunate enough to be stuffed up in the attic, where the sounds were somewhat muffled and there were no little feet storming over their beds to demand breakfast. That was the benefit, Adlai supposed, of being too old for any family to want to adopt you: you got to be tidied away.

Penna took the tidying away a little too literally and kept her side of the room as undisturbed as possible. There were no personal items, despite having lived at the orphanage longer than Adlai. Her clothes were folded and hidden away in a chest of drawers, and on top of that single piece of furniture she kept only what was needed: a comb, a small mirror, some lotion, and a soap bar that smelled of lemon. If she left tomorrow, there wouldn't be a hair or thumbprint to say she had lived there. Adlai's side, on the other hand, would take a few trips up and down to sort through.

She headed over to a pile of clothes to dress. Unless she could bring herself to wake before the sun, which she wasn't likely to, she knew the washroom wouldn't be free again until nightfall.

She pulled on white pants in a shiny fabric and a wrap top the color of an atomic sun. It was bright and garish enough. Adlai had plans to play the Shadow Game herself today, and wearing something attention grabbing had always been her father's advice. It was the folk who covered themselves up in hoods and tried to melt in the background who garnered the suspicious looks in the desert market.

Sliding her sandals on, she let Penna climb down the ladder first. A mistake, as her friend was wearing a long green dress with fine stitching she was careful to protect as she climbed down the rungs. Adlai's stomach was growling by the time Penna finally dropped to the floor and the ladder shook, ready for her. She slunk down it, realizing at the same time that the crying she'd heard had finally stopped. A door opened, and Mother Henson, cradling a sleeping newborn, looked at them.

"Well, at last. While you two have been dozing, I've had the whole morning full of things to do. Couldn't count them to tell you," she said in that offhand way that told Adlai nothing had been done. Especially as she followed it up with, "I'm going to need some extra help today."

Adlai rolled her eyes at that, but Henson pretended not to notice. Every day she needed help with something or other, and it was always for jobs she was supposed to do.

"What do you need?" Penna asked. Adlai wanted to hit her for so easily offering.

Mother Henson smiled. It looked odd on her, more so as she must have been at the mirror moments before the baby started fussing and had makeup on only one eye. It looked like a dark, dusty bruise, while her other eye shrank in comparison.

"You're a good girl, Penna, dear. I'll just need the meals cooked and some of the rooms cleaned. Gilly has a potential match, so her area will need tidying up the most. And if you could make her presentable too—you know she's always running wild with the boys." The baby whimpered slightly and she rocked him closer to her chest. "Perhaps you can make some honey cakes? The family will love that."

Penna had work in the afternoon and all those tasks would take most of the morning without any help. She side-eyed Adlai, hopeful, but Adlai shook her head. She was done scrubbing floors and cooking for an army of ingrates. Mother Henson might have given her a roof over her head, but that was all she did these days.

"Leave it to us," Penna said brightly. Adlai sighed and wondered why Penna still bothered to stay on Mother Henson's good side. As soon as the baby started to whimper, Henson forgot they were even there.

Only the helpless, screaming babies could stir the mother in Mother Henson. Once a child started talking and walking, the mistress of the orphanage could easily forget the child still needed food and attention. Adlai, at least, had been old enough when she'd been forced through the doors to know not to look for love from such a woman, but some of the younger ones learned the lesson harder.

"You know you don't have to always help," Adlai said as they walked down to the kitchen. There were three other kids inside, picking at corn muffins that looked like the runts of a baker's litter.

"I don't mind." Penna's eyes swept over the open cupboards and she started putting things back in their places. Her busy hands stopped on a pile of mangoes. "What I do mind is good fruit going to waste. If I were to make a big fruity mash, do you think there'd be enough to satisfy the greediest little monkeys?"

Adlai sighed, knowing Penna wasn't really talking to her and that she'd be distracted making breakfasts for a good while. She took some fruit for herself and headed to their usual spot out on the balcony.

Outside the air was warm but not the sticky, sweating kind it would turn to later in the day. She jumped up to sit on the banister ledge and swung her legs over the dust path below. People were starting to head to their work or make those early-morning purchases, as much a part of a routine as getting dressed. The same sight as always.

She looked further ahead. The Arbil pyramid shone golden in the distance, creating a three-sided sun with the morning light glinting off its massive walls. They were ancient walls, older than the city gates, but the gold brick made it look brand new. Like the trinkets from her father, the pyramid was the city's treasure; a place of birth, healing, and death.

Adlai took a bite of her pear; it was overly sweet but cooler than a glass of water. She was on to the second one when Penna arrived. Her dress had wet stains on the front and one of the kids must have pulled at her headscarf, as her tight curls were showing underneath.

"You know it's Henson's job to cook the meals and prepare the kids for their appointments. She's *paid* to look after us," Adlai said.

There was a small crooked table and two creaking chairs on the balcony. Penna sat down on one and stared dreamily out to the same horizon Adlai overlooked. "Mother has her hands full with the little one. It used to be fun." She turned to Adlai. "Remember that game we'd play? Tell Me How...? We could play that again this morning."

Adlai laughed. Penna had round dark eyes that were hard to say no to and one of those genuine smiles that a child might make when presented with a treat. The problem in this was that the treat was a stupid game she'd invented to pretend they weren't cleaning up vomit or peeling their lives away in buckets of potatoes.

Penna had been her best friend these last seven years. Her only friend. But while Adlai wanted to flip the page to when they could get out of this place, she sometimes thought Penna wanted to freeze time and stick her feet into the foundations.

"I'm not staying here all morning," Adlai said, already regretting it.

THE BATHWATER HAD warmed to a level that, while it wasn't exactly hot, was at least pleasant to run her hand through. Adlai was sweating from hauling several buckets up and down the stairs and could do with sinking into a clean bath herself, but the water wasn't for her.

Not that Gilly was grateful for their effort. Adlai turned over the empty bucket and sat on it as she watched Penna fight with the girl to remove her muddy clothing.

"I washed yesterday!" Gilly argued. Adlai didn't believe her. Some of the kids might splash water on their faces and rub soap through their hair, but not many of the kids bothered filling a bath. Gilly looked, and smelled, as though she had been many days without even a cursory wash.

"Come on," Penna said gently, "you want to look your best for your appointment, don't you?"

Gilly snorted but let Pen pull off the last of her underclothes. Naked, the girl looked even more wild. Her dark hair ran long down her back in a tangled mess and she had an assortment of cuts and bruises, some healing, others fresh from a recent fight. They could hide most of them in nice clothing, but Adlai didn't like her chances.

There were more boys than girls at the orphanage. There always were because when people wanted a child, what they really meant was a son. Mother Henson turned girls away like they were rotten food she didn't want dumped in her kitchen, only occasionally adding one or two to her collection for the rare couple who actually wanted a daughter over a son.

Gilly, wild and unruly, was unlikely to be the girl the couple were coming for.

"We still have cooking to do," Adlai said, "so unless you want to help out with that, get in the tub and let's make this quick."

Gilly scowled at Adlai.

"Ignore her," Penna said. "She's in a mood. You can go back to playing later. But right now you have to be clean."

Gilly scowled again, and made sure the water splashed over Adlai as she climbed into the tub. At least she was in, though.

An assortment of bottles and soap bars lined a shelf by a small glazed window. Penna took a few items from there and handed Adlai nail files as she poured in oils that smelled of jasmine and smoke. Gilly wrinkled her nose but didn't complain. That came when Penna dipped the girl's head back and started work untangling her hair.

"Owww!"

"Why don't we play the game?" Penna said. "Tell me how . . ." She looked over at Adlai as she dug the comb through a particularly large knot ". . . you learned to swim."

"I don't need to swim today, do I?" the girl asked, confused.

"No," Penna answered, smiling. The knot loosened, and more water splashed over the edge of the tub and gathered by Adlai's feet.

Adlai reached for one of the girl's hands and began picking the dirt from her nails. "How I learned to swim?" she repeated, thinking for a moment. It had been a while since they played this game. "I never had to learn to swim. My mother was a mermaid, you know, so I was born with a fishtail. Before I could talk, I could swim." She looked down at Gilly's confused expression. "I know what you're thinking: 'Where's your fishtail now?' Well, fishtail scales are worth a lot of money, and when I was very young, three or four years old, I was kidnapped for them. They peeled off my scales like I was a vegetable for a summer stew."

Gilly yanked her hand away. She had the look of someone who'd long ago stopped listening to fairy tales, probably right around the day her parents didn't come home. Had Adlai once been this child? The girl's features seemed to be screwed up permanently in anger, her frown as deep as claws.

"Don't worry," Adlai said, grabbing Gilly's other, equally dirty, hand. "My father saved me. I wouldn't have legs at all if he hadn't brought me quickly to the desert market. Everything is sold there, you know. Including a magic potion to grow limbs. He had to use his blood for it and that's why I have his knobbly knees, and I have to shave every day or else I break out in man hair. Though"—she lowered her voice to a conspiratory whisper—"sometimes I still get the odd scale . . ."

A tooth of the comb became stuck in another big knot, but both Pen and Gilly ignored it. "What color were your scales?" Penna asked.

Adlai thought for a minute. Her eyes drifted over every color in the room—the blue tiled floor, the white tub, the cracked gray walls. She discarded them each in turn. "They were colorless. They picked up all the colors in the light, like glass does."

She could tell Penna liked this idea. Her pretty dark face was entranced, and even Gilly loosened her frown, staring wide-eyed from one to another. They were adults in her eyes, albeit adults talking nonsense about mermaids, but for a moment all three forgot what they were doing in the room. Playing the game could sometimes make Adlai forget this was an orphanage, or that Pen hadn't always been family to her. The thought tugged at something she wished it hadn't.

"Have you ever seen a mermaid?" Penna asked. She pulled the comb loose and smiled down at Gilly. "They look so beautiful in the picture books, don't they?"

Adlai finished cleaning the last nail and dropped Gilly's hand. She stood up and came away from the tub. "How many mermaids you expect to come across in the desert, Pen? It's not like orphans, where we're two a dozen."

Penna shook her head. "But there are other places. Oceans and mountains out there. Places with snow, even. Do you think they really exist?"

"Mermaids, or other places?"

"I don't know. Both, I guess."

Adlai didn't answer her. The truth was she wanted it all to be real. If she could leave Libra and travel the kingdom, she thought she might see things just as impossible as her shadow that could steal. She stared down at Gilly. "What do you think?"

"I think this game's stupid, and I don't see why all this fuss has to be made every time one of us has an appointment. I don't want to be adopted. I'm going to move into the attic when you two leave."

Adlai shook her head. "Then you're even more stupid than if you'd believed I was half mermaid. Don't you get it? You have a chance at a family today. Take it."

2

Nothing but Dreams

THE WAITING ROOM WAS THE only part of the orphanage that had a homey feel about it. There were two plump sofas with feathery cushions, a bookcase with little animal ornaments, and a feature wall of drawings that the younger kids added to periodically. Even the tiled floor was of a happy, bright orange.

This was where the adoption appointments took place. Adlai and Penna were busy setting the stage for Gilly's potential new family, while Mother Henson had taken the girl to her office to run through the script of what to say and do, as well as what *not* to say and do. That was important too. Adlai had messed up each and every one of her appointments through some perceived slip.

Once, she'd stolen the watch off a woman who'd made her open her mouth to check her teeth. Another time she'd spilled the coffee a man had demanded she serve. She had never been able to be the girl a couple wanted. She doubted Gilly would either.

"How is it you were never adopted, Pen?"

Penna had been a light in the darkness. A sister when she'd had no family left. Always so kind and patient, she had the sweetest temper Adlai had ever known. If anyone was going to be adopted, Penna was the model child.

"Oh, I was close once," she said with a fake kind of breeze to her voice. "Everything was going well and then they asked me if I liked to read . . ."

Adlai frowned. "But you do like to read."

"Because you taught me." She took a small, well-worn book off the shelf. The cover's title was written in a playful, childish script: *Fantastical Fables of Glories Gone—Heartfelt Heroes and Irredeemable Ignobles.*

"I was eight," she continued. "I could only understand the pictures and so I made up what I thought the stories were. Mother actually apologized for presenting such a simple-minded child to them." She put the book down. "After that she had me helping out with the cooking and I didn't get any more appointments."

"You mean she saw you'd do her work for her." Adlai dropped the cloth she'd been wiping the end table with. She was starting to wonder if the same thing hadn't happened with her. Weren't they always the ones doing Mother Henson's work for her? "Maybe we didn't screw up as bad as we thought, Pen. Maybe this whole show with Gilly is just to groom her into our replacement."

Penna shook her head. "You don't really think Mother would play with our futures like that?"

"I think *Mother* doesn't see us as having any futures."

Penna started to defend her, as she always did, but Adlai wasn't listening. She came over to the book and flipped through the pages. Some of the stories were as familiar as if she'd written them herself: smoke dragons living up in the clouds and causing droughts, firebloods who died and were reborn again, and of course the shadow wielders. Tales that people had once believed as fact were now written as myth. She'd read the tale of "Menko and the Shadow Wielder" a thousand times as a kid.

Menko was the hero, sworn to save a princess whose land had been ravaged by disease. The tale featured three gallant princes, each using knowledge from their lands to try to solve the crisis. The Capri prince grew better crops to feed the people, the Libran prince brought superior medicines to cure the people, and the Piscetian prince built an array of freshwater spots to cleanse the people.

But the crops died, the medicine failed, and the water grew dirty, and the princes died with the people. Only Menko could see what others had failed to, for the princess was a shadow wielder. To keep her youth and beauty, she'd been sending her shadow out across her land and stealing from her people. Not riches—she had plenty of those. Her shadow could steal the rosy complexion of a young maid or the strength of the strongest man.

To end her reign, Menko searched the sky for wisdom and came across a fallen star. In his hands it became a dagger with flame like a comet's tail trailing the blade. He plunged it into the princess's shadow and trapped it there, where it would never harm another soul.

There were other tales that showed shadow wielders at work. Some were just petty tricksters, but most played the part of villain. It used to make her laugh to read of these great powers they supposedly had. She knew the stories were made up for children and that, as fantastical as her shadow was, it certainly couldn't steal youth or beauty. The only thing it could harm was a person's pocket.

The door to the waiting room opened and Mother Henson came swooping in with an almost unrecognizable Gilly at her heels. The girl's wet hair was braided back and she wore a light, frilly dress with long sleeves that covered up the scrapes and bruises. Gilly plucked at the frills and shot both Penna and Adlai a look, daring either of them to laugh.

"You look lovely," Penna said, and no doubt meant it.

"How she looks will hardly matter if everything else is out of place," Mother Henson said, brushing her finger over the table Adlai hadn't finished wiping. "What have you two been doing all of this time? Where are the honey cakes? They should be by the sofa for the guests."

"Would you like us to pick fresh flowers too?" Adlai said. "Or hand sew a welcome flag?"

Mother Henson eyed Adlai with her usual coolness.

"Do try not to ruin the girl's chances today. We all want this to work out for Gilly."

"Do we?"

The coolness left Mother Henson's eyes. For a moment she looked at Adlai the way she did when a small child was being led through the doors for the first time.

"You think I turned people away from adopting you, don't you?" Henson said softly. "Simple girl. I wouldn't ruin your few chances in life. Yours might not be the saddest story to come my way, but I still felt for you when you arrived. A father walking out on his child is a sad thing."

"My father didn't walk out on me." Adlai gripped the book so tightly her nails punched through the leather.

Henson arched her brow. "Of course not. Mystery night intruders, wasn't it? Strange they didn't take you too."

It wasn't the first time Mother Henson had mocked Adlai's version of what happened the night her father went missing—the city guards hadn't believed her either. There had been no blood, no sign of a fight, no items stolen. And no body. Her father had simply vanished. Only Penna had listened to her, and probably she was just being nice. Like how she was now, coming over to Adlai and resting a hand on her arm to calm her.

"Don't you have anything else to do?" Adlai said, her voice steady. "I know how busy you are."

But Mother Henson didn't leave. She came closer. Close enough that Adlai could smell that sickly rose perfume sticking to the air like hot vapor.

She looked down at the book she was still holding.

"It always surprises me how many children come to my home with dreams fogging up their heads. They have nothing but dreams, even after life has already been so cruel to them." She turned to Gilly. "Let these two be a lesson to you, child. Almost full grown and living like rats in my attic. If you have any sense, you'll take this adoption seriously. There are so few chances for girls like you."

She looked down at Adlai and Penna, her gaze lingering on Adlai as her voice became soft as a whisper. "You think I ask too much, but I could turn you out to the street tomorrow, and then you'd see how generous I've really been. You have a bed here and food. Neither of which come for free."

Adlai didn't answer. She couldn't. Penna's hand gently pressed down, reminding her again to stay calm.

"You're very good to us, Mother," Penna said. "I'll have those cakes warm and ready."

Mother Henson nodded. "You're a good one," she said. "I know if I extended *your* stay here, you'd appreciate it."

She took a last appraising look around the room and then at Gilly, whispering something final to the girl before leaving.

After the door shut, the air seemed to thin out between them. A boy rushed past the window and tapped on the glass, making them all jump. He laughed and stuck his tongue out at Gilly.

"Eat sand, Billun," she yelled. She looked like she wanted to run after the boy but stared down at the frills of her dress again. "I hate wearing this thing. And I don't want to meet any strangers."

"You want to be a rat in the attic then?" Adlai said, still bothered by Mother Henson's words. The girl's eyes widened and she looked to Penna for comfort.

"If the family takes you, it'll be because they want you, Gilly," Penna said. She came toward the girl and brushed a wild strand of hair behind the girl's ear. "Prettying yourself up like this is just a nice way to meet them for the first time. You'll still be able to run outside and make friends and do all the things a child should, only you'll have a family to love you and take care of you. That's not so bad, is it?"

"What if I don't like them?"

"Then you can always come back here," Adlai said, again with force but this time the girl relaxed.

She really did look pretty. Adlai unclasped the necklace she'd put on this morning.

"Take this," she said, putting the bee pendant around the girl's small neck. "For luck."

Gilly stared down at it and grabbed at the wings. "Is it real gold?"

"It's real luck," Adlai said. "Bees are like faeries; they fly around making flowers grow, and their sting keeps away anyone with bad intentions."

Gilly fingered it uncertainly, then tucked it under her dress collar, out of sight, as all good magic should be. Her eyes jumped back to the window and she tugged at her sleeve again.

"Best not to risk your pretty dress running about outside," Penna said, seeing what the girl was thinking. "Why don't you check over your room? Make sure you have everything tidy and ready to go."

The girl nodded. Amazingly, when she left through the door they didn't see her immediately pass by the window outside. Perhaps she would be good and stay indoors. Or perhaps she'd head out through the kitchen.

"Gilly won't be as foolish as us," Penna said in the silence afterward. "She's not the type to mind what anyone says, and she doesn't talk nonsense. She doesn't even believe in mermaids."

"Sensible girl."

"Yes, there's no good reason why a family won't want her."

Adlai wasn't as confident for the girl, but she stayed silent on that point and went back to wiping the table.

"Pen?" she said after a moment.

"Hmm?" Penna was taking down the books from the highest shelf, as though anyone would check for dust that high.

"You don't still believe in dragons and . . . and shadow wielders, do you?"

Her friend laughed. "No more than I believe you ever had a fish-tail." She brought the feather duster down. "But . . ."

Adlai looked up. "What?"

"Well, it's just that if I ever have a child, and they want to believe in those pretty tales, I wouldn't tell them otherwise, or call them simple." She smiled. "In fact I'd have their Aunt Adlai play several games of Tell Me How and really get them dreaming."

Adlai let herself smile at the thought, but her chest was heavy, as it always was when she wanted to—but couldn't—tell Penna her secret.

You can only teach your shadow one trick, Little Drizzle. But that trick isn't worth your life. Others can't do what we can, so others can't know.

Well, her father was gone. Disappeared. Dead. She didn't know, and yet his voice stayed in her head. Sometimes she wanted to rebel against it.

Other times listening to him and keeping this secret just between them kept him near somehow.

Shadows and secrets.

Her shadow didn't have the kind of power that could save or destroy kingdoms, not like the stories. But it was enough, she hoped, to make the kind of money needed to leave this place.

It was a small dream, but it was a start.

By late afternoon the usual crowd was flocking around the city gates. Adlai slipped among them, letting herself be herded down the stone-slab road that curved out toward the desert.

The first place to visit was the Stalls of a Thousand Suns, where everything shone from the high heavens. From jewelry to saucepans, knives to chains, the desert sun sweated beads of light off every item.

Of course Adlai wasn't in the market to buy. She fingered the signet ring she'd stolen last week during the Rain Festival and hoped that enough time had passed that not too many questions would be asked over it.

"Ms. Adlai." Izel, one of the nicer stall owners, grinned at her. He was a big man with a Gem accent that clipped each end syllable as though he hadn't the time to finish the word.

"I have jewels as bright as lemons just waiting to adorn your lovely hair." He held up a long hairpin with decidedly ordinary yellow beads. "The very latest in fashion."

His stall had an array of mannequin heads dressed in badly combed wigs and displaying similar cheap hair accessories, necklaces, and earrings. A single arm hung off the table, sagging from the weight of many bracelets.

"You know fashion best," she said with a smile, but she didn't stop. She'd rather put real lemons on her head than his tack.

The stall she stopped at seemed to merely sell a haphazard collection of knickknacks: used candlesticks with wax stains, and cutlery that made their clay counterparts look sharp. But Vima made his real money off the black market, peddling items Adlai stole for him.

"If it's a haggle you're after, this time it had better be worth it," he said.

Vima was dark-skinned and had his bald head wrapped in an even blacker scarf with the ends slung over his shoulders like two coiled snakes. He had thick lips, a strong jaw, and watchful eyes. If he wasn't always moaning about their deals while he cheated her, Adlai might have thought he was attractive.

"You're telling me you didn't sell the headdress? It had phoenix feathers."

He shrugged. "The plumage was very faded, I had to add a discount or I would have lost a good customer."

"A customer who doesn't pay enough is a bad customer," she said.

"And a thief who asks for too much is lucky to have buyers."

"Fine. Maybe I'll find my own buyer for a ring worn by one of the prince's personal guards, then?"

Vima leaned forward and regarded her coolly. "How did you get a knight's signet ring?"

"How could I not when they wandered in the market for last week's rain celebrations?" She pulled out the ring. The silver band had markings—words of obedience and loyalty—but it was the red cut gem that spoke the loudest.

"Hmm, you don't get more money for daring," he said, but from the flash in his eyes she thought she would get a good price on it.

⟡

She'd had to haggle for half an hour before she got a deal she was happy with. It was enough to rent a bed for a month or so but it wouldn't be enough to live on for much longer than that. Stealing like this was like feeding her future one spoon at a time when she really needed to feast.

But wanting to steal something monumental was like wishing on a star or praying to the gods: it didn't mean it would actually happen. Adlai walked through the crowds, assessing and discarding marks, hoping to find some worthwhile trinkets to steal. She wasn't expecting to see the flash of metal that winked at her from a nearby fruit stall. Not gold. It looked more like copper, only she knew it wasn't copper.

Suraci. It had to be. No other metal had that bronze, fiery sheen, and it couldn't be faked like everything else in the market. She'd never seen it with her own eyes before, but her father had told her about it. Specifically to stay away from it. Some silly superstition that the metal was cursed, but nothing had looked more beautiful to her. She could feel it weighing heavy in her palm.

She smiled, thanking the god Himlu for her luck.

It was time to play the game.

3

The Shadow Game

THE SHADOW GAME HAD RULES. Like, *Don't get too close to your mark*. They weren't stealing with their hands, after all. Her father could play from as far as twelve feet away, but he'd had more time in the game than she had. Adlai didn't need to be in touching distance, but she did need to be at the same stall. She maneuvered her way through the shoppers and stood over by the fruit.

The stall was small, clustered with wooden crates that were bursting in sweetness. Here, she had to be careful not to get in the way of real shoppers. There was a trick to it, she knew. Too far away and she'd have little chance of success, but being too close to the mark could be just as risky.

A family was getting a basket thrown together and she slipped to the other side of them. Finding a corner where something was happening that didn't involve herself was the best cover. Her mark was just a few paces from her. Up close she realized he was just a boy. She couldn't see his face; it was shadowed by his hood. But he was around her height. A similar age, perhaps. How had he come in possession of suraci metal? A prize so rare it had its own myths? She watched him with extra interest as he tossed some coins to the vendor and took an apple.

Ultimately it didn't matter how he'd come across the item; it would be hers soon enough.

She eased her shadow out, letting it become darker and longer. As she stretched it, nice and slow, she picked up a fruit and questioned the owner on price.

"Two turns," the vendor answered, distracted as the family settled on the last item they wanted. She shook her head, putting it down.

Meanwhile, her silhouette followed the stranger and climbed the crates. The longer Adlai had it out, the more she could feel her body complain and start to heat up. It was best to do this fast; she'd fainted before from taking too long.

Yet something was bothering her. She sensed movement behind her and held her shadow in place.

Turning, she saw someone hovering near her coin purse. He smelled like cheap booze and had muscles fit for hard labor. From the way he edged forward, Adlai could tell he was just the sort of thief her father had hated the most: the clumsy kind who brushed up right by their victims, breathing down their necks to steal. What they did was different, an art, he'd always say.

She looked past the pickpocket and moved subtly away, still keeping her shadow frozen.

The mark was leaning against the side of the stall, eating his apple and sticking around like a pretty dangling fruit she just needed to grab. Adlai closed her eyes and focused before letting her shadow rush in. It passed over him for the briefest of moments, and she felt the prize drop in one clean shot.

She could breathe again.

Her shadow crawled back to her and she knew it was time to leave.

Luckily, she already had the perfect escape route.

The small-time thief was persistent, she had to give him that. He'd followed Adlai all over the stall and was this moment fiddling with the clasp of her coin purse. She waited, pretending to take notice of the cheaper fruit below as his sweaty fingers continued to struggle with the clasp. When at last it clicked open for him, she chose that moment to turn around, and caught him dead in the eye.

Thank you, she wanted to say, but instead she opened her mouth and screamed, "THIEF!"

Adlai knocked into a crate of oranges as she made herself stumble back. Onlookers saw her open purse and the boy with the outreached hand. The idiot didn't even run, but she did. Adlai rushed into the crowd, weaving her way quickly through and letting them eat her up.

I'm safe. No, I'm rich, she thought as she ran. To the right buyer she could sell this for tens of thousands of turns. She and Penna could walk out of the orphanage today—tonight—and stay out. It was a whole year's rent. Maybe more. Adlai could even set her sights beyond Libra. With this kind of money, Penna could get settled and Adlai could get unsettled—she could lift off the anchor and see more of this world than a dusty desert.

She stopped at the center fountain and splashed some of the good fortune on her face. The water was warm, but as it ran down her neck it turned to ice.

Something was wrong, she realized. All the heat from running slipped away and now she was cold. Freezing. She gripped the stone edge of the fountain to stop from shaking. Her heart pounded in her chest, the sense of danger prickling her skin as time seemed to slow around her. It was a new sensation. Something she'd never felt before. A feeling of being watched.

Of being hunted.

She turned to look around and . . .

. . . her mark was coming toward her. He'd tracked her through the crowd, perhaps chasing after her the moment she'd run. But why would he have followed her? How could he have known she'd stolen from him?

She swallowed and backed a few steps away, but he wasn't interested in closing the short distance between them. Instead he bent down and laid his palm out on the sand.

Impossibly, her shadow stretched out again and moved toward him as though being pulled. But she'd hidden it away, and it wasn't possible for someone else to control it. So how could it be reacting to this boy?

The whole world turned cold as her shadow reached him. He was shouting distance away, and yet he felt as close as a whisper. Her shadow was at his feet. She couldn't pull it back. His hand disappeared through it and it was like a punch to the stomach. She fell down. Something twisted inside her, as though he were reaching into her insides and turning them. She was going to be sick. Somehow he knew what she'd stolen from her, and he wanted it back.

She was on her knees fighting back the vomit. She didn't see him stand up, she didn't see him move at all, but when she looked up again he was standing right above her.

"Please . . ." she begged.

The stranger looked down at her. "That's funny. You actually do sound scared." His voice was cold, detached, as though seeing something unexpected crawling under his foot.

She tried pleading again, but her voice caught in her throat when she saw what he was holding. It was the thing she'd stolen.

Up this close the metal was even stranger. It formed a simple pocket watch, the chain wrapped over the stranger's fingers and swayed slightly in the desert wind. Ordinary, if not for the

WITHOUT A SHADOW

impossible light engulfing it. The dazzling sheen of orange and red and gold made the watch seem to be alight with fire. It roared from his palm, and the sight stunned her, transfixed her, frightened her.

Then the stranger opened the watch and the sickening sensation grew worse. She cried out, not knowing why, until she saw what he was doing.

In his other hand he held her shadow. He was pulling and twisting it up from the ground. Her shadow was like smoke in his hands, breaking apart and reforming. Spitting and vanishing. It was solid and vapor-like at the same time. The pain ripped straight from her heart, and her chest screamed from the weight of the pull.

She tried to find the face of this stranger, this boy, who was going to make her heart explode, but his face blurred inside the shadow of his hood, and it was too late; she was going to pass out . . .

Then the pressure was gone, the cold with it. The market shifted back, as sweaty and bright as before.

She felt relieved. She felt like herself again, and then she heard him whisper something close to her ear, and she saw another flash of metal. But it wasn't sucari or gold. Her heart jumped, and she thought how unfair, how wrong it was that this would be her end as she watched the plain, simple steel knife arc toward her.

❴ 25 ❵

4

The Black Desert

THE DESERT MARKET WAS SILENT. The throb of the crowd, the trickling fountain, the flapping of tent coverings—all of it had stopped and left nothing in its place. No screaming, no yells for help. Adlai's eyes were shut and she kept them closed, afraid of the silence.

Hot sand rubbed against her palms. She remembered clutching it as a sharp pain tore through her neck and her breathing became tighter, her world blurrier. She grimaced and tried to force the memory away. Instead, the memory grew louder. A chill ran down her back as a hooded face filled her mind, his heated breath against her cheek . . .

Enough. She opened her eyes. Blinked, and waited for the scene in front of her to adjust to reality, for everything to start making sense. She wasn't in the desert market. The tents, the people, everything had vanished. Even the sand she was lying in had transformed. Where there should have been sloping, golden dunes, there was instead shadow, like nightmarish giant beetles glittering under a hazy horizon further on. And there was something on that horizon. The silhouette of a city was in front of her. One that looked as if it had been plunged into night as everything was cast in thick, black shadow.

She looked up, expecting stars and moonlight. But it was day. Blue sky hung above her, the sun scorching as it bore down on this strange world of darkness.

Where in god's circle am I?

For a wild moment she considered she still had her eyes squeezed shut and all of this was deep in her mind. A dream seemed more likely. She was imagining the ink-black sand as it rolled over her feet, or remembering the feel of the sun heating her back.

As she got closer to the city, Adlai noticed movement from the gate. Someone was coming out of them. From this distance she couldn't tell if it was a man or a woman, only that they were heading her way with purpose. She wondered who her dream would conjure up. The figure was as black as the surroundings and Adlai shuddered, imagining a faceless blur headed toward her.

The hooded boy, perhaps. Her feet stopped in their tracks, and coldness crept over her.

But no—closer, Adlai could make out a woman's shape. She wasn't a mass of shadow either. The woman was wearing a dark gray dress with billowing sleeves, and around her neck were shining silvery necklaces that were strung together and winked with each step. Hypnotic and regal. The woman was beautiful with dark black skin and unnatural deep blue hair braided high on her head.

Adlai shaded her eyes and nodded to the gate. "What city is this?"

"The sun bothers you?" the woman asked.

Adlai kept her hand cupped and it masked her frown. The woman was being serious. "It's hot and I'm thirsty," she said, and because

H. J. Reynolds

she didn't want the woman to get the wrong idea, she added, "I have money. If you tell me where I am, I can sort myself out."

The woman smiled. The severity of her face with its sharp angles softened as she studied Adlai.

"I don't need any money," the woman said finally. "I'm Yaxine. I—" She stopped herself. Shook her head. "I really can't believe I'm meeting you here of all places."

Suddenly her hand was reaching out to Adlai's face. Adlai jerked away. Knowing the woman's name didn't make her any less of a stranger. There was an awkward pause. Howling wind rushed by them, snagging more black sand in the air, and Adlai got the eerie feeling that it was just her and this woman for miles and miles.

"Sorry." The woman Yaxine said and dropped her hand. "It's just so unexpected. You look so much like—" her voice caught again.

"Like who?" Her eyes narrowed. "Who exactly are you?"

"I was . . . I am married to your uncle."

Adlai let out a breath of relief. This woman had mistaken her for someone else. This was all a misunderstanding. She smiled at her. "I don't have an uncle."

Yaxine glanced up at the sky, an uneasy look crossing her face. "We shouldn't be talking out here," she said. "Please, come with me, Adlai."

Adlai took a step back. Her pulse flared.

"I didn't tell you my name."

Yaxine's gaze turned soft. "You didn't have to. I was there when Leena had you wrapped in your first blanket and your father turned to us and said you were a girl. You were Adlai." She smiled. "I remember that moment so clearly. And all the times after, but you were such a little thing that I suppose you really don't know me." She took a step toward Adlai. "I only want to help you."

"Help me?" Adlai didn't believe this woman and she didn't need help. "I'm fine. I just need to get back to . . ."

{ 28 }

She shook her head. She needed to wake up. That's what she really needed, because the only way this woman could know her name and her mother's name was if this was a dream. A nightmare. Adlai didn't know why, when she dreamed up family, she'd given herself an imaginary aunt, but she would wake up soon.

"You don't remember dying, do you?" Yaxine said. Her voice was gentle, but the words shook through Adlai.

"I didn't . . ."

"You did," Yaxine said. "But that doesn't mean you have to stay dead. The sun only bothers the ones who can go back."

Adlai couldn't speak. Yaxine began to walk away, not to the city gate, but out into the desert. She shouldn't have wanted to follow her—the woman was crazy, and this place of light and dark . . . Adlai was dreaming it all. She had to be. Yet Yaxine's words were like rope coiled around her, and as the woman walked away, her words tugged her to follow.

Dazed, she followed.

A black tent was camouflaged in front of a low sloping dune. Adlai slipped inside, relieved to be out of the sun's gaze. A bare mattress took up most of the space, with two cushioned seats at the foot of the bed and a table between them. It was the table Adlai's eyes fixed on. A jug of water was on the top and two cups were stacked next to it as well as a bowl of fruit. She ignored the fruit and helped herself to a cup as the woman sat down.

"What's the last thing you remember?" Yaxine asked. She'd taken a cushioned seat and sat with her legs crossed, watching Adlai with hungry fascination.

She isn't my aunt. None of this is real.

And yet she could feel the rough clay of the cup and taste the warm water in her mouth. She shook her head. "I was in the desert market," she said. "The one outside Libra. But I can't be dead. I can't have just . . . I'm not . . ."

Hers weren't the hands or tongue of a dead person. Not even a little bit. And dead people didn't sweat, or take in big, deep breaths to calm themselves down. Breathing was not a dead person's problem.

"It's all right," Yaxine said, leaning forward. "I told you I can help you, and I wasn't lying. Just tell me what you remember."

Adlai took in another deep breath and put the cup down. She told Yaxine about the boy. Her mark. And how horribly wrong everything had gone.

"Could he manipulate your shadow?"

Adlai was dumbfounded again. "How did you know?"

"Shadow powers are rare in the world of the living, but not here."

"But where is here?"

Yaxine looked down, her voice quietening. "This is the death shadow of Libra. Those with shadow powers come here when they die."

Her pulse flared. *Those with shadow powers* . . . "My father." She swallowed, and the words came out in a rush. "You said you knew my father, do you know if he's, if he . . . He has shadow powers, he should be here if—"

She nodded slowly. "He's here." Yaxine sighed, staring at Adlai as if she were a thing of wonder. "He talks of nothing but you. All he wants is for you to live and love and be his little kid. He won't believe that I've seen you. That you grew up so much."

Little Drizzle, she thought. That's what he used to call her. Her head swam. She'd said for years that he hadn't left her. Not by choice. She'd known he would never have left her. And yet she hadn't *really* known. There had always been that small part of her that doubted.

He died. All those years she'd been in a world where her father couldn't reach her, she'd been waiting for someone who was never coming back.

Her surroundings blurred. Every childish hope she'd had fled from her in a choking sob. Her father was dead.

But so was she. If her father really was just beyond the city gates, then surely he was right now waiting for her. The thought sparked something bright in her. She had found him. She had to go to him . . .

A hand brushed her arm. Yaxine's hand wasn't clammy like hers but the touch was warm.

"I know what you must be hoping for, but I can't take you into the city."

"Why not?"

"Because you can return to the living, your parents won't want you here with them, not when you can still live. You said it was a boy that manipulated your shadow? That's lucky. He must have been newly trained, or this path wouldn't still be open to you."

Adlai pulled her arm away. "I'm going to see my father."

Yaxine sighed. "I'm sorry, I really am, but he wouldn't thank me for taking you to him."

The flap in the tent shivered, and a strange, cold wind blew in.

"Then I won't ask you to." Adlai turned and ripped the tent's sheet back. Black desert and a shadowy city stretched before her. The gate was a good distance away, the kind of distance it would be mad to run while the sun was so high and there was no shade between her and her goal.

But Adlai was dead, wasn't she? Her fingers clenched on the fabric of the tent as she let the insanity of everything she'd heard pass through her. Fuel her.

She ran.

Yaxine yelled after her, but whatever she was saying didn't matter. The sun, the sand, the distance, *the being dead*—none of it mattered because her father was somewhere near, just behind those city walls that looked so much like home, as though the shadow of Libra had been reforged for the dead.

Sweating, she reached the city gates. Her hand flew out to steady herself against the walls, but she met with nothing and stumbled to the ground.

What had looked like a solid city wall from a distance wasn't so solid-looking up close. Libra's walls were made of stone, but these ones … She reached out again. Unlike the sand at her feet, the walls weren't physical. Her fingers passed through them as if they were made of smoke, and yet the blackness didn't chase away from her and it didn't disappear. It was strong. Cold.

She remembered her shadow rising from the ground like smoke and the hooded stranger holding it in his hand.

The memory shot fear through her, but also curiosity. She wasn't in danger now, and before that moment in the market she had never seen shadow rise from the ground and *be* something. Her shadow took things; it wasn't an object itself, and yet these walls, she was certain, were made of shadow.

There was nothing but shadow separating her from her father. She laughed, still breathless from running, and got up.

The wall looked thick, the shadow endless, and once she stepped through, she wasn't sure what would happen. Would she be able to find her father in this world? Was he waiting for her to take the final steps?

"Adlai."

It was Yaxine's voice. She'd followed her. Turning, Adlai saw the woman's jewelry was in disarray and her braided bun had come apart.

"If you go through there, it'll be too late. You'll never leave. I told you already: you can go back. This doesn't have to be your end." Yaxine met her eyes, an intensity behind the gaze. "You don't trust me, but please, let me save your life."

Adlai took a step back; her hand glided over the shadow behind her and the cold brush of it clung to her skin.

"I don't want to go back," she said. "I died. I'm dead. It's really not as bad as I thought it would be."

She turned away from Yaxine. She sensed movement in the shadow, a ripple that hummed against her skin, making it seem alive.

"You're not dead, Adlai. Not truly. You have no idea what it's like when death is made permanent." Yaxine's voice had a hard edge to it. "I know this feels like your body but it's not. Your body is somewhere out there. Maybe in the market, or maybe your body has been moved already. Wherever it is, you'll have to act fast when you return to it. The person who attacked you is a trained killer. You aren't safe, and the longer you stay here, the less time you have to run. And you do need to run."

But Adlai didn't want to run. She took a step forward, passing her hands through the shadow first, wondering how far the darkness went.

"Don't! Please. He'll know if you go through it."

Well, that was what she wanted—for her father to know she was here. Home. And yet she hesitated to take the full step into the dark.

The shadow drifted through her fingers and tugged at her to move forward. *Come*, it beckoned, like a whisper in the dark. But instead of urging her forward, it froze her in place. That wasn't her father's voice but someone—*something*—else. There was a growl underneath the word. Adlai swallowed, her body tense and unmoving.

"You're not alone up there," Yaxine said. "You have family."

Adlai snapped her head back, her foot sliding through the sands, away from the shadow. "I don't have any family left."

"Your uncle," Yaxine started to say, but Adlai cut her with a look.

"If it's true, why did my father never mention an uncle to me?"

Yaxine wrung her hands, and her finger trailed a wedding band.

"That was wrong of him. It should be him telling you this instead of me. Or your mother. She'd steal a thousand shadows for the chance."

Adlai looked away. She didn't want to admit it, but she might not have recognized her mother if it had been her at the gate instead. She had no memory of her, only stories from her father—and in none of those stories had he mentioned she'd had shadow powers like them.

Maybe she didn't. This woman was no doubt lying about knowing her, and lying about Adlai having an uncle.

It wasn't fair. Nothing Yaxine said made any sense, and Adlai was tired. She wanted her father to come find her. She imagined her mother, some faceless woman running in with him and holding her so tight she couldn't breathe, and it wouldn't matter because she would be home.

When she could speak again, she said thickly, "Does he know about me?"

Yaxine stiffened.

"I live in an orphanage," she went on. "Does your husband know that?"

"Things are complicated for people like us. Shadow powers . . . they complicate a lot of things."

It wasn't a good answer and Yaxine seemed to know it.

"You have to leave here. You understand that, don't you, Adlai? The longer you're here, the more likely your shadow will be taken and then you'll have no way back. Your parents want you alive. I understand life's been tough, but my husband's a good man, you can trust him to keep you safe."

"Like he kept you?" The words jumped out of her before she could think. Yaxine drew away, her eyes flashing as if there was a tirade of things she'd like to say.

But then she turned back. She breathed in. "He does the best he can. He runs a safe haven for people like us. Without it, we wouldn't have a hope of surviving. Please, child, go to him. You don't have to be alone anymore."

Adlai closed her eyes and hated that there were tears behind them. She forced them away. Worse was the image she had of her father, his back turned to her as he played the Shadow Game in the market. She could almost hear him telling her not to look. You were never supposed to draw attention to the game. Adlai had always thought it was because they were thieves, but now she realized that was stupid. Her shadow powers were wanted by other people, and they were prepared to kill for them.

They'll hunt you and kill you. Over and over.

It was that voice again. The growl from the shadow. Adlai looked wildly around. Yaxine did too—she'd heard it as well.

The sunlight dimmed. A huge shadow emerged from the sky, its shape distinct and frightening. A black beast with wings was flying overhead, blocking out the sun as it came toward them.

"He's here. He must have felt you at the gate," Yaxine said. Her words were jumbled and she pulled Adlai behind her. "You have to go. Now."

Her fingers pressed into Adlai's arms as the beast swooped down closer. The sun was back in her eyes and she could only make out a huge black shape sending a cold wind from the beat of its immense wings.

"How . . . how do I go back?" Her voice was pitched as a whisper. A fearful thing scrambling to get out of her throat.

"It's just like stealing," Yaxine said. "You have to steal your body back."

The beast landed ahead of them, and as it dropped down it whipped up the sand at their feet. It was like no creature Adlai had ever seen. Too giant to be of her world. Wind roared around it, swirling power.

It was death. Facing it, she realized that she didn't want to die.

"When you're back in the living, run to the desert," Yaxine said. "Follow the King's constellation. Your uncle will come for you there."

"I can't—"

"Go, Adlai!"

The beast was padding toward them, a moving shadow with a pull she couldn't escape.

Adlai didn't have her shadow, and she didn't know where her body was right now, but she knew she wanted to live.

She closed her eyes and prayed.

5

The Boy in the Cell

Reaching for her shadow wasn't as easy as Yaxine had made it seem. Focusing her mind, the black desert disappeared and in its place there was a new darkness that stretched on and on. A void with no end. And yet as she searched through it, she felt a thread leading her upward.

Her shadow called to her. It was a hungry blaze, urging her back to life, but instead of warmth it radiated coldness. The sense of truly being alone. She'd never felt lonely with her shadow before, but reconnecting with it now was like walking into an empty room, expecting someone to be there who wasn't.

Her father, who taught her the Shadow Game, really was gone. She was going back to a world where he wasn't in it. She was going back to being alone.

But Adlai had chosen to live, and Yaxine had promised her that she did have family out there. She took hold of the connection, ignoring the emptiness, and willed herself forward.

When she opened her eyes, everything was still black, but the blackness was something physical. She could make out a slight shift in it each time she breathed and realized it was fabric being sucked in and out from her face. She wriggled around, her body her own at last, and found an opening in the side of whatever the thing covering her was.

Pulling it off, she sat up, blinking quickly at finding herself in a dimly lit room and—stranger—laid out on a table. She looked down at the cloth she'd pulled off and saw what the thing actually was.

A body sack. She'd been laid out inside a black cloth sack reserved for wrapping the dead.

And suddenly it wasn't so strange, because that was what she'd been: a corpse. She reached up to her neck and found dried blood stuck to her skin. She swallowed. Her mouth had the taste of burnt copper, and her skin was taut where more blood had dried down her chin. She shivered at the thought that she'd probably choked on her own blood.

A part of her denied it. Even if it was her blood, perhaps she'd only passed out and whatever she'd experienced with Yaxine and the blackened desert had been a dream. No, a nightmare.

I didn't die . . .

Movement caught her eye. She froze, unsure whether to lie back down and cover herself again or find out where she was. The handle to the door turned before she could make up her mind, and a man walked in.

Stupid. The door hadn't even been locked; she should have tried to get out the moment she'd come to. Yaxine had warned her to run, and instead she'd wasted time staring wide-eyed around the room, wondering what was real and what wasn't.

The man coming toward her now seemed more nightmare than real, his face nothing but a skull. The air turned sharp, an overpowering perfume cutting through it that made her head spin.

He was wearing a death mask. The mask was laughable, a mix of dried paper and flaking white paint. And yet she couldn't look away from the pitiless skull where only the man's eyes were visible. Healers only wore those when handling the dying and the dead. She shivered. He was here for her.

"Dying gods . . ." His eyes widened from inside his mask, and in that moment Adlai knew the blood, the memory of being stabbed, waking up in that strange other world . . . all of it, it had happened. There was no room for doubt in the horror that was playing out in his whitened eyes: she was supposed to be dead; she was the corpse he was here to collect.

The nightmare backed away from her. His gloved hand reached for the door and he stumbled from the room. Panicked as he was, he didn't forget to lock it—she heard the click a moment later. She rushed to the handle anyway and shook it for all its worth. Yaxine had warned her she wouldn't be safe here, and even though she'd made it back from death once, Adlai was in no hurry to discover if she could make it a second time.

She gave up on forcing the lock and instead searched for a weapon. She couldn't be caught helpless again.

Adlai looked around the room in a blind panic, discarding a paperweight she found on a messy desk that was covered in harmless—and distinctly *not sharp*—objects. A coat hung by the door on a wooden coat-tree, and she considered using it to swing with, but what good would it really do against the swords the guards were sure to carry?

She was still searching when she slipped on the cloth she'd been wrapped in, only registering the fall when her back screamed out in pain. Tears welled in her eyes. She felt stupid again and stayed where she was, forcing herself to think. She wouldn't let herself cry. Crying was too much like giving up. She breathed in deeply, and when she looked around again, calmly and slowly, her gaze lit on one of the guard's own weapons. Incredibly, a broken *dja* spear was lying on the ground. It must have rolled under the desk and been forgotten about.

She went over to it. Adlai had never held one in her hands before. On duty, patrolling the streets, a *dja* was as much a part of a guard's uniform as their white cap. Holding even a broken one now, she realized it was heavier than it looked; she'd always assumed the spear would be hollow but there was weight to the slim body. She had very little idea of how to wield the weapon, but the bronze tip was polished and sharp enough that she assumed merely pointing it at a guard's chest would work.

She waited in the dark room for a guard, or anyone, to appear. She waited for so long that she contemplated breaking the glass in the door and crawling out. But before she could decide if this was a brilliant idea or a very stupid one, guards appeared down the corridor. Four of them. All with swords hanging from their hips and spears in their hands. Adlai took a quick step back and angled herself so she wasn't immediately visible through the glass.

They don't know I'm not helpless.

The guards entered the room and brought with them a draft that sent shivers through the torch flames along the walls. Thin lines of shadows from the guards and their spears stretched over the tiled floor.

If shadows could cut, Adlai was now facing a maze of knives, each one blocking her from the exit.

But Adlai was leaving this room. She was getting out of here; it didn't matter if there were four guards or a hundred. She'd come back from the dead, hadn't she? Her hand gripped her weapon tighter as a wave of invincibility pulsed through her.

She took a deep breath—it drew the attention of the guard closest to her and she lost the element of surprise. Panicking, she struck out at the guard, the bronze tip of her weapon aimed at his face.

He blocked her move with lightning speed. Pain ricocheted down her arm with such force that she fell back and nearly dropped the *dja*.

The next hit wasn't defensive. The guard slammed his fist—another weapon she hadn't counted on—into her face.

Adlai was stunned. Her cheek warmed and throbbed and she became suddenly aware that behind skin was bone—acutely, painfully hard bone. She didn't notice which of the guards took the *dja* from her, but when she next looked down, she was weaponless.

The fight was over. Adlai's untrained swing had been easily swept aside. She wanted to laugh at herself. Or hurl the paperweight if she could reach it in time. She was desperate enough to try. They'd sent four guards when one would probably have been enough, and it was this thought, rather than the pain in her arm and cheek, that burned through her.

But she didn't have to think for much longer. Two sets of hands pinned her down, their fingers digging into her arms with strength that could break bone. But more than the physicality of their grip, she saw in their faces the fear that caused them to be more brutal than necessary.

They didn't want to touch her.

The guard who had punched her stood over her, bringing up his *dja*. She flinched, expecting to see the bronze tip, but instead he held up the opposite, blunted end. In the next moment he brought it down fast, connecting perfectly with the side of her head.

WHEN SHE CAME to, she found herself in another dark, though much smaller, room. A lantern swung from the ceiling and cast a dim, fiery glow over three brick walls. The fourth wall was not really a wall so much as a collection of steel bars with a heavy lock trapping a door in the middle. She was in a prison cell. This was an improvement, she realized, and wanted to laugh. A prison cell, not a body sack.

Himlu's luck won't stop shining on me.

She assessed her wounds as much as she could without a mirror. For the most part, the blood covered her neck and collarbone, though some had made it onto her top, giving the garish green color muddy brown patches. Her pants had smudges she supposed from being dragged across the floor but otherwise her legs were unharmed, and although her arms hurt—her right more than her left—the marks didn't look like anything serious.

It was the lack of a wound that worried her. She remembered the knife from the market, the one that had killed her. Yet as she scrubbed herself clean at the water basin, she couldn't feel any wound there.

The sound of the water splashing in the bowl reminded her of a more pressing need. A clay pot was underneath the basin. She took the lid off and recoiled from the smell of overuse. But as she turned away she became aware of a figure lying in the cell opposite her. Adlai rushed to put the lid back on and her cheeks flushed. The longer she stayed down here, the more likely she'd have an audience when she was forced to use it.

"Hey, I know you." The voice spoke out from the cell, and a boy Adlai didn't recognize sat up in his bed. His voice wasn't rough like she expected from a hardened criminal and it wasn't slurred like a drunk's, but it was never a good idea to start talking to boys behind bars.

She slunk back further in her cell, hoping the less visible she was, the less interested he would be in talking to her.

Or at least that her silence would give him the hint to leave her be.

"I know you," he repeated, louder this time.

She wasn't in the mood.

She was a mess. Her chest was wet from washing her neck and she brushed her unruly wavy hair back, wishing she had something to tie it with.

"You're the reason I'm in here!" The boy was insistent. He sprang from the bed and gripped hard on the bars of his cell. Light flooded his face, and she saw that he was about the same age as she was, or perhaps a shade older. He had light brown skin and dark chestnut hair. Handsome, Adlai thought, with his darker still brown eyes and long face that had a shadow of a beard starting to grow.

Handsome and stupid. Now the face came with a memory, and she realized he was the thief from the market whose fumbling hands had tried to steal her coin purse.

"They arrested you?"

"Yeah," he answered, frowning. "That's what happens when you cry thief to a crowd."

"Well, but you were trying to steal from me," she said.

He pressed his face up against the bars. "Whereas you were just innocently shopping, eh? What happened to you? You look like death."

She shot him a dark look but didn't answer.

"All right, don't tell me your troubles. What do I care, anyway?" He leaned back. "But I'll bet you're here for the same reason as me: for what you were trying to steal."

"What?" Adlai stepped closer and narrowed her eyes. "What did you just say?"

Adlai looked into the other cells on either side of the boy's, but they were empty. She suspected her neighboring cells were as well—she listened out but heard nothing.

"Are we the only prisoners?" she asked.

"In the holding cells?" The boy shrugged. "This is just where the city guard keeps petty criminals until a judge is bothered to hear us out. A formality. We'll be taken to the city prison after, I've no doubt of that." He smiled. "Why, do you have friends waiting for you there?"

"Of course not," she said, then considered him. The smile. The cockiness. "You don't seem overly worried about the situation."

"Maybe I don't plan on being taken to the city prison."

Silence passed between them. The boy began pacing, and Adlai remembered the need to pee but couldn't bring herself to use the pot. She sat on the creaky mattress instead and tried to calm herself. Could she risk waiting here? Yaxine hadn't been very clear on who exactly was after her, or how they knew anything about her shadow, but she'd been clear on one thing: Adlai wouldn't be safe until she left Libra. Sitting in one of the city's holding cells was definitely the opposite of what she should be doing. But how to get out was a question she wasn't sure how to answer.

"Hey." She was distracted from her thoughts by the boy again. "I'm sorry I was being such a sandlicker. It's my fault I'm in this cell, I own it. And you . . . you look like you've had a far worse day."

She wanted to laugh. Or cry. She definitely couldn't speak.

Footsteps sounded from upstairs. Adlai and the boy froze and turned their attention to the stairs leading up to the door. Someone was coming.

"Look, you don't want to tell me anything, fine. I don't want to know whatever you've got going on," he said in a rush. "But when that guard comes down, distract him if you want to get out of here."

She snapped her head back at him. "What are you going to do?"

Before he could answer, the door opened and a guard came down the stairs holding a tray of food.

Adlai frowned. The guard was bringing her raisin bread and water. He had to bend down to push the tray through a rat-sized hole at the bottom.

Behind the guard, the boy was making signs at her and mouthing something.

"Wait!" she called out.

The guard paused. He wasn't the same one who'd knocked her out. This one was as skinny as a new-grown tree, his head bowed low as he muttered to Amansi, the goddess of life, to preserve him. He wouldn't look at her.

Either the guard was the religious type, or knowing a young dead girl was breathing again had awakened his faith. It was something to grab on to.

"Please," Adlai said. "I need to talk to someone. A priest? Do you know a temple priest I can talk to?"

The guard's stare was fixed on the stone floor, but his shoulders tensed and he turned partway toward her as if her helplessness drew him back. Her eyes flickered to the opposite cell, and of all the shocking things that had happened today, she found something else to wonder at.

The boy's shadow was climbing out of his cell and creeping toward the guard. Like an outstretched hand, his shadow passed over the keys attached to the guard's belt, and then the keys were gone. Adlai locked eyes with the boy. He winked at her, but despite his bravado it was obvious that it was taking all of his concentration to pull his shadow back.

Her heart raced. She felt dizzy, and it took effort to focus back on the guard.

For the first time the guard faced her directly, and his eyes weren't cold or fearful. There was pity in them. Somehow that was worse.

"I'll pray for you," he said, "But the gods aren't always merciful."

6

As Bad as It Looks

ADLAI WATCHED THE BOY PLUCK the keys from his shadow and unlock his cell door. Casual. Like it was a trick he'd done before. Yet Adlai had never known anyone else besides her father who could move shadow.

Who is this boy? And why had he been fumbling with his hands to steal in the market?

She doubted she would have the chance to find out. The boy darted from his cell and rushed toward the stairs. He hadn't even left her the keys.

The seconds were ticking away, but Adlai was numb to her options. All she really wanted at that moment was to be back at the orphanage. She hated that place, but she needed Pen. She would gladly spend the day peeling potatoes and making up childish stories. She'd stick her feet in the foundations if it meant having her friend with her right now.

"Something really bad happened to you, huh?"

Adlai snapped out of her thoughts. The boy was back, shaking his head as though already regretting what he was about to do.

"You can run, right?" he said. "You aren't injured?"

She wondered what he would do if she said that she was. Leave her here to rot? Weakness wasn't an option. She didn't know how long she'd been knocked unconscious, but she knew she was ready to run.

"I'll keep up," she said.

He turned the key in the lock and pulled back the cell door. She should have leaped through it, blindly following this stranger who had freed her, and yet . . .

"Your shadow . . .?" she said, hesitating.

He grinned at her. "What, you thought you were the only one?"

He knows about mine. She tensed. He must have seen her stealing with it in the market. Was that why he'd targeted her?

"Come on," he said, the smile gone and impatience replacing it. "You promised to keep up."

Unease filled her stomach that this stranger knew her secret. But she knew his too. For now, they each had to trust the other.

The door out was up a narrow set of wooden stairs that creaked like a secret alarm for wandering prisoners. Her heart thudded as they waited at the top, ears pinned to it, listening for what could be on the other side. After an excruciating long silence, the boy turned the handle. It was unlocked. He must have unlocked it in the moments before coming back to her cell.

Outside was a long corridor with a sliver of light beckoning them forward. Adlai and the boy stepped quietly across the stone floor, the need for caution countering the urge to run.

Adlai didn't know which way would lead them out. The patch of light grew stronger to one side and looked promising, but when they came to the end of the corridor, the boy veered in the other direction. She trusted his knowledge of the place. Unlike her, he'd probably been very much alive when he'd been brought into the building and conscious when he'd been placed in his cell. She hoped he'd paid attention.

"Wait," he said. They paused in a new, darker corridor and bent low behind a drinking fountain shaped like a lion's head. Here, there were three doors with the unmistakable sound of activity behind them.

"Which door?" she whispered.

He shook his head, about to say something when the door furthest from them opened and two guards came out. Adlai stilled, becoming statue-like next to the fountain. With any luck they wouldn't turn this way.

But Adlai and luck were not on good terms that day.

She went cold: the shorter guard was the same one who'd hit her so hard she'd seen black. She must have gasped or made some involuntary movement, because both guards turned to the fountain like predators hearing a twig snap.

There was a good running distance between them and the guards, but their hiding place was as fragile as glass; the slightest movement and they'd be seen.

The boy looked up at the window above them, then to her. She gave a slight head shake. It was too high. They wouldn't make it. But perhaps he hadn't seen her head shake. Before she could stop him, the boy climbed on top of their hiding place and yanked her up with him.

The guards were thirty paces from them. The shorter one's face broke out in fury at the sight of her.

"PRISONERS OUT OF CELLS!"

All three doors snapped opened and five more guards peeled out. Boots slammed the stone floor.

Adlai had nowhere to run, and fighting hadn't done her any good before.

She looked down and caught a glimpse of her own panicked reflection. The fountain's water supply was a wooden pail hooked behind the decorative stone. She grabbed it, nearly falling over from the weight.

The angry guard's curved blade whooshed through the air, his eyes locked on Adlai.

She lifted the pail, arms trembling, the water slow and heavy as it swayed back and forth. It was nothing to their blades. Nothing to their strength. She threw it anyway, savoring the shock and outrage as water splattered across the floor and sprayed their pristine uniforms.

Now she had a step. She leaned the pail against the wall and with quick understanding the boy bore his weight on it. He was slightly taller than she was and reached the window latch.

Click. A sweet breeze rushed down to them. Their eyes met. She expected him to pull himself through the window, but instead his hands were around her waist and she was lifted up, up, up.

The window was the size of a crouch and a drop of about ten feet. She didn't think about that though. Her hands dug into the frame and she rolled through the opening, landing heavily on the gravel below.

Dazed, she tried to push herself up. Tiny rocks stuck to the sweat on her skin, cutting into her painfully. And then she was forced back down. A huge weight—the boy—crashed into her. Limbs everywhere, rocks everywhere, and a few choice words before they were both finally on their feet.

And then they were running. Really running. Lungs burning, feet pounding the ground, and wind tearing down her throat. She heard orders being yelled out behind them. Her neck ripped in pain as she caught a glimpse of the guards' gray tunics and glinting steel barraging after them. The boy was fast but she was faster, and she soon stopped looking to see if he was keeping up. All that mattered was putting enough distance between herself and those curved swords. She wasn't about to die a second time today.

Only when she thought she might be sick if she kept running did she start to slow down and blink in her surroundings.

It had been late afternoon when she'd been killed in the market. Now, the coolness of evening settled in and the lethargic pace of the people around them signaled the day's end. Bars had their tables out where customers sleepily drank their beer, shops were closed, and children stuck close to their parents on their way home. In this dwindling down of the city, running seemed jarringly out of place. A few eyes peered her way. She slowed to a walk, wondering what street she was on, before a sweaty hand grabbed her and pulled her down an alleyway.

The boy had kept up with her. She hadn't exactly been trying to lose him, but the degree of sudden closeness between them sent Adlai panicking.

"What are you—"

"Shh!" He leaned in closer, his hands flat against the wall and acting as a barrier on either side of her. They were literally eye to eye and nose to nose—the tip of his nose brushed against hers. She jerked away. But as she looked past him, she saw what had caused him to yank her aside. A city guard was on the opposite side of the street, looking curiously where she'd just been. He could be one of the guards chasing them, or he could just be patrolling. It didn't matter either way, as Adlai remembered the blood spotting her top. She shrank back and let herself be covered from the guard's view.

"Maybe we don't want to be running out on the street right now," the boy said, casting a patronizing look down at her.

"All right," she snapped. "I haven't escaped from prison a whole lot."

He laughed and it blew wisps of her hair from her face. "Well, I'm glad not to be standing so close to a criminal mastermind then.

I'm Erikys, by the way," he said. His voice was steady, and it pulled her back from the growing panic she was feeling. "I'm not always a thief, and you're the only person outside of my family that's ever seen me use my shadow."

He seemed less of a stranger with a name, which was good considering his breath was brushing her cheek.

Adlai didn't know if the guard was coming over to investigate or not. She heard shouts in the distance but her eyes were fixed on Erikys. His were a deep brown, like his skin. His hair was lighter, chestnut in color, and it fell over his forehead in messy curls.

"Adlai," she said. Her voice sounded more breathy than usual. She cleared her throat. "I am usually a thief, and you're also the only person, except family, that's seen my shadow."

He smiled. It was all teeth, and she caught a playful glint in his eyes. "Isn't it nice we could be each other's firsts?"

She glared at him. His arrogance tore her attention away from his stupidly handsome features to just over his shoulder. The city guard was moving in another direction, and the streets were calm. Peaceful.

She took the opportunity to stomp on his foot and force some distance between them.

"Ow! What was that for?" he yelled.

"Breaking out of prison together doesn't mean you can act so familiar."

"All right. But we should get moving," he said. "Separately," he added, "if you find my jokes or saving your life a bit much."

The street's golden light was beginning to fade. It would still be hours until it was fully dark though. They would have to find somewhere to hide in the meantime. *They.*

She sighed, realizing that despite her misgivings she was counting Erikys into her plan. He'd helped her escape twice now. Once with the keys and then all but pushing her through the window.

"We stick together," she said. "For now."

WITH A BLOODSTAIN all over her top, Adlai desperately needed a change of clothes. And since she couldn't risk going back to the orphanage, there was only one other place she could think to go.

Penna worked at a dressmaker within walking distance from the orphanage. It was near a popular lake where children often played, women washed their clothes, and lovers came to meet.

Adlai looked past the silky darkening waters and gestured for Erikys to follow her around to the back entrance of the shop. A staircase led up to where Penna worked on the third floor.

They hurried up the steps and Adlai knocked on the glass window. Several heads turned her way, and her friend jumped up from her workstation, hurrying over to the door.

As Penna's gaze swept over the brown dried spots on Adlai's top, the mud tracks on her pants, and the boy standing behind her, a speechlessness seemed to take over her.

"It's not as bad as it looks," Adlai said. Though maybe it was. Maybe her situation was just as bad as the horror Penna seemed to be imagining as she waited for Adlai to explain. But the six women cutting up fabric at the nearby workstation made no attempts to hide their curiosity. She lowered her voice. "Is there a room we can talk in?"

Penna glanced behind and then nodded, understanding.

"I'll go on break," she said.

She led them through the busy room of twenty or so women doing half a dozen tasks. Some were draping fabric over wooden frames, others painstakingly sewing beads in elaborate designs, some more cutting up fabric or drawing out patterns, and a very few seemed to be doing nothing more than overseeing the work.

One of these overseers called out to Penna.

"We don't allow friends up here, Ms. Lo."

"We're customers," Adlai said with as much conviction as she could muster. "Paying ones." Though truly she didn't have a coin on her—the guards had taken everything except her clothes. But Erikys made a point of jangling his pocket. For a moment Adlai thought that he actually *did* have a bag of coins in there. Then she remembered the keys and smiled to herself.

The overseer narrowed her gaze on Erikys.

"Five minutes," she said to Pen.

Her friend still had a dazed look on her face as she led them into a mini kitchen.

"I'm sorry to come to your work like this, Pen, I really am, but I didn't know what else to do." Exhausted, Adlai sat at the first table she came to. Discarded pieces of fabric were littered like crumbs and she played with the frayed edges of a rag.

Penna took a breath and sat down next to her. "It's okay. Just tell me what happened."

Erikys left them to talk and wandered over to the cabinets, scoffing when he came across only crackers.

"That's Erikys. He's a petty thief," she said.

He turned around at the mention. "Untrue. I was arrested, thanks to you, but I didn't actually steal anything."

"Right." Adlai found herself smiling in spite of the situation. "He's a failed thief. We just escaped the city guards together. My arrest was a little different from his."

"You were arrested? For what, stealing?"

Adlai gave her friend a long look. "You've been working since you were twelve, Pen, and you still haven't saved enough money to leave. You haven't even paid off your training debts. If I'd done the same, we'd be out on the streets by the end of the year. But what I do, it's gotten me some savings. Enough for you."

Her friend shook her head. "What do you mean, enough for me? We're moving out together."

That had been their promise. If they didn't find a family by the time they were eighteen, they would be each other's family and find a place of their own. Even with the revelation of having an uncle somewhere out there, Adlai wanted nothing more than to carry on with her original plan and live with her friend.

Adlai swallowed. "I can't stay in the city anymore. I have to leave."

She pushed the fabric she'd been fiddling with aside and told Penna what she could. She kept most of the details to herself and told only parts of what had happened in the desert market. Erikys supplied an unlikely story of overpowering a guard and stealing the keys from him. Penna looked incredulous, but the truth would have been harder for her to believe.

"Can you get us some new clothes?" Adlai asked afterward.

Penna had taken pity on Erikys and was making him a sandwich over by the counter. It didn't take much to get food from Penna.

She paused in making the sandwich. "He's going with you?"

"I am?" Erikys turned to Adlai.

They both stared at her in surprise. But too much time had already passed. She wondered if the guards had visited the orphanage yet, and a sinking feeling hit her chest.

Mother Henson would sell her out in a heartbeat, and she'd start by telling them she was friends with Penna, which would lead them here, at any moment.

"Guards will be looking for both of us. The city isn't safe," she said. "Being here right now probably isn't safe. We have to go away until they stop looking for us." Adlai couldn't be certain, but she thought it doubtful that previous dead thieves had come back to life, only to then slip through their hands again.

"But where will you go?"

Adlai bit her lip. Even if she knew, she couldn't risk telling Penna. The less she knew, the better. "I don't know," she said instead.

It wasn't a great answer, and she could tell Penna wasn't satisfied. Not even a little bit. But instead of arguing, Penna handed Erikys his sandwich and sized him up. "We have some traveling clothes that might suit. I'll be back in a moment.'

Erikys nodded.

Penna left and an awkward silence followed until Erikys sat down.

"You really think we have to leave Libra?" he asked.

She sighed. "It wasn't a city guard that caught me." She lowered her voice despite there being no one around. "There are people out there who know about us. About shadows. You wouldn't stand a chance against them and I won't be caught by one of them again."

He studied her, perhaps trying to imagine how bad the threat was. The bloodstain spoke for her. When she'd gone through the events with Penna, she'd explained it away as spilled wine. But Erikys had seen her cleaning up in the cell. He knew what it was really; he just didn't know that it was her blood.

"But do you have any plan? Anyone you know outside the city?"

The answer was no . . . and yes. Adlai wasn't sure she could explain it well enough, or if she was making the wrong choice to leave, trusting in family she'd never met. How did she know her uncle even existed? Yaxine and everything she'd promised could have been the work of a dream.

And yet the black desert had to have been real. The power that had swept over it when the black beast arrived was as sharp in her mind as when the blade in the market had pierced her throat.

"My plan is to survive," she said.

Penna came back holding a bag full of clothing. For Adlai she had a fresh white top ("Don't spill wine on this one."), loose gray pants, and a long sand-colored jacket that came with a heavy hood she could fasten over half her face.

Erikys was given a sleeveless vest in olive green and tan baggy pants. His jacket was shorter in an off-white and came with a similar hood.

Penna also pulled out some underwear with a blush as she handed Erikys's his, but Adlai noticed the bag was still not empty.

Her friend had another outfit.

"Pen, no."

"If you're leaving, then I'm coming with you."

For a moment, Adlai looked at her friend and imagined taking her with them. The plan had been to move somewhere together. So what if that somewhere wasn't in the city?

But Penna wasn't like Adlai or Erikys. She could have a normal life. Her friend didn't dream of being chased by guards with swords, or corpses coming back from the dead; she dreamed of romance and growing old with a herd of grandchildren to dote on. This was Adlai's nightmare, and she couldn't drag Penna into it.

"No, Pen, you're staying here. And when you go back to the orphanage, you're going to remove the clothes pile under my bed and lift up the loose floorboard. There's money there and a few things I haven't sold yet."

Penna tried to interrupt, but Adlai continued: "There are trinkets in my bedside table too. Some worthless, but others will sell in the desert market. Go to Stalls of a Thousand Suns. Ask for Vima; he runs an antiques stall. He'll try to swindle you, so don't sell on the first offer."

She wasn't sure Penna had heard her. She repeated the name again and where to find him, but her friend had a strange look in her dark eyes, like she was far away.

Adlai grabbed her hand. "You'll be okay."

"Tell me how?" Penna looked her dead in the eye. "How is it you have to leave and I have to stay here? And no fantasies about mermaids. The truth, Adlai."

It seemed like days or weeks had passed since they had been making up fanciful tales for Gilly in the bathroom.

"You wouldn't believe me. Honestly, the story about the fishtails is more believable than anything else I've experienced today." She pulled Penna into a hug. She smelled of lemon and family, and Adlai didn't want to let go. "If I had time, I'd explain everything, I swear it," she whispered. "You have to trust me that you're better off here."

Out of the corner of her eye, Adlai could see Erikys shifting uncomfortably. Doubtless he believed her even less than Penna.

The overseer shouted Penna's name from the other room. Penna looked over her shoulder and then back at Adlai, her dark skin wrinkled with worry.

"The floorboard under my bed," Adlai repeated. "Take the money and sell the items. Will you at least do that?"

At last her friend nodded. She smiled, but it didn't quite reach her eyes. Penna still looked dazed, and Adlai hated that her leaving would mean abandoning her friend. They'd had enough of that; they were supposed to be able to count on each other.

"How will I know where to find you?" Pen's voice trembled, as if she knew the answer already.

"I'll come back," she promised. "When it's safe."

When no one was looking for the girl who'd come back from the dead.

7

The City Gate

LEAVING THE CITY MEANT THEY would need to get their hands on supplies. Adlai had stolen the signet rings of knights, pearl-rimmed astradials, books in dead languages, and coins enough to drown in. Some food and water shouldn't be a problem.

They were crouched in an alleyway opposite the back entrance to a popular bakery; Adlai listened for the approach of guards, but the only movement on this side of the street came from the haggard and hungry. She looked sideways at Erikys. He'd wanted to do things his way. The "normal" way. But as risky as it was to use their shadows, Adlai knew it would be quicker and they could take more than their hands could carry.

A baker's apprentice came out and discarded moldy loaves into a waste bin that the small, hunched crowd waited to dig through. It was as good a distraction as any. She edged forward. The back door stayed open. Adlai could smell the wet dough of tomorrow's bread being prepared and she arched her neck to look further in. *There.*

A store cupboard. She looked back at Erikys with meaning and he nodded. They could take some of the fruit preserved in jars of lemon water, and there were plain biscuits stocked in tins, honey in pots—there were even bottles of wine. The wine wouldn't be of much use, she thought, but they could fill the empty bottles with water.

She didn't check if Erikys had his shadow out already; she had to concentrate on her own. Panic rushed through her at the thought that it might not respond. It had brought her back from the dead, but before that it had failed her in the market. The memory of the hooded stranger's grip on her shadow and the cold feeling that came with it clouded her mind. For a moment all she could see was his hand on the ground, pulling her shadow toward him.

She forced her breathing to calm and closed her eyes. She wasn't in the desert market. Her shadow was her own. Adlai reached for it and was hit by a rush of cold. Her chest tightened like ice had glazed over it, and she gasped, eyes flashing open to see her shadow spill onto the ground around her until all there seemed to be was blackness.

Her shadow stretched out in wild directions. It climbed over the alley walls, pushing against them as if it needed more space, to be larger. And inside the darkness: claws. She felt them scratch through her shadow, searching for something or trying to get out. She didn't know. But she remembered the sensation. As a child she'd been afraid of her shadow because of this very feeling. As though a beast had control of her shadow. Her father had taught her how to control the fear, how to think of her shadow as no more than an extension of her arm. She ignored the fear, pushed past it, and forced her mind to move her shadow as she had a thousand times before. But her shadow hit back at her. It slammed her against the alley's brick wall.

"Adlai!"

Erikys was suddenly by her side. He was sweating as if his own shadow had been causing him trouble too.

Her shadow went quiet. Its burst of energy retreated the moment she'd been hurt. Instinctively she pulled it back, clenching her hands into fists to stop shaking.

"I need a minute," she said. "Just give me a minute, then I'll—"

"You'll do nothing," he said. He stood above her. "Gods alive, Adlai, we're trying to escape the notice of the guards and you're out here making your shadow large enough to steal the whole goddamn store." He shook his head, as if he couldn't believe what she'd been thinking. As if she'd been in control. "Keep that thing out of sight and stay put."

She watched him take a discarded crate from the floor and head toward the back entrance, his shadow nowhere to be seen. He'd do things the normal way. His way.

<hr/>

His way took longer and ended with him running back to the alley, shouts ringing out behind him.

"Let's go!" he called. The crate he was carrying looked full, but she couldn't see of what exactly as he ran past her and she was forced to follow. But whatever he'd managed to steal was more than she had.

They twisted through busy streets, cloaking themselves in crowds until they ducked behind a badly lit tavern, aptly called the Stolen Star. Or it would be apt if Erikys had stolen stars and not, as it turned out, moldy bread and biscuits. He'd had the sense to get them water bottles at least, she thought, as she caught her breath.

"Not bad, eh?" he said, dumping his spoils on the ground.

She bit back the honest answer. If she'd been able to use her shadow, she could have gotten so much more . . . but in the time that he'd been gone, Adlai had attempted to use her shadow again, and the moment the cold had crept through her bones, she'd tensed and pulled it back. She tried to convince herself that the feeling would go away. It was just the strangeness of the day. Her body might not show signs of having died, but her shadow, like her mind, probably needed time to process what had happened to her. If her shadow was acting this way now, it was just because she was letting the fear take over.

But she wouldn't let herself think of her failure right now. Getting out through the city gate was what she needed to focus on.

Drunken laughter sounded through the tavern's window. She crouched against the wall, but they were well hidden if anyone did choose to look outside. They were next to a wagon piled high with barrels. She got up and took a closer look. The barrels stank of booze but they were empty. Empty and fairly large.

She turned to Erikys. When she'd first seen him in the desert market, she'd thought he was drunk and had the look of a farmer. Now she thought he could pass for an apprentice of most trades. He was strong, and every business needed a pair of strong hands.

"Could you pull this wagon?" she asked him.

It had wooden planks that could be lifted and pulled or tied to a horse's saddle. Men that couldn't afford livestock were often seen pulling wagons like this in the market. It wouldn't look so strange.

Erikys had his back to her and didn't answer immediately. He was watching the street, and as she came closer to him she saw what was drawing his eye.

The dusty streets were darkening and mostly empty, but there was a spot of white in the distance. She went cold. A city guard was knocking on doors. If the guard was searching for them, Adlai felt sure he'd come to the tavern. Crowds were the best hiding places, and drunks had the loudest mouths; they couldn't really be sure no one had seen them run here.

She pulled at Erikys's arm and repeated her question.

"Are you suggesting we steal this?" he asked.

"I'm suggesting *you* steal it." She took a deep breath, already hating what her part of the plan would have to be. "I'll be riding in one of these." She tapped a barrel. "Try not to pick a bumpy path."

Erikys looked at her as if she were insane and then laughed. "Of course not, princess. Should I steal you a plush cushion so you can take a nap while I get us to safety?"

Adlai clenched her hands. He didn't get it. He hadn't died today; he didn't know how dangerous it would be for them to be caught again.

"What do you suggest?" she asked. "That we outrun another guard? Or maybe we pretend to be lovers having a drink inside the tavern?" She got closer to him. "The guards will find us if we stay here. They'll be searching for us all night. Either we split up and try disguising ourselves, or you pull this damn wagon to the gate and we get the hell out of this city."

Adlai hadn't realized she was shaking until she stopped talking. She hugged her arms over her chest and looked quickly away.

She expected Erikys to joke or argue some more that her plan wouldn't work, but when he spoke again, his voice was soft.

"I don't think we should split up," he said. "And I can pull that wagon."

She nodded, not trusting herself to speak again. There was a dirty canvas bag under one of the barrels that they could put the supplies in. It would make them easier to carry than in the bulky crate, and she could hide the bag with her in the barrel. She started filling it, her hair covering her face so that she didn't notice Erikys bending down to help her. His hand brushed hers and she froze.

Whether it was from being attacked in the market or from being attacked in the prison hold, Adlai was on edge, but Erikys wasn't her enemy.

To clear the awkwardness she felt, she turned back to him and smiled.

"Once we're past the gates, you can complain about my plan all you like."

The gate was close by, and the tavern was busy enough that it might be a while before the wagon was even noticed missing.

She lifted the lid of one of the barrels toward the back and climbed inside. Erikys looked entirely unconvinced at the meager space it gave her to move and the single hole on the side as he placed the lid over her head. Then he was at the front of the wagon and she was lurched forward, the barrels shaking around her as he pulled it off and away into the fast-approaching night.

SHE STARED AT the city walls through the small hole in the barrel: the walls were smooth gray stone that was impossible to climb or even comfortably touch during the day. Five guards manned the main entrance: three by the gate and two on the wall. Perhaps they wouldn't yet know to look for any runaway prisoners; perhaps they would get through without the checks.

"You there!"

Adlai stopped breathing. She stilled completely as the wagon jolted to a stop and she heard Erikys being called away by one of the gate guards.

He moved so far away that she couldn't hear what they were saying.

Thump.

A barrel was knocked over. Then another. Adlai saw a flash of a hand as a lid was removed from the barrel next to her.

They were checking the barrels. Of course they were. But would they check every single one? And what was Erikys saying? She wanted to know exactly what was going on, but she had to be still. She closed her eyes and prayed that the goddess of whispers was listening.

Keep our secret, she begged. *Don't let us be caught here.*

Not when the gate was right there.

The lid above her shifted. Light peeked into her barrel. She could only see the guard's hand but soon she would see everything. Soon *she* would be seen.

Coldness crept out of her, but it wasn't just fear: her shadow pushed against the barrel and the tight walls around her trembled. She couldn't pull it back. She couldn't breathe.

Hush, child. The words were soft, but the voice in her head was a growl. Her shadow wrapped around her. Claws sank into her. *Let go.*

Was she going mad? Had dying affected her mind as well as her shadow? Adlai stopped thinking, she stopped struggling—she didn't want any part of what was about to happen next, because either the guard was going to yank her out of this barrel or some kind of madness was taking root.

She heard the barrel lid drop. Then the guard's voice.

"Nothing here."

The heaviness in her chest lifted. Everything was dark. She was still in a barrel, but somehow it wasn't the same one she'd put herself in. This one was shut. Through the side hole, she could glimpse the guard, but the perspective was different. He was further away from her.

She swallowed. Her shadow had moved her. The voice had come from her shadow, not her mind, and it had somehow taken over and saved her.

"Like I said," Erikys was saying, "they're all just empty barrels."

He was hurrying back to her, a confused look momentarily crossing his face. But whatever he might be thinking, he didn't miss a beat. He picked the planks up again and with a grunt the wheels rolled toward the gated entrance.

The gates were open to them. They were leaving Libra. Adlai was leaving her old life behind, and already she was so very lost.

ERIKYS PARKED THE wagon by the small dirt track that most travelers took when leaving Libra. Adlai waited a moment, then pushed the lid off the barrel and climbed out.

"I thought you were in that last one!" he said, relief palpable in his voice.

"We were lucky." Adlai looked down as she wrapped the canvas bag with all their supplies so it hung heavy from her hips. She wasn't sure she could explain what had happened. She wasn't sure she knew.

Erikys grinned. "We did it, little thief."

"Not quite," she said. She gestured for him to follow her, but he hesitated, the grin sliding from his face.

"There's nothing that way," he said. And it was true; Adlai was walking away from the dirt track, away from the paths to other towns and cities.

She stopped and looked back at him.

"We'll be safe this way," she said. It came out breathless and unsure.

"Safe in the desert?" Erikys repeated dumbly. "Who told you this?"

A dead woman told me, while I was dead. It sounded crazy enough in her head. So much of her head seemed crazy right now.

"You don't have to follow me," she said. "But no one will come for us out there."

Erikys stared at her blankly. Then he gave a small, nervous laugh. "No, I don't 'spect they will."

8

A Singular Woman

A ROYAL MESSENGER ARRIVED LATE IN the afternoon for Dressla. Bosma, her oldest and most trusted guard, showed him into her small, cramped office.

"Long-lived Thelan Cario Kingsblood of the Gleaming Sands, second-born prince, heir to the throne of Zodian, guardian of the desert and all of Libra, commands you to his court for an audience with His Radiance."

The "second-born" bit must irritate Thelan, she thought. Lost the throne by being born a few minutes after his brother. And now, having outlived his brother, he spends his days searching the stars for a way to steal the crown from his nephew. Stars couldn't give power though.

He needs me.

Royal stargazers and their charts were nothing but charlatans pretending to read the future from the gods. Dressla's research was different. Here, in this very office, she had files upon files of true, tangible results. Her office was on the top floor of the Arbil pyramid; a small room with pinprick windows and walls overcrowded by books. Her life's work was here. It was home.

The messenger was young and earnest and barely took a breath in between giving the grand address.

She sighed. Going to court would mean abandoning her work for the rest of the day, something she was particularly loath to do after reading her assistant's latest report.

"It wouldn't happen to be an optional request for my presence, would it?" she asked, fluttering her eyelashes and angling her face up prettily to the messenger.

Dressla was undoubtedly a beautiful woman. Her light brown skin was flawless, her hair sleek and black, and her wide-set eyes were likewise dark with glittering gold across the lids. A large nose ring with a fine chain looped across her cheek to a matching gold earring. On her other ear was a red jewel hanging like a fat raindrop, if rain were made of blood. In most rooms, she would be considered striking, but compared to her fellow researchers, she was, quite simply, breathtaking.

The messenger managed to breathe again, however.

"Madam Dressla, you are summoned—" he began.

"No, messenger," she said, dropping her demureness. "You may leave and summon someone for me."

"That is not—"

Dressla moved past him and knocked lightly on the door. Bosma appeared without hesitation. Of course she could send her guard out for this task, but then she'd be down a guard. Besides, she knew the prince would want his messenger to have properly snooped around before returning.

She turned back to the messenger. "Bring my assistant, Farnell, here."

"This is an urgent summons!"

"Indeed," she said. "And the longer it takes you to understand this, the longer our illustrious prince waits."

She would have liked to have sent the messenger out of her office with a similar, equally grand and ridiculous address as the one he'd come to her with. Something like, *Beauty personified, Lady Dressla, head of research in Arbil, master of shadows and chaser of death, commands her humble servant to explain the most unexpected findings of his recent report.*

DRESSLA'S ASSISTANT ARRIVED a moment later, bemused but used to her ways by now.

"That was a knight, wasn't it?" he said as the door shut behind him.

"A royal messenger," she corrected. "I've been summoned."

Farnell frowned. He was the same age as Dressla and yet he looked much older, with lines wrinkling his pale face and an unkempt beard he continually scratched. "Then what are we doing in your office?"

Instead of answering, Dressla picked up the report on her desk and turned to the page that had grabbed her attention. "Was the shadow truly undamaged?"

"We did the experiment several times to be sure," he said, with a touch of defensiveness.

Dressla put the report down, but her fingers traced over it.

"Have you checked to see if any shadows are unaccounted for?'

Farnell nodded. "There isn't a single one missing."

That wasn't strictly true. It sparked an idea in her.

"Have you dated the shadow?" she asked, keeping the excitement from her voice.

"It's fully mature."

Dressla suppressed her annoyance. Farnell could give her the information, but he couldn't translate it into an original thought.

"Dated," she said. "Have you aged the shadow?"

"Oh." Farnell stared at the report, wrinkles creasing his forehead as he considered what she was asking. "I didn't think that necessary."

Dressla never liked to spell out her ideas, and she usually didn't give voice to them until she had the results to back them up, but here was an unusual case.

Adlai Bringer, a recently matured shadow wielder, was supposed to be lying dead in the cold chambers. Her shadow was supposed to be trapped in a suraci watch. In normal circumstances, Dressla might not even have bothered to run any experiments yet; another dead shadow wielder was of little consequence when she had collected dozens of them already.

But Adlai Bringer was not dead. She had been killed in broad daylight, with plenty of eye witnesses to corroborate the equitor's story, and then, miraculously, she had brought herself back to life. That part in itself wasn't all that miraculous—Dressla knew it was entirely possible if her shadow was still attached. She had seen shadow wielders pull the same trick plenty of times before and it was why equitors were trained to take their shadows the moment they killed them.

Which left the question of whose shadow the equitor had brought back with him?

At first Dressla had assumed it must have been a damaged part of the girl's shadow, and that somehow not all of it had been collected. It would have been interesting to know that even with a damaged shadow it was possible to come back from the dead. But the shadow that was collected was healthy and complete.

It had also crossed her mind that the shadow itself wasn't Adlai Bringer's. That after failing to take hers, the equitor had sought to trick them by stealing one of the shadows they stored in the cold chambers and claiming it for the girl's.

But if none of their shadows were unaccounted for, and the shadow was whole and undamaged, Dressla was forced to come up with a new theory.

"Age the sample and release the equitor. If I'm right, he wasn't lying: that shadow did come from Adlai Bringer."

"But we already know the girl still has her—"

This time her annoyance showed, her eyes flashing quick as a viper. "I am aware of all the facts, Farnell."

Dressla often felt a lack of patience. Sometimes she thought she hadn't risen to her position for any of her virtues, she'd risen simply because everyone else was so goddamn stupid.

She opened her door a crack and saw the messenger standing in the hall, a reflection of her own impatience. She turned back to Farnell.

"The prince waits for me," she said. "You have your orders; I trust you don't need me to repeat them."

THE INSUFFERABLE MESSENGER set a marching pace down the echoing corridor. He was the reason she was having to walk the public paths down Arbil. It was Dressla's habit to stick only to the cold chamber, the experimenting room, and her office, leaving through a secret corridor when she absolutely had to go home. The rest of the Arbil pyramid was a series of floors she chose to ignore.

Well, she was forced to see them now.

The floor below hers was a training center for equitors. They walked swiftly past a library that had a few of the weedier students bent over books, and moved down the hall where they could hear a series of grunts and sticks connecting in the air. Equitors were either all brain or all muscle: Dressla hadn't come across one that had talent for both.

But it was the lower floors that made Dressla the most uncomfortable. To most citizens Arbil was a hospital. People traveled from all over to be treated here; it was said to be a place of miracles and that if your child was born in the pyramid, they were blessed.

All Dressla saw were the sick and the dying. They were nothing like the corpses she had in her cold chamber. Shadow wielders died perfectly. Their bodies didn't decay, they didn't even keep the wound that killed them. Their skin was always so beautifully unblemished, and with their eyes peacefully closed they could be mistaken for sleeping.

There was no sweat. There was no smell. No release of gases or uncontrolled excrements. Death was made beautiful in the cold chamber, beautiful in part because it wasn't permanent, and really that was the only death Dressla was interested in.

<hr />

To reach the palace, they'd had to ride to the other side of the city.

Though an impressive building, as all palaces must be, it was nowhere near the splendor of the Arbil pyramid. Its bricks were white, not gold, its height low and stretched rather than climbing upward. The only height came from two turrets on either side of the palace, where Dressla knew the official stargazers would be waiting on the rooftops for nightfall. The sky was already darkening, and she smiled to think of those stargazers, desperately hoping that tonight the stars would show something of worth to the prince.

Many believed the gods wrote the story of humans in the stars— as though the sky were pages of a book; but Dressla didn't require her fate to be written in a sky that could only to be seen at night. Her life was one that would be great regardless of the gods, regardless of stars, and regardless of princes. Dressla was known at the gate and with the messenger shadowing behind her, she made her way uninterrupted inside the grounds.

It was only at the steps leading into court that she was stopped.

"You've arrived late." The guard's eyes were directed at the messenger, then turned to Dressla. "The prince will see you in his chambers now."

He's retired to bed already? Dressla thought. *Things must be desperate.*

She lowered her hood and let the guard escort her down the opposite corridor. He stayed closer than necessary and more than once she felt his eyes travel down her. She unclasped her cloak and let him look longer; it made no difference to her what a guard thought of her summons.

At the door to the prince's chambers there were more guards. Two of them pulled back the heavy door and she quickly bent down to a curtsy; it was important that the first sight the prince had of her was humble.

It made Dressla want to laugh sometimes. The little humiliations men thought they were making of her.

"My summons was urgent."

The prince's voice sounded weak in the echoing chamber, like he was too small for the room. In a way he was. Though he was covered in jewels and the finest silks, Prince Thelan was as skinny as a peasant and shorter than Dressla. She made sure to keep her head low as she approached him.

"I came as soon as I could, my prince."

"Hmmm," he grunted. "Perhaps we do not have the same notion of urgency."

Thelan was sitting in a heavily cushioned chair that Dressla knew helped ease his back troubles. He was approaching seventy and had never been a handsome man. Without strength and youth his features looked harsher and more drawn out. His lips puckered, his nose turned downward, and his skin seemed to sag even more under his fine bands of jewels.

"Perhaps not, but I did bring what you asked," she said. She took off her traveling cloak and knelt by his side. "Would you like it now, or later?"

"I would have liked it two hours ago, when my wife wished to dance. Instead I had to sit like a fool as she twirled around with my son." He fidgeted in the chair and winced at a sudden spasm.

Dressla hid her smile. Thelan had four sons, all of them closer in age to his new wife than he was.

She made to rise but Thelan's hand shot out with more speed than she thought possible. He grabbed her wrist with surprising force. Dressla stumbled and he brought her close enough to spit on. "You'll do better next time. I shouldn't have to summon you to attend me. There can be nothing more important than servicing me."

Dressla waited for his grip to break. She felt the slackening of fingers and he slumped back from the effort. Giving him the tonic now would give him what he wanted: the strength and vigor of youth.

He needed it to keep up with a young wife and sons who wished to take over his lands. But the tonic's effectiveness was weakening. He needed it more and more. It wouldn't be long before he ordered her to stop her work and live full-time in the palace.

Dressla took her earring off—inside was the tonic that she always kept on her person.

His shadow was cast away from her; ordinary and gray and faint across the stone floor. Huddled as he was, his figure was lost in the looming chair.

Carefully, she poured the tonic into his shadow. The red liquid hissed and smoked as it hit the stone and sank into the ground. Where it landed, a deep black bled out and slowly filled the rest of his shadow, leaving a strong man's silhouette inside the faint chair outline.

She looked up and saw palpable relief in his face. He sighed and clasped her hand that still held the empty vial. "You are more intelligent than your predecessor, I can admit that. The leaps you have made show that quite clearly. But still, you lack something," Thelan said. He let go of her hand and leaned back in his chair, his movements already smoother and more at ease.

Dressla ignored him and fastened her earring back in place, ready to rise again.

"I have my own spies, you know, that tell me how infrequently you obtain fresh subjects," the prince said. "Even today you allowed one to slip through your fingers. A girl, I believe. It caused quite a stir among my people."

"We are working on locating the subject."

The prince laughed and drank wine from his goblet. In the firelight his wrinkles seemed to lessen and his eyes brightened.

"Just as you are working on finding their hideout? That, at least, your predecessor was better at doing." He tilted his head. "You think calling them subjects dehumanizes them and makes it easier to do the things you do, but I have found it's better to not pretend in these matters. I name and hand-feed all my prize animals. Come feast time, I find satisfaction in having known the food on my plate." He swirled the goblet around and appraised Dressla. This time he took in her body with an almost youthful hunger.

"What you lack is ruthlessness. That's what's needed to get results. It's not your fault. Women have maternal instincts. Men are more primal. We can act selfishly and do what's necessary."

Dressla stood up. The torch on the wall beside her warmed her face, and whatever emotion passed over it was taken in by Thelan's watchful gaze.

"You don't agree?" he asked. "Come, say what you are thinking."

"You forget, my prince," she said quietly, "that I have no children. And if my predecessor was truly ruthless then it would be him standing here before you, not me."

And if you *were truly ruthless, you would be king already.*

Thelan had watched his father, then his brother, and now his nephew wear the Zodian crown. If he was given his youth back, he believed the gods would finally weave ruling this kingdom into his fate. As if they hadn't already overlooked him enough times before.

"Ha!" Thelan drained what was left in the goblet. He'd looked weak and tired when she'd entered the chamber; now a restless energy took hold of him. His fingers danced with their gleaming gold. "Then I am lucky you are a most singular woman as you make for a far prettier sight."

She smiled, the sight just as pretty as Thelan could hope for.

"What a queen you would make," he said.

He wasn't entirely wrong, but she knew his promise was conditional on her experiments working and improving, if his youth fully came back and he could do all that he dreamed of doing.

But if the stars truly had Dressla as queen in them, then she knew it would be because she'd wiped the skies of all the princes and kings before her.

9

Spilling Secrets

ARKNESS HAD SLOWLY TAKEN OVER the desert, bringing the cold with it. In a way, it was a relief. A distraction. With each step Adlai felt her shadow itching to be released, but the drop in temperature made her forget about that and of wanting to rest. Instead she began to worry how much colder it would get before they were rescued. If they were rescued.

She shivered. A new kind of misery to add to the silence pricking the air after she'd told Erikys she was *following the stars*. As though she were some god-appointed stargazer.

He hadn't argued or called her crazy, and he was still following her. Perhaps he thought it was too late to turn back. Or maybe he was good at persuading himself that everything would work out.

Under the gleam of starlight and a crescent moon, large dunes sloped across the horizon and had turned a bluish black, as if the land were bruised. Or dead. Her steps faltered, remembering the shadowy black hills she'd seen all too recently. Had she really been dead? The scene in front of her now was unnervingly similar, so much so that she half expected to see Yaxine walking toward her again to tell her she'd failed.

"You okay?" Erikys asked.

After walking for so long, and after experiencing such a day, all Adlai wanted to do was lie down and sleep. Forget food. She wished she had a soft, warm blanket to curl up in.

"Could we rest for a bit?" she asked. Her voice came out scratchy after so much silence.

"Sure." He looked around with a raised brow. "Think there'll be a hotel nearby?"

He had his jacket fully fastened, the fabric at the front covering the lower half of his face so she couldn't tell if he was trying to joke or simply pointing out how foolish this whole journey was. The fact that she didn't know how much more desert they'd have to walk through didn't help. If only they could see something on the horizon: a building, smoke, something to be walking toward rather than staring up at the damn crown constellation.

She hated looking up at those seven stars. It was like she was walking on a plank with her eyes closed and eventually her feet would step on air, just as eventually the night would end and her guide would disappear.

"Okay, so we'll make camp where we want," he said, distracting her from her darker thoughts. "We shouldn't rest for too long though. Stars are kind of a night thing."

"I know, I'm just . . ." She pulled the fabric of her hood up as well and wrapped her arms around her chest. "Today has been a lot. You're not meeting me at my best."

"You mean you don't have a habit of wandering into the desert at night?"

"No, funnily enough I don't have the least experience in any of this," she said. "I've never even built a fire before."

Erikys was silent for a moment and she wondered how many times since they'd left Libra he'd regretted following her.

"Well, we have wood, so we can try for one," he said finally. "I used to go camping when I was a kid. I doubt making a fire has changed since then."

Erikys had brought the empty crate from the wagon and he began breaking it apart. She watched him from the corners of her eyes. His arm muscles flexed under his jacket and she wondered about how and where exactly he'd been raised. He can't have been just a thief. Thieves needed quick hands, not muscle.

Adlai sat down as Erikys got sparks kindling from some broken pieces of wood. The flames became larger and brighter and she thought how impossibly stupid it would have been to be alone in the middle of the desert. A rush of warmth came over her, not just from the fire, but at finding herself not alone.

"Something on your mind?" he asked.

Her eyes were fixed on a gold anklet hanging off Erikys's left foot. There was a black gem attached to it that looked like a cheap trinket from Izel's stall. The jewel was clouded, and she could see the gold chain's paintwork flaking off to show the copper underneath.

Conscious that she was still staring, she nodded to it. "Nice anklet," she said.

"Thinking of stealing it?" He said it jokingly, but there was something uncomfortable in the way he sat down and covered the space between them with the remains of the crate. Perhaps someone important to him had given him the anklet. Someone he'd rather be sitting under the stars with right now.

Stars were made for spilling secrets—for saying the things you didn't dare to under the harsh glare of the sun. How many nights had she stayed up late whispering nonsense and dreams with Penna?

"Can I tell you something?" her voice was almost a whisper. "It's going to sound crazy."

"Crazier than where we are right now?" he asked.

"A lot more." She took a deep breath. Erikys's face was bathed in firelight as a harsh gust of wind blew, shaking everything but his eyes from her. She let the words out.

"I think I died today."

He didn't dismiss her or laugh. His steady gaze took her at her word, and it was like looking up at the night sky, as though she could spill all her secrets to this boy.

"You mean you had a near-death experience?"

"No," she said. "I really died."

His eyebrows arched. "So . . . this is your afterlife? Running from the city guard and hiding out in the desert with a stranger? Which god did you piss off to get my company?"

She sighed, the magic of the moment lost. He didn't believe her, of course.

"I'm not dead now," she said. As if that was the insane part that needed clarifying. "Dying and coming back hasn't happened to you then?"

"You're serious, aren't you?" Adlai didn't answer. Erikys frowned suddenly. "Is that why you were covered in blood earlier? Did someone hurt you?"

"It was a knife. He had a knife. I felt . . . I died and then I . . . went somewhere."

Erikys was very still, like he was holding in his breath.

"I know I sound crazy. But so does having a shadow that can steal. Or maybe it really was just a dream and I'm leading us to our deaths by acting on it. We could get bitten or stung, or we could run out of rations before we realize there's nothing out here, and by then it'll be too late to turn back."

Just saying it made her want to turn back. Despite the fear that gripped her heart when she thought of the desert market, she couldn't only link it to danger. It was a place of excitement too.

Endless opportunities. Her father had made her feel as though the world was hers for the taking, that she could slip anything she wanted into her shadow. There was nothing to take out here.

"*Adlai.*" He said her name with such force that she came back to herself. "It's all right. Just tell me exactly what happened today. From the moment you screamed thief at me and ran into the crowd."

"You won't believe me."

Erikys turned to her. He was an arm's length away, a distance the open desert had made seem natural and necessary, but with the fire crackling between them it now felt a degree too intimate.

"I grew up on a farm," he said. "My father and his father and his father before him were all farmers, so that was what I was supposed to be. But I never wanted that. Sometimes I would dream about telling my friends about my shadow. Showing off, really, and proving I wasn't just some farm boy. But something always held me back. The fear of seeming crazy, maybe, or of them thinking something was wrong with me. It isn't natural, you understand?" He looked across at her. "Look, I know I was joking around before, but if you're serious, I'll listen."

So Adlai told him. She told him all about the boy from the market who she'd stolen suraci metal from. How the boy had found her by the fountain, put his hand on the ground and pulled her shadow toward him. What that had felt like: seeing her shadow sinking into his watch. Then his face inches from her. A sharp pain from his knife as he buried it in her neck. How warm her blood was in her mouth as panic filled her lungs and her breath came out in painful, hot bursts. Like her life was being squeezed out of her. She was stabbed, but as she died, it was as though her own body had been strangling her.

Erikys was turned away from her, yet she could see his expression clear in the firelight. He looked like he was going to be sick. The flames spluttered in the silence.

"I'm sorry," he said. His voice was thick and he suddenly seemed very different from the cocksure boy from the cell, the one who'd swiped the keys from the guard as he'd winked at her.

She frowned. "You didn't do anything. And I'm fine now. That's the other part I haven't told you about yet. Where I was when I woke up."

When she was done describing the shadow world, meeting Yaxine and repeating most of what the woman had said to her, Erikys still looked queasy.

"You brought yourself back the same way you pull an object from your shadow?"

She shook her head. "It was more like my shadow brought me back."

"But you said your shadow was stolen. How did you get it back from the boy in the market?"

"I don't know," she said honestly.

"Didn't the woman know? The one you met in that shadow world?"

Adlai shrugged. "She didn't believe it had been taken from me. I guess she was right about that. I have my shadow and I'm here. I'm alive."

"Yes." Erikys was looking at her strangely. Of course he was. She was crazy: what she was saying was crazy.

"And that woman, Yaxine, she told you there are more of . . . of us out here?" Erikys asked, not quite meeting her eyes. Probably he was beginning to understand that her reason for being in the desert was based on a near-death experience.

"She said to follow the king's constellation and I'd find them."

Adlai didn't add that Yaxine had told her she had an uncle. That still felt too strange to her. She'd been without family for so long, and she knew he wouldn't understand that point. Erikys still had a family.

"Your family will be worried about you, won't they?" she asked.

"I doubt it," he said. "My parents have enough going on right now with the farm, and they have my brother to help out. He's younger but far more responsible," he added at Adlai's questioning gaze. "They're all used to me not being around. It's better that way. What about yours?"

Adlai put on the face she was used to projecting whenever someone asked about her parents. The one that made her look as though she was mildly interested in the topic but not enough to elaborate. It helped to think of her mother more than her father in these instances, as she had no memories of her that could hurt.

"Orphan," she said. "I don't remember my mother. She died when I was three. My father raised me until he . . ." She swallowed, unsure of the word. Unsure of everything about what had happened to her father. He hadn't abandoned her; she knew that now. But how had he died?

The last time she'd seen him had played out in her mind over and over again; it was an itch, a wound she ripped open every time, but no matter how hard she scratched, it never healed.

They'd both been asleep in the little apartment they'd rented over the top of a shoemaker's shop. She remembered the leathery smell and how the sound of little hammers, like rainfall, used to wake her up every morning.

But that night she was woken up by something else. Voices and footsteps out in the hall. Then her father came inside her room. She'd been so sleepy, she couldn't remember how he had looked at her, or what he had said. She just remembered looking past him and hearing strangers at their door.

Sometimes she thought she'd imagined the strangers. When she was feeling really low, her mind whispered to her that he'd simply left. It explained why she couldn't remember anything else of that night. Her father had been standing in her doorway and she hadn't even looked at him properly, hadn't even tried to listen to him, she'd been so focused on the other voices and footsteps. Imaginary or real. Blackness was all she remembered after that, and when she next heard the little hammers at work, her father was gone.

"I was ten when I was brought to the orphanage," she said finally.

"I'm sorry," he said. They were both quiet for a moment, the only sound the crack of wood being added to the flames.

"It wasn't all bad. Pen is like a sister to me."

"For what it's worth," he said, leaning back on his arms, "you were right not to let her come. There's no way I would have let my brother come either."

She nodded. If there was one thing she was glad about right now, it was that she hadn't dragged Penna into this. She'd be safe in their attic room right now, warm in her bed.

Adlai wrapped her arms around herself. It was growing colder in the desert, as if the moon radiated ice the same way the sun radiated heat.

"Doesn't your brother have a shadow though?" she asked. "If he uses it in public—"

"He doesn't have one." Erikys had an edge to his voice. She frowned and he swallowed hard before adding, "He almost died last winter. A harmless cough that turned into a fever we couldn't stop." He sat up straight, messy curls falling over his eyes. "Every day we waited for it to break but it wouldn't leave him. I'd watch him sweat in that bed, his eyes not seeing me, and wherever his mind went, it felt like he was taking me there with him. Like I was dying in that room."

Adlai tried to speak. To imagine what it would be like to watch someone you loved drifting away from you like that. It seemed an impossible weight.

"Healers?" she asked tentatively.

Erikys scorned. "No healer would help us without the proper coin. That's why I started stealing in the market. Eventually I got enough to buy him the medicine. My parents thought it was a miracle. As if Descon himself had listen to their prayers and swooped in to stop his plague."

"You saved him."

Erikys shrugged. "I saved myself too. Now my brother will inherit the farm, and I'm free to do as I please."

She sensed his shift and the lightness he forced into his tone. He was the carefree boy again.

"And right now, I think we should get moving," he said. She didn't disagree. Warm as the fire was, they couldn't stay out in the desert all night. Wherever Yaxine had wanted her to go, Adlai had to find it.

Erikys grabbed their scant supplies. They began walking in silence, neither of them wanting to admit how dark and cold and hopeless their journey was turning out to be.

She was grateful when, a little later, he turned to her and she caught a playful gleam in his eyes. "So if your story about dying is true, that makes people like you and me immortal."

She relaxed and found herself easily smiling.

"I wouldn't bet my life on that. One death is enough for me today," she said. "So if a snake is drawn to us, remember to offer out your arm first."

Erikys grinned as he shifted closer, their arms almost bumping as they matched each other's pace. "I promise to protect you from snakes."

"And scorpions."

His face clouded over and she laughed. "Don't tell me you're afraid of scorpions but not snakes?" she asked, incredulous. "What does it matter if you can't die anyway?"

"I don't know if I can't yet."

But his words sounded faint as a prickling sensation climbed her skin. She stopped in her tracks, vaguely aware that Erikys hadn't noticed anything. He was still smiling, his stride uninterrupted, calm.

Her shadow crawled out of her unbidden.

Can you smell them?

The voice was a growl. Her breathing hitched. It was the same voice she'd heard in the barrel. The same one as in the shadow world.

One, two, three.

"Adlai?" Now Erikys stopped, head tilted and a frown forming as he watched her shadow grow larger. "What are you—"

She shook her head, unable to speak. In the distance she registered movement coming toward them, but it wasn't another person or an animal. It wasn't a living thing at all.

10

Uncle Lou

IT WAS SHADOW. BUT NOT as she'd ever seen it before. The shadow was split into three, each part moving quickly and silently, rising from the ground as fire. Fire that was completely black and eating its way through the sands as it licked all the way up to the stars and blocked their guiding light.

Erikys turned. He saw what was heading their way and dropped down to a crouch, as if he could attack the flames or perhaps run from them. Like hers, his shadow leaped out in response to these strange, burning shadows.

Yet when the shadows reached them, the fire became smoke, and the smoke thinned out to reveal three very real, very *not burned* strangers. The smoke rolled off them and dropped like a weight to form their shadows. But even stationary, each of the shadows flickered, a layer of black trailing off them, as though at any moment they might burst back into flame.

You can only teach your shadow one trick.

Her shadow could steal, but these . . . these had been *fire*, or something like it. Cold fear ran through her as she stared at the strangers.

One boy and two girls. A moment ago they had been running down the dunes as black flame; now they were awash with colors and gemstones. They were beautiful. One of the girls wore the kind of dress Penna would spend days making; it was all shades of blue with white gems draped over the sleeves and a hem like seafoam. The other girl was dressed more like the boy: both were in baggy trousers and silk tops with fine embroidered collars. Rich garments, not at all suited for walking through a desert. But of course they hadn't walked anywhere.

"Adlai Bringer?" The boy spoke first. Tall, dark-skinned, and unnervingly handsome, he spoke with an accent she couldn't place. Not Geman or Cantha, and certainly not Libran. "Your uncle said you would be alone."

"Uncle?" Erikys stared at Adlai. She ignored him.

"Why didn't he come?" The question came out sounding pathetic and she bit her lip. What did she care about a man she'd never met before?

The boy studied Erikys and Adlai, taking in their shadows and perhaps the exhaustion written across their faces. He turned to the others. "He won't like this complication."

"Another person isn't a complication," one of his companions answered. The one in the pretty dress. She had deep brown skin and thick dark hair that was braided and reached down to her hips. "Honestly, Kanwar, you do talk nonsense sometimes."

Kanwar didn't seem to agree and looked to their third companion. Her shadow was the one flickering the most, smoke like kindling meeting the air, and yet she was so ordinary to look at. Her hair was a dull brown that looked slept in, and she had tanned, freckled skin and flat features.

"He has a shadow," the freckled girl said. "Lucky boy." She laughed. "Without one, we'd be leaving you in the middle of the desert."

"No, we wouldn't," the taller girl said sternly.

But Adlai wasn't so sure. She moved closer to Erikys.

"I don't know who any of you are," she said. "But he's coming wherever I'm going."

Erikys smiled at her for that. A small one—underneath it she saw the same unease she was feeling.

"You sure? This is a perfect opportunity to be rid of me," he muttered to her.

"Don't tempt me," she muttered back.

She could feel the gaze of the strangers on them and wondered again why her uncle hadn't come himself to find her.

"Who are you people?" she asked. "What was that fire?"

The boy—Kanwar, his companion had called him—turned to her and she realized how little she liked those dark eyes that settled on her.

"We've wasted enough time looking for you," he said. "You can ask all your questions once we have you back safely."

"Back where?" Erikys asked.

"Somewhere that isn't desert," he said.

Before either of them had a chance to object or ask what exactly he meant, the freckled girl cracked a wicked smile and disappeared. Her shadow rose from the ground and swallowed her in black fire again. Now that Adlai was closer, she could see it had a physicality to it. Or rather she could sense the physicality. As though if she reached out and touched it, there would be something to feel.

Adlai was too amazed to notice anything else. She only had a moment more of shock as the smoke swirling inside the fire sprang into something like a hand, or a claw.

It leaped out of the fire and came right for her.

ADLAI WAS FALLING, but she wasn't alone. Something dug into her skin. Claws pulling her down, down, down into the dark. She cried out but it was soundless. A rush of wind stole her breath, and Adlai was jerked forward through some force she couldn't name. The sensation was too strange. She tried to feel around for something familiar, but there was only blackness and a buzzing that thrummed through her body.

Then the buzzing stopped. She was lifted and the darkness peeled off her like a curtain being drawn.

The first thing she realized was that she was no longer outside. The desert and the starlight were gone. In its place were white-washed walls and sparse wooden furniture. An overhead fan swirled loudly above her, startling her.

She looked further around the room and saw Erikys equally confused. A kitchen filled the space behind him, all white rock surfaces and gray wood cabinet doors. A simple bowl sat on the countertop with a towel over it.

The freckled girl was standing next to her, her shadow gone but a dangerous glint in her green eyes nonetheless.

"Shadow's the fastest way to travel," she said.

Adlai didn't doubt her. She had no idea how far they had just traveled, but moonlight peeked through the window in the kitchen. *It's still night.*

"You can steal people?" she asked, her breath still catching up with her. She thought of all the objects she'd stolen with her shadow, and of what her shadow had done when it had moved her from one barrel to another.

It had stolen her. Shadows could steal people.

Kanwar was beside Erikys, and he gave her another steady look that made her feel small and stupid.

"Not everyone can," Kanwar said. "Some shadows can't be taught. Some are weaker than others." His gaze moved from Adlai to Erikys, as though he didn't think much of either of them.

Her jaw tightened. It was hard to imagine being able to control that kind of power. Impossible, in fact. Yet the way he said it made her want to prove him wrong. But before she could say—or do— anything stupid, she felt a shift in the room. The freckled girl's smile vanished and the taller girl seemed to shrink. Kanwar had already looked serious before, but now he was so stiff it was as though he'd been slammed against a wall. The alertness between them was unnerving. She looked to Erikys and saw him likewise confused, likewise wary. Watching him, she missed the moment the door opened.

At first all she saw was an ordinary man. He walked toward them in long strides, moving with a purposefulness that snapped her attention to him like a gust of wind had blown through the room.

It was her uncle. It had to be. He had the same golden wavy hair, the same wide mouth and dark brown eyes. But more than sharing some physical features, Adlai knew it was him from the way his gaze clung to hers.

"Adlai." His voice was deep and cut with emotion. He spoke to her, and only her. Like there was no one else in the room. "Gods, but you look just like your mother. Exactly like Leena."

Adlai was struck dumb. The comparison made her uncomfortable, and she was glad when he stepped forward and clapped a hand on Kanwar's shoulder instead.

"Thank you, Kanwar, you've done brilliantly. As always."

His eyes fell on Erikys for the first time and he frowned, his hand now digging into the boy's shoulder.

"He was with her, Caster Luth," Kanwar said, and there was no mistaking the apology in his voice. "He has a shadow."

The room grew tense. Adlai got the sense that her uncle wasn't used to surprises.

"A moment, if you don't mind," her uncle said. It was said politely, but Adlai could feel the coldness as he pulled Kanwar aside. The two girls followed, and Adlai couldn't make out what any of them were saying.

She moved closer to Erikys.

"I'm sorry," she said.

"What for?"

"This is weird."

"What's weird? Your uncle, or the traveling through shadow thing?"

"The uncle thing mostly. I've never met him before."

Erikys stared at her oddly. "Never? Well, I'm not sure I was invited to the reunion. In fact I'm pretty sure he's telling one of them to dump me back in the desert."

Adlai shook her head. She didn't know anything about her uncle, but she knew she wasn't going to let him do that.

"You're staying here," she said firmly.

"Where do you think *here* is?" Erikys asked.

The front door still hung open and they both turned toward it. Outside, the sand was bathed white in the moonlight. A breeze that was sweet and fresh had palm trees swaying in the distance. This wasn't the desert. They'd left Libra behind for somewhere entirely new.

A thrill like a brush of feathers ran over Adlai at the thought and, wherever she was, it was so much more than a simple hideaway. From the furnishings to the glass windows, to the coolness spiraling down from the fan . . . all of it was so homey, so comfortable.

Her uncle turned back and addressed Erikys. "We weren't expecting you, but you are of course most welcome." His smile stretched wide, a ray of white teeth gleaming, and for the first time Adlai felt somewhat at ease.

"Um, thanks." Erikys caught her gaze; he was still nervous.

She tried to look reassuringly back at him. She'd led him here and she wasn't going to abandon him.

"Would you mind if I speak to my niece alone?" her uncle asked. "Kanwar can show you around. Whatever you need, he's at your disposal."

Kanwar hardly had the appearance of a friendly guide. His face, full of sharp angles from his cheekbones to his jawline, was set with a permanent stiffness. For a moment no one moved.

"He doesn't have to go, does he?" Adlai asked.

"I'd really prefer some privacy. It's been many years since I last saw my sister's child."

The others were waiting by the door. Erikys hesitated, but then he grinned at her. "I'll stick my arm out first," he said, "but if there are scorpions, you owe me."

She smiled back at him; at the ridiculous boy who'd followed her into a desert. "I'll pray for snakes."

The others looked from one to the other as if they were crazy or speaking in a suspicious code. Adlai didn't care. Everything about today had been crazy, but she was glad she hadn't been alone for it.

Erikys left with the others and she turned her attention back to her uncle. His eyes hadn't left her.

"Are you hungry?" he asked.

She was. Desperately so, but she was also feeling sick—whether from the dizziness of traveling so fast or from being suddenly in front of a family member she didn't know anything about.

She nodded instead. Her uncle pulled out a bar stool for her to sit down on and took the towel from the bowl. Inside were several flatbreads, still warm from the oven. She watched silently as he opened a cupboard and prepared an unnecessary spread; copper plates instead of clay ones, a glass of freshly squeezed juice, little pots of yogurt and honey and a plate of dried nuts.

She picked at the nuts first, dipping them in the honey and making a mess of the countertop and her fingers.

He smiled at her. "Still addicted, I see. I remember Den used to call you Little Drizzle."

She swallowed hard at hearing her nickname again. Her father had called her it because of the way her hair drizzled down her back like honey, and also because he was forever cleaning her hands and face of the sticky treat.

"And what did he call you?" she asked.

"Dendray never mentioned me?" The smile faded, but her uncle didn't look all that surprised either.

She shook her head.

"Well, I'm sorry for it. I suppose we didn't see eye to eye on many things. You, for one. Especially after your mother . . ." He sighed. "Leena was my twin. Some used to say the better half of me. I'm Luth, but you never used to be able to say it. Uncle Lou was what you called me."

She frowned. "That boy Kanwar called you Caster Luth."

"Yes, we have a system here," he said. "You'll get to know it, but "Caster" is simply the title of a fully trained shadow caster. It's a term of respect."

"Fully trained?"

"I'm sure your father taught you as well as he could, but here you'll learn everything."

Adlai considered what her uncle was saying. It went directly against what her father had told her.

You can only teach your shadow one trick.

"Why did he leave?" Adlai felt a sudden dread in the pit of her stomach. Maybe her father wouldn't want her to be here. If he'd chosen not to tell her about all these other tricks, and especially not to tell her about having an uncle, perhaps it was because he hadn't trusted him and had never meant for Adlai to come to this place.

"It was complicated," Luth said, a little too vague for Adlai's liking. He sat down on the stool next to her. From this side she saw he had five small black rings running the whole way up his left ear. He sighed again. "Grief was the main reason. But he was wrong to think he could keep you safe in Libra of all places. When I heard of his passing, I was very tempted to bring you here."

He left you all alone.

Her shadow trembled as the beast's voice rumbled in her head. She wanted to ignore it. Her shadow couldn't talk to her. What she was hearing wasn't real. She'd left the shadow world; the beast couldn't touch her here.

But a cold rage burned through her because she knew the voice was right. She stared down at the copper plate. It was just the kind of shiny thing she'd steal in the desert market. All those years of stealing to scrape together savings, and here was her uncle with plenty of money and plenty of time to have helped her. "He died seven years ago. I didn't think I had any family left."

"I'm sorry, Adlai. Believe me, I wanted you here. You have no idea how glad I am to see you again at last. And not only that, but to see you've grown to be so much like your mother . . . But your father was very clear. He wanted you to live away from this. Frankly, I'm surprised he even taught you any shadow powers. I thought he'd ensure you wouldn't be a target."

Adlai shifted in her seat, uncomfortable at the idea that her father hadn't done enough to protect her.

"You're wrong. He taught me rules. The only reason I was attacked was because I tried to steal something I shouldn't have." She looked down at the copper plate again. The sheen was similar to suraci metal but without flames licking through it. "He told me suraci was cursed, and I didn't listen."

"Did you try to steal one of their watches?"

She looked up sharply. "How did you know that?"

"Your father really should have warned you. Suraci is a strange metal, but it isn't cursed," he said. "It's a weapon. Only trappers have suraci watches. They trap shadow in them."

Adlai frowned. She saw a flash of the hooded stranger leaning over her, her shadow like black smoke in his hands as he pulled and pulled.

"They hunt people like you and me," her uncle explained. "Steal our shadows." There was an edge to his voice. He tapped a finger against the countertop. One, two, three. As steady as a drumbeat. His other hand stroked his jaw. "I'm inclined to think you were both lucky and unlucky in that regard. The trapper you dealt with can't have been well trained, or you wouldn't have had a shadow to return to." He stilled suddenly and his gaze stuck on her, though it was as if he were seeing someone else. "It was a trapper who killed Leena, your mother. Trappers," he said bitterly, "are responsible for most of the deaths here."

Adlai drew in a sharp breath. Her head swam, as though she was racing through shadow again, her whole body disconnected from where she was.

"My mother had shadow powers too?"

Her uncle's eyes were as dark brown as hers and set in a familiar shape. She wished she could feel warmth in them, but he was a stranger to her. As much a stranger as her mother, yet there was a flicker of something in her chest to know him. Like a match trying to light.

"Your mother was very powerful," he said. "She could have been a leader, if such things were decided by sheer power alone."

She looked away. The countertops gleamed white; her hands looked dirty in comparison. She gathered the crumbs of dried nuts into a pile, trying to absorb what he was telling her. Her mother had been powerful. She'd had a shadow. The ache in her chest intensified. She'd spent years pretending she didn't need a home, that all she needed was enough money to leave the orphanage, and yet suddenly she was facing an uncle and he was offering her a place of belonging.

She closed her eyes and ignored the ache.

"You let me live in an orphanage for years because my father said he wanted me to live a normal life?" She opened her eyes, anger rooted in them. "It isn't normal to be without anyone. It isn't *normal* to not have anything of your own, except what you can steal."

Her uncle tried to interrupt but Adlai stood up, her stool scraping across the floor. "Even if it's true you were respecting my father's wishes, why wouldn't you come yourself? I *died*. Then followed stars in a desert like an idiot. All to be brought here by more strangers, into this ridiculous house that looks like it repels dirt. And the thing is," she continued, "you really don't owe me anything because I don't remember calling you Uncle Lou. I don't remember anything about you."

Adlai's voice had slowly risen, anger coursing through her, but when her uncle also stood she found herself stepping back. He was silent, and yet she felt a weight pressing the air between them. An oppressive power he wielded as he looked down at her.

Cold. Her uncle's shadow wasn't anywhere to be seen, but she felt a coldness radiate from him. It was the same coldness she'd felt in the shadow world when the beast had ripped through the sky and come down with its terrible power of death.

"I don't expect you to understand," he said finally. "You've been ignorant. You've been scared. You've been alone. But I'm not asking you to forgive me. I didn't bring you here to be your mother or your father. Here you can learn. Your powers can be what they were meant to be." His expression softened. "And you need never be alone again."

She looked down at the floor. Tiles the color of the sky with bits of white marbled through them were laid out under her feet, but she saw only the black sands of the shadow world and remembered the strangeness of being lost from her body, from life.

"You've died before," she said. "You've seen the shadow world."

He gave her a curious look.

"It's a hard place to leave, even when you return from it," he said. "But never think of yourself as having died. Not when you're so young and your shadow so strong."

"My shadow isn't strong," Adlai said automatically.

"You're Leena's child. You don't have much choice in the matter." Her uncle said it in a way she thought he meant to be humorous. Instead she found herself glaring back.

"I have plenty of choices. If I stay here, it'll be for one reason only: I want to know how to fight them. Trappers. I want to find the one who made me feel so weak and helpless, who tried to take my shadow from me. And I want to find the ones who took my father. I want to find them and be so powerful that they have no choice but to try and run. Only I won't let them escape."

Her uncle stepped toward her. This time she didn't back away. This time she met his gaze and held it.

"I'm sure of it," he said finally. "As I said, you're Leena's child. You don't have a choice in the matter." This time it was said without humor. Instead he looked sad and placed a hand on her shoulder.

"Teaching you how to use your power, to learn about your heritage is what I've always wanted for you," he said.

Adlai tensed under his touch and pulled away. She had everything to gain from staying. Here she would be safe. Here she would be powerful. Here she finally had family. These were things to be grateful for, to celebrate. They were impossible things. And yet a nagging part of her wanted to find Erikys that very moment and leave with him. Her father hadn't wanted her to stay here, and her uncle hadn't done anything in the past seven years to change that.

This place, wherever it was, wasn't home.

11

The Missing Shadow

RESSLA SAT ALONE IN THE cold chamber room awaiting Farnell's new report. She often came to this room to think. It was much more spacious than her office, and though a cupboard would also be larger than her office, this was a genuinely large room. A blank page of a room—entirely gray from the walls to the ceiling to the floor, and as cool as stepping into a river.

It was also full of dead bodies. Each one had its own small table with a fabric cover that hid the body from view and gave the appearance of floating tombstones, line after line of them. There were over a hundred bodies to date, of various ages. It was the work of many years of collecting. More than she'd been alive for. Since Arbil's inception two hundred years ago, the goal had been to study shadow and to do that, shadow wielders had to be collected.

An inscription was written under each body, naming and dating the subject, and next to that was a suraci watch that stored the subject's individual shadow. Some of the older subjects, the ones the first equitors had caught, had had to be burned. Shadow wielders could only come back from the dead when their connection with their shadows was strong, and this seemed to deteriorate over time.

Dressla had burned more than a dozen since becoming head researcher; her predecessor had never thought to keep checking the shadow connections and hadn't seemed to have given a moment's thought to their dwindling resources.

The prince only funded her research because he'd seen the benefit in his own preserved youthfulness. But it was short term. She needed better results. She needed—

Her thoughts were broken by the door opening, but it wasn't her assistant who entered.

A far younger man with flame-red hair and a long, pinched face strode in. She frowned for a moment and then recognized him as the equitor who'd brought her the mysterious shadow. The shadow that was definitely not Adlai Bringer's, the girl he'd so brutally killed in the market. He was just a boy—he couldn't be older than twenty—and he was badly injured. As he came toward her, she saw bruises on his face and long cuts running up his arms, and though he walked with confidence, he couldn't quite mask the limp in his step.

"Madam Dressla," he said, inclining his head. "I hoped to be able to say my thanks." He pointed to his left cheek, where the largest bruise bloomed. "If you hadn't spoken up for me, they'd still be interrogating me about that damn shadow I took." His gaze turned sharp. "I never lied about it. I really did take it from the girl in the market."

She glimpsed the wounded pride in the way his shoulders rolled back and his chin rose as if daring her to contradict him. She smiled humorlessly. A boy like this could never grasp the true significance of what had happened in that marketplace; for him it was simply a matter of his honor as an equitor. She sighed. "It might not look like it, but I am actually rather busy."

"I know. I want to help with that."

"You?" She looked around the room, half expecting to hear laughter come from the bodies under their covers. "You'd better clean yourself up and report back down to the equitors department. This isn't the place for you."

The boy walked slowly over to her instead.

"My best friend was the one scouted to be an equitor," he said. "He's the reason I got this position. The higher-ups wanted to reject me, but I think you'll find I'm hard to shake off."

Dressla didn't say anything. He didn't seem to be threatening, at least not in a violent way, but there was an edge to his voice. *Desperation.*

There was nothing more dangerous than a desperate man.

But would he still be desperate to help if he knew about her work? She pulled a cover off one of the tables and revealed the dead child lying underneath. The subject was three years old, still with a baby face and one tiny hand clutching a sock, leaving a foot bare on the metal surface.

"He looks sweet, doesn't he?" she said. "He could be sleeping. And in fact it's easy enough to wake him. His shadow is just here," she said, and tapped the suraci watch chained in place. "Shall I wake him and show you the work we do up here?"

He glanced at the child and then back at her. His face betrayed no fear or disgust, no reaction at all. "Teachings say that these are demons, cursed and unnatural. A skin with shadow but no soul." He nodded down at the child. "An equitor brought you that kid. What makes you think I can't handle the rest?"

"And is this child a demon, do you think?"

"It doesn't matter either way."

"I see," she said. "So you kill for pleasure then?"

His eyes were black and unusually bright in that moment. "I kill for myself. If I don't, someone else will, and I don't plan on letting anyone take what's mine," he said. "Here, I get an opportunity. Being an equitor, working in Arbil, it means something out there."

"Arbil tortured you after your first assignment."

"It punishes, and it rewards."

She cocked her head. "What's your name?"

"Corwyn," he said simply. He didn't offer a last name. Perhaps he didn't have one.

"And what reward do you seek, Corwyn?"

"To work for you, Madam Dressla."

Dressla put the cover back over the child and shook her head. "This floor is a place of research. What position did you finish your classes in?"

"Low in the areas that books were a feature. Top in survival and combat."

She began moving to the door, thinking the best way to be rid of him was to go back to her office and wait for Farnell there. "I already have guards," she said. "I've no need for more muscle."

He matched her step with a forced effort and she turned on him sharply. "Why should you even want to work for me?"

"You're researching how they do it, ain't you?" Corwyn gestured around the room. "The shadows, bringing people back to life. What man wouldn't want a chance to be invincible?"

His answer wiped the smile from her face.

"Arbil has been studying shadows for centuries," she said, her tone serious now. "The bodies you see in this room, they aren't like us, and we can never be like them."

"You aren't like most people, I'd wager."

Another answer that stunned her, but she was distracted by the door opening again, this time with her assistant behind it.

Farnell stopped and blinked at the boy—a boy he probably thought should have been on the hospital floors of the Arbil pyramid and not up here at the top level.

"I . . ." Farnell cleared his throat. "I have the report ready," he said and scratched his beard, usually a sign that he had more to say but wasn't sure if he should.

"This is the equitor who captured the shadow," she said. "Do you have it with you?"

"Oh, yes." He brought the suraci watch out from his jacket pocket. In the dim light the metal glowed up at the three of them, seeming to burn brighter.

"Very good," Dressla said. Seeing the watch and sensing the shadow inside prickled an excitement in her that she hadn't felt in a long while. It was the excitement every scientist felt when on the verge of a discovery. For a moment she forgot about the other two in the room.

"Would you like me to read you the results?" Farnell asked.

Out of the corners of her eyes, she saw Corwyn smirk.

"What?" she asked the boy.

"You think you already know the results of whatever experiment your lackey's been doing."

Farnell bristled at the description. He glowered at the boy.

"You captured the shadow, that doesn't warrant you to be a part of the research that follows," he said. "You shouldn't even be on this floor."

"It's all right, Farnell," she said. "The boy's right. I do have a theory."

Dressla moved past them and walked to a table with a long gray cover over it. This one wasn't of a child. The body under this one had been brought to Arbil seven years ago and had remained a mystery ever since. A shadow wielder, captured, killed, but his shadow had disappeared. The two equitors who'd killed this subject had been imprisoned for weeks and tortured to no avail as their stories had never made sense. After they were executed, the mystery of the missing shadow continued to plague researchers.

Now Dressla thought she understood the mystery.

"What age did you date the shadow?" she asked, looking down at the handwritten plaque in front of her.

Subject 187.
Male, Libran, thirty-six at time of decease.
Died Year Axel sixty-one.
Special notes: shadow unaccounted, zero resurrections,
married to Subject 179.

"Between thirty to forty years old," Farnell answered. "You don't think . . .?"

Dressla turned back. They'd both followed her to the table and were reading the plaque, Corwyn with mild interest, and Farnell with slow but understanding eyes.

"Would you say it was possible for the shadow to be thirty-six years old?" she said, smiling because she was sure she was right.

Corwyn hadn't captured Adlai Bringer's shadow. He'd captured her father's.

12

An Unusual Case

ADLAI WOKE EARLY THE NEXT morning. For a moment she couldn't place where she was. She expected a low angled ceiling, sunlight filtering through discolored scarves, and Penna getting ready for the day over on her side of the attic room.

Instead, she was in the bedroom her uncle had shown her to yesterday, one he claimed was entirely her own. Adlai had never had a room to herself, and she wasn't sure she liked it. Certainly there were good points: the bed's mattress felt like a hundred cushions had been squished and melted together for her comfort, and the quilt was a light, silky dream. But she'd tossed and turned owing to the strangeness of it all, waking several times during the night to look around.

She had a wardrobe where already a handful of clothes were hung up inside for her. A big wood-framed mirror featured near the door and a soft cream rug filled the middle of the floor. Over by the desk there were books and papers arranged neatly. Even the walls were something to look at. They were painted a pretty light green with gold flowers spiraling up and down the length of them.

It was overwhelming. All this stuff that was supposedly hers. Funny that. When she stole something from the market, it felt like her own possession the moment it slipped into her shadow, but to be given things?

She got out of bed and drew back the curtains, thick gray ones that fitted the windows perfectly and hadn't even whispered it was morning. Her own restlessness had done that. Some of it was excitement to be here, somewhere new at last, and to have family—that was something she hadn't imagined for herself since her father had disappeared.

But the other part, the part that had kept her on edge the whole night, had less to do with excitement.

She had died. Falling asleep wasn't easy to slip into when she couldn't control where her dreams would lead her. The ones that whispered that she couldn't cheat Death—it would come back. She thought she could feel it cling to her shadow and she remembered that voice she'd heard. But she had to remind herself that her shadow wasn't something to fear; it had saved her. She was safe. And here, she might learn not just how to survive, but how to be powerful too.

HER UNCLE WAS sitting in the living room in a loose white shirt and gray pants. She supposed she had him to thank for the lack of color in her own wardrobe.

It was an ungrateful thought; having fresh clothes to wear instead of dressing back in her traveling ones was a good thing. Yet the very bland sand-colored dress she'd found among the whites and grays and blacks was not the kind of color she tended to pick for herself. Or really a color. *I'm not stealing in the market today*, she reminded herself. She didn't need to stand out in order to distract from her shadow. And blending in might not be such a bad thing.

"I'm glad you're awake, Adlai," her uncle said. "There's breakfast in the kitchen and I've arranged Nadir to give you and that boy a tour around the place this morning."

"Can't you show me around?" She shouldn't be so eager to spend time with him. After all, he hadn't even bothered to come to the desert when she'd been fleeing for her life. But he was family. It seemed miraculous to her when she thought about it. To have family you never knew existed.

Luth put down some papers he'd been reading and came over to her with that careful, assessing regard he'd shown her yesterday.

"Unfortunately, I won't be here," he said. "This morning I plan to be in Capri, and this afternoon I'll be seen in Aries."

Adlai laughed. He was being absurd. "Those are on two opposite ends of the kingdom."

"Yes, well, Zodian is a large kingdom that has a whole host of trappers in each of its provinces. Part of how I keep everyone safe here is making sure trappers think we could be just about anywhere in the kingdom."

She blinked at him. "You intend for a trapper to see you?"

He smiled, looking down at her indulgently. "It must seem mad to you. You don't know what your powers can be yet. Once you start to learn you'll look back at your trouble in the market and wonder how you let a single trapper lay a finger on you."

Adlai's eyes darkened. He made it sound as though it was her fault for being killed. That she'd been too weak.

She must have shown her anger. Luth crossed his arms and turned serious.

"Don't mistake me, Adlai," he said. "Trappers are a threat to us all. Why else would I go to such lengths to keep them from finding us? But their threat lies in numbers. A single bee's sting kills the bee, not the person. A swarm of bees, however, now that's not something you want to experience. And they would swarm here if they knew where we were."

She shook her head. "He had a knife and he could manipulate my shadow. He wasn't some insect I could swat away."

Actively seeking out trappers didn't just seem mad, it *was* mad. This couldn't be something her uncle just did casually in his day-to-day routine.

He reached out and put a hand on her shoulder, as if sensing her anxiety. "I'll be back for dinner." He smiled, the shape of it so achingly familiar. It was her smile, or perhaps, buried deep in her mind, she still remembered her mother's. "You have nothing to worry about."

She nodded. Her uncle was powerful. She had to believe that. To trust in him.

As if to prove his point, he stepped back from her, and a false wind suddenly swept around him, trailing wisps of black smoke. They quickly engulfed him. It happened so fast she seemed to feel it more than see it. This was a roar of nature. Of power ripping through the air.

And then he was gone, but the air still trembled. She reached out with her fingers and felt them numb, as if she'd touched a block of ice.

Yes, her uncle could take care of himself; his shadow was something else entirely, and he was in total control of it. But could he really expect her powers to be like his?

⋅—◦•◦—▸—◂—◦•◦—▸

SUDDENLY ALONE IN a strange place, Adlai tried to distract herself while she waited. Breakfast was a collection of cream-filled pastries, and she ate two of them while she went from room to room. It was a one-floor house, which was odd to her as Libra was full of apartments that climbed the sky in their bid to match the grand height of the Arbil pyramid.

Leaving the kitchen and living area, she discovered a meticulously kept study with leather-bound books, abstract paintings of storms, and a bar. Down the hall was her bedroom and a bathroom opposite. Her uncle's bedroom she left alone, but there was a room next to it. One that she couldn't puzzle what it would be, and when she went for the handle, she found the door locked. Luth hadn't locked his study—he didn't even lock the front door.

Adlai pressed her eyes against the keyhole, though of course she saw nothing but her own eyelashes. She pulled away, biting her lip. There were no female touches in the house. His wife's existence wasn't anywhere; no stray earrings left lying around or scarves on the cloak hooks. Perhaps this was the room he kept her possessions in.

She shook her head and turned away from the door. He'd given Adlai her own bedroom. She wouldn't snoop in a room he didn't want opened.

NADIR, WHO KNOCKED on the door half an hour later, was thankfully not the freckled girl whose shadow had felt like claws digging into her. Instead she was the tall girl with the long thick braid and far kinder eyes. Just as she had been yesterday, the girl was dressed in fine silks, her skirt flowing white and a wrap top in pale pink. She looked like a princess forgoing jewels to blend in with the commoners.

"Your uncle suggested I show you around. There won't be as much to see here as in Libra," she said, tugging on her braid as if the settlement's lack of entertainment was a personal failure of hers, "but there are some very pretty spots."

"As long as there aren't any guards with swords or trappers with knives, I'm sure I'll like it just fine."

Nadir laughed, a soft breathless kind that made her seem almost embarrassed by what Adlai had said. "The ocean does have sharks, and there are some berries you definitely shouldn't try, but a tour of the island should be safe enough."

An island. Adlai followed Nadir out of her uncle's home and took in the sight before her.

The houses weren't tall like in the city, but they were sturdy looking, made of sandstone brick and painted in bright colors with flat tiled roofs, glass windows and little homey touches that gave a permanence about the place. Clay pots were filled with herbs or flowers, stone pathways led up to elaborately carved doors. She saw people, strangers, walking over the sand lined by rocks as though these were streets to follow.

And then there was the sea. The houses weren't built close to the shore, but you could still see the water from up here: blue-green waves streaked the horizon and brought a coolness to the air she had never tasted before.

The sight both shocked and thrilled her. She smiled to think of Penna and what she would say to that horizon—a part of her wanted to run down to the beach and start looking for mermaids. This place was like something out of a storybook.

"How many people live here?" she asked.

"About twenty families or so," Nadir answered.

"All with shadow powers?"

"No." She shook his head. "Not everyone here has powers, but most do."

That puzzled her even more. She'd grown up hiding her powers, and yet here was a place where she wouldn't have to. "Why wouldn't my father have wanted me to grow up here?" She said the thought aloud without really meaning to.

Nadir smiled sadly at her. "Fathers don't always know what's best."

THEY PICKED UP Erikys from a small house set a little further out from the rest of the homes. Nadir said it was owned by an older couple who looked after Kanwar and had agreed to take Erikys in for now.

Adlai merely nodded. She was anxious to see Erikys. Everything was new and different here. Adlai had died and been reborn into a brand-new life. One she'd dragged him into.

But she needn't have worried. A few moments later, Erikys came grinning out the door, the grin only fading when he reached Adlai.

"Did you not sleep well?" he asked. She wasn't smiling back, she realized. Erikys was in a loose white shirt and shorts. His brown curls were pushed back by a headband and his face was clean and bright. He looked dazzling. He looked like he was born for adventure. Life beamed out of him, and she was ready for some of that light to hit her.

"Better than if we'd had to camp in the desert," she said finally.

He laughed. "Ah, but then you could have slept under starlight next to yours truly."

"And listened to yours truly snoring?"

"The most soothing sound you'll ever hear," he said with a wink.

Adlai rolled her eyes. Nadir was smiling at them both and then blushed when they turned to her.

"The stars are, um, very nice here too," she said.

THE ISLAND WAS beautiful, that much Adlai could see. Everything was so much greener than she was used to; torrents of wild grass shot up through the sands, spilling over the rocks and even seeming to grow on trees, their long-fingered tendrils swaying like vines. Palm trees were the most common sight, bending over them and granting shade on every path they walked.

Down one of the paths, Adlai caught sight of a tent just like the desert market ones with a series of oddities displayed underneath.

"That's Caster Mai's business," Nadir said. "She gets new things every few weeks and can sometimes bring back something specific if you ask nice enough."

Adlai shot Nadir a strange look.

"Where does she get her stock?" she asked.

"Oh, well, some casters leave the island for supplies."

"In boats?" Erikys asked, his interest likewise piqued. "Or that other way?"

Nadir looked unsure. She tugged at her hair. "Trading with outsiders can be dangerous," she said at last. "Mostly our supplies come from using our shadows."

They were already headed to the tent, but now Adlai approached it with more curiosity. It sounded like this woman, Mai, was a thief.

She looked ordinary enough. A woman of around fifty with thin black hair swept up and starting to gray. Her clothes were layered and light, fluttering in the breeze the same as her tent's covering. She squinted in the sun to greet what might be her first customers of the day.

"Caster Mai," Nadir said respectfully, "this is Adlai Bringer and Erikys Sandtree. They arrived yesterday. Please welcome them kindly."

It was a typical greeting. Banal, even. But Caster Mai wasn't smiling. Her squint was gone as Adlai stood under the shade and the women's gaze turned to her.

"Leena's child?" Mai stared blankly at Adlai's face, as if seeing something there that she couldn't look away from. "Here?"

Adlai moved closer. Mai's table was full of treasures made to entice, but Adlai could only stare back at her.

"You knew my mother?" she asked, her heart thudding against her chest.

Mai seemed to shake herself out of some thought. Her eyes turned sharp again, looking at all three of them in turn. "I've nothing for you here," she said. "Nothing I can part with."

Adlai had seen market stall owners try this tactic as a way to increase interest in their stock, but the woman's eyes darted too wildly, and she was so clearly eager for them to leave that Adlai couldn't see it as a negotiating trick. Her father had been similarly cagey when she'd wanted to hear stories about her mother. She'd thought it was grief that made it hard for him to talk about her. But that didn't explain this woman's reaction.

Nadir tried to laugh it off and appease the woman with promises that Caster Luth would be pleased to learn his niece had been well taken care of.

"Is that a threat?" the woman spluttered.

"No, no of course not!" Nadir appeared mortified, but Caster Mai was glaring at Adlai as if the threat was coming from her. As if she were afraid of Adlai.

They left the tent with Nadir apologizing simultaneously to Caster Mai, Adlai, and Erikys.

"She really isn't normally like that," Nadir said when they were further from the stall.

"She knew my mother," Adlai said quietly. "And she turned me away. Why would she do that?"

Nadir seemed just as unsure. She tugged on her braid. "We probably just caught her at a bad time. My mother can tell you all about yours when you meet her. They were good friends."

Adlai nodded. Erikys smiled at her reassuringly and the three of them continued down the path in silence for a while.

But Caster Mai proved not to be an unusual case where Adlai was concerned. They entered a community food hall, taking in the spread of tempting pastries and sliced fruit and warm, inviting atmosphere, until the people eating there turned their heads and noticed Adlai. She watched their eyes skim passed Nadir and Erikys to fix on her. Some of the gazes were merely curious. Only a handful of looks had a colder, accusing edge. As though she shouldn't be there. As though she wasn't welcome.

Or perhaps she was imagining it all. Adlai tried to listen to more of what Nadir was saying as they helped themselves to some food.

"Classes are quite important here," she said. "We have them in the mornings, but it's encouraged to always be practicing." Nadir pointed to a pastry with coconut shavings on top. "That's the best one. On the way back, I'll show you where the classes are."

Erikys yawned, still loading his plate with more food. "Classes are optional though, aren't they?" he said.

Nadir frowned for the first time. "Yes," she said at last. "But everyone has to learn to control their shadow. It's our responsibility."

"Your responsibility." Erikys pointed a cream puff in her direction. "Me, I'm just trying to stay out of trouble."

13

The Sun Room

CLASSES WOULD START THIS MORNING. Adlai stood in her bedroom in a plain white dress, her hair piled up high, and felt as though a ghost stared back at her from the mirror. She wasn't sure why she was so nervous about going to class—she should be excited to learn more about her powers, to strengthen them and become the caster her uncle thought she could be.

She drew her shadow out carefully. Reaching for it was like diving underwater; her mind seemed to slow as a force rose up to meet her. It didn't literally knock her back as it had in the alleyway in Libra, but she felt something strong pulling and pushing against her. Unbalancing her. She took a steadying breath and let her shadow settle around he

Why do you feel so different?

Was it because she'd pulled herself back from death? Or had her shadow been damaged in the trapper's hands?

But her shadow didn't feel weaker. If anything, it felt stronger.

She tried to move it slowly around the room. A gold hair clip caught her eye on the desk and she pushed her shadow out toward it.

Crash!

The entire desk fell over, and a moment later her uncle knocked on her door.

She righted the desk and grabbed the clip from the floor. It was time to go to class. She needed it.

———

CLASSES WERE LOCATED on the second floor of a temple. It stood away from the rest of the settlement, hemmed in by a rocky cliff and jungle overgrowth. There were more rocks out this way and less sand, and although the top floor was called the Sun Room, as Adlai approached the building, she was drawing further away from the sun and walking instead into shadow.

A shiver ran through her as soon as she entered. The downstairs was devoid of much light: only a couple of torches were lit to show black walls and black floor. A bone-white staircase curved upward and she could hear the rustling of sand falling but she couldn't see from where. A hazy aroma of musk told her incense was lit from further inside. It clogged at her throat as she climbed higher and higher.

A huge fire blazed inside the actual classroom, sending warmth into the large space. A space that seemed to be cut from glass.

The room had windows fitted from top to bottom. Each wall was a sheet of colored glass depicting scenes that looked like pages from a storybook.

On one side, the glass was shaped to show a woman with sun-gold hair lounging under a tree in a dress as pretty as the night sky. On the opposite wall the glass showed a laughing man with black skin and dreadlocks fanning in the air around him. He was wearing nothing at all, but a roaring wave crashed at his feet, the spray *just about* covering his lower parts. The third one, in the middle between the man and the woman, showed a single, very familiar black beast with striking blue eyes.

She froze. In Libra, the temples showed the god of Death as a man with a hood always shadowing his features. But none of these figures were of the Manni she'd grown up praying to. The Libran temples must not know the real gods, she thought. The priests hadn't been to the shadow world. They hadn't looked Death in the face, because now she realized she'd seen Manni herself. And he wasn't a man. He was a beast.

The beast in the glass was watchful, its eyes an unnerving blue that seemed to see straight through her. Which was ridiculous because this was just glass. *She* was seeing through *it*. Yet she couldn't shake the feeling that she was somehow thrown back to the black desert, and Death was watching her again.

"Beautiful, isn't it?" Nadir came to her side. Adlai knew she was trying to be nice but beauty was the last thing she thought of when looking at the god of Death.

She gave a small smile back and looked around the rest of the room instead. Kanwar and the freckled girl from the desert were in the class, as well as two younger boys and an older woman with a ribbon of tattoos snaking along her arms and legs.

"Adlai Bringer." The woman beckoned her forward. "I'm Caster Shani, the instructor for the older levels. I understand you haven't had a great deal of instruction?"

"My father taught me," she said. She didn't add that he'd only taught her to steal, or that she'd heard voices from her shadow since coming back from the dead.

"Well, why don't we do a quick exercise and see where you're at?"

Adlai started. "Like a test?"

Shani tilted her head, perhaps sizing up Adlai's nervous energy. "I won't put you on the spot. We'll do it as a class," she said. Turning away, she clapped her hands and called the room to attention. "Everyone to me."

The two young boys came quickly, but Nadir was talking with the other girl and the pair seemed heedless of anyone else.

"Don't make me resort to embarrassing nicknames, Babbi," Shani said.

"Ma!" Nadir shot daggers at Caster Shani. She crossed the room with a scowl that made Adlai better see the resemblance between the instructor and her daughter.

Adlai swallowed. So this was Nadir's mother. The woman who had been friends with her mother. Class wasn't exactly the place to ask for stories about her and she wasn't sure how she would even approach the topic. Or if she wanted to know the answers. There had to be some reason for the stall owner's rudeness when she'd realized she was Leena's daughter.

"Farrin, Kanwar, you two as well." Adlai was brought back to the room as Shani gestured snappishly for the freckled girl and Kanwar to join them.

"Now then, class," she said, "we have a new student today. I expect you all to welcome her warmly. This is Caster Luth's niece, Adlai Bringer."

The girl, Farrin, smirked at Kanwar. "You won't be the best in the class anymore," she said. "We've got Luth's little niece now to show us all up."

"That's Caster Luth to you," Caster Shani said sternly. "And you're right. If Adlai is anything like her uncle, or mother even, then you're all going to have to work harder."

Kanwar was leaning against the wall. A strip of red light from the window pooled over his dark skin as he scowled at her, accepting the challenge.

Which was just great, after Caster Shani had promised not to put her on the spot.

She tensed as Kanwar moved from the wall toward her, his shadow already out in front of him, strong and impossibly black; it seemed to eclipse the light and everything it touched, concealing the very ground from view. Like her uncle, he radiated power.

Adlai didn't feel powerful. She felt like a thief who'd stolen something she couldn't sell.

He stopped two arm's lengths away from her and she took an instinctive step back. His shadow was smoking from the ground. Why was it smoking? Kanwar wasn't the only one with a smoking shadow. Farrin and Nadir had their shadows out too, both leaving the same flickering trail a few inches off the ground.

Caster Shani noticed her confusion.

"These three"—she pointed to the trio—"can travel with their shadows. That's how they were able to get to you in the desert and bring you here."

"Which wasn't exactly easy," Farrin said. She glared at Adlai. "You picked an annoyingly faraway place to get stranded." She side-eyed the teacher. "You'd think a rescue mission like that would mean we'd mastered the skill enough."

Shani smiled. "Unfortunately, your shadow shows otherwise." She looked at Adlai. "The wisps you're seeing are their shadows in the before state of travel. They should only be like that if the caster is about to travel. Not as a natural state.

"Now, how about we practice a different skill today?" Her voice became louder, addressing the two younger students as well. "Detection. I'm going to hide objects in your shadow, and you're going to tell me what they are."

Suddenly, a cold wind shot through the air. Adlai blinked, looking around for its source, but there were no windows open and the fire crackled on calmly.

"Look down," Caster Shani said softly. The comment was aimed at her, the only one confused in the class. Adlai made the connection. The coldness had come from Shani's shadow; she'd sent it over all of theirs so fast that Adlai hadn't even seen it, only felt it.

The other students were bent down, their hands feeling over their own shadows.

"What . . . what do you want me to do?" Adlai looked back at Caster Shani.

"Detect," Kanwar said. He glared up at her as though she were stupid.

Shani came over and put her arm on Adlai's shoulders, gently guiding her down and then passing her hand across her shadow. "Feel through your shadow and you'll see the object I've put in there."

Adlai shook her head. That was impossible. Not only had she not seen Caster Shani's shadow but there was no way anything had dropped into hers without her feeling it.

Her fingers brushed over her shadow hesitantly, as though afraid of finding teeth in the darkness ready to bite her. But there was only the cold and a sense of a deep, dark void shivering below the surface. She used to think of it as the perfect hideaway for the things she stole, but now it seemed to hum with a power that had a will of its own. Her fingers froze. A flash of something gold flickered in her mind, and for a moment she thought that maybe she had left one of her stolen goods in her shadow. But no, this was . . .

"Coins?" she said, confused.

"How many?" Caster Shani asked.

"I don't know."

"Keep searching then," she said, rising. Kanwar was already standing. He looked at Caster Shani.

"Mine is a chair. Metal wire back with a blue fabric covering," he said.

"Very good," Caster Shani said, smiling. "Does it have a pattern, this blue fabric?"

Kanwar frowned. "An outline of a face, I think. The eyes have ... flower petals for eyelashes." He said the last part like it was a bad taste in his mouth.

"Exactly so," she said. She winked at Adlai. "A very ugly chair I made myself."

The others were all starting to get up, each student detailing the strange object or objects their shadow had. Only Adlai remained on the ground, her hand no longer brushing but pressed firmly down against her shadow and searching for the image of those coins again. But they had dropped out of her reach. She closed her eyes and tried to block out how stuffy the room was becoming and the dizziness settling over her. The heat of the sun radiated through the glass windows.

This is mad, she thought. *How am I supposed to know what's in my shadow if I didn't put it in there myself?* It was like being given a box and being told to guess what was inside. An impossible riddle.

Her shadow shifted under her. Suddenly her hand was yanked further down, into the depths, and her face was brought inches from the dark. She was at the edge of a cliff, forced to look down. But even as she looked through her shadow, she didn't see what she was supposed to because it wasn't coins inside.

Two blue eyes stared back at her from inside of a beast's face.

Power has to be seized, child.

She gasped, pulling herself free and getting thrown back in the process.

"Adlai?"

She was lying on her back. Caster Shani and the others gathered around her with looks of confusion.

"Are you all right?" Caster Shani bent down beside her. Adlai sat up, shaken. Blinking, she saw that the other students had managed to get their objects out. Just behind Shani was the ugly chair Kanwar had described. There was also a stack of books, a marble rolling pin, a tea set, and a single shoe without the laces.

"I . . ." Everyone was staring at her. Even the damn chair had its eyes on her. "I couldn't see the coins again," she said finally. She couldn't tell them what she'd seen instead. The god of Death couldn't really be in her shadow. He couldn't really be talking to her. It had to be the shock of dying.

"We can't move on to the next task without the coins, Adlai," Caster Shani said. "Would you like a break? I can have the others start a new task while you take a breather."

Adlai shook her head. She didn't need to rest; she needed to take back control.

Power has to be seized.

She gathered her shadow to her, hand steady and determined.

Ignoring how tight her chest was and the weight of the stares, Adlai focused only on the coolness of her shadow. *Her* shadow. There was nothing else in there but coins. She imagined plucking each one out. She smiled. Relief flooded her as the familiar weight of coins filled her palm. It was hardly a fortune, two domes and six turns, but each coin sent a thrill through her as though she was holding precious jewels.

"Excellent." Caster Shani beamed at her. "Now to trick your partner."

Caster Shani paired the class up. Adlai had hoped to be with Nadir but was partnered with Kanwar instead. If possible, he looked even less happy about the pairing, and not for the first time she wished that Erikys had come to the class.

"Nadir, Adlai, and Jacs," Caster Shani said, "turn around. The rest, take an object. And mind, you can change them up. Take the cover off the chair, put a coin in the pages of a book. Do something or nothing, just as you please."

Adlai turned to face the window, squinting at the ghostly reflections to try and see what Kanwar was picking to hide in his shadow. She couldn't, of course. She would have to rely on her shadow doing as she wished, or for Kanwar to be unoriginal enough that she could guess.

But his face gave nothing away when it was time to turn back around. She took a breath and drew her shadow out. An icy feeling passed over her but she ignored it, standing more steadily than before. Inch by inch, she moved her shadow forward, toward his. She imagined his shadow as an object. Not something she wanted to steal, but a coat pocket, perhaps. A very large, smoking coat pocket. Inside was the shiny thing she needed.

Her shadow overlapped his and she stumbled suddenly from the physical pull her shadow attempted. As though it had wanted to pull his shadow into hers. Kanwar locked eyes with her. Anger flashing in them.

"What are you doing?" he snapped from across the room.

It felt like her shadow had tried to seize Kanwar's. She shook her head, bewildered. Clenching her hands into fists she forced herself to concentrate on the task. It wasn't his shadow she wanted but what was inside it. Images flashed through her mind: the chair cover, the cups from the tea set, the coins. Only these came to her in the normal way images came to mind—by *thinking them*. It wasn't the same as when she'd seen the coins in her mind's eye. That had been real. Something she'd known, like focusing on her heartbeat or hearing her own breath.

From the corner of her eye she saw that Nadir had retrieved two books and the shoe. Those could be eliminated at least. The other student was struggling like her though. She paused to see the young boy frown, mystified by whatever Farrin had hidden.

Turning back to Kanwar she saw him with his head cocked to the side, apparently bored of waiting.

Adlai redoubled her effort. She searched through the endless black, only his shadow was . . . well, it wasn't a coat pocket: it didn't have a bottom to it, she couldn't just slip whatever was inside of it out.

She eased her grip on her shadow, pulling it slowly back.

"I don't know," she said. She had the feeling she'd said that a lot in this class. "Did you stuff a rolling pin in a teapot?"

He glared at her. "A guess as idiotic as the idea."

From out of his shadow, he brought up two coins.

Her jaw clenched as she stared at them. Just two coins. He hadn't even tried to make it difficult for her. Had he chosen something simple because it was her first class, or because he thought that was her skill level?

If the latter, he was wrong. Her shadow was a mess. *She* was a mess, and she was far, far below that low bar.

14

The History of Shadows

ADLAI SEARCHED FOR ERIKYS AFTER class and finally found him lying in a hammock outside a building that was covered almost completely by books. Books were piled as high as walls around the door and more framed the windows. Erikys himself had a stack in easy reach on the ground below him.

"Enjoying yourself?" she asked, not quite able to mask the irritation at find him so relaxed. Pushing and tugging her shadow had exhausted her.

Erikys smiled over at her. "You look terrible," he said.

Her eyes narrowed and then settled on the book he was reading. "If you aren't interested in going to the classes, why are you reading a book called *The History of Shadows*?"

"Oh, this?" He slammed it shut. "Just a bit of light reading."

The book was leather bound and gleamed with gold-sprayed pages. So much gold as there were so many pages—it was thicker than Adlai's fist.

She didn't know how he hadn't fallen asleep; she felt tired from just looking at it.

"Will you come to class tomorrow?" she asked.

"After all the fun you look like you've had, I think I'll pass," he said. "I told you I'm not interested in using my shadow."

"Why not?" she cried, exasperated. How could he just ignore his shadow? Hers was a constant presence, like goose bumps creeping over her skin. "Your shadow is the reason we got out of the cells."

"And yours was the reason you were in one of them."

Adlai's jaw tightened. Erikys wasn't wrong, but he wasn't right either. He didn't understand.

It wasn't fair that he could just—

Her shadow clawed over the sands, becoming darker and larger as it pushed up from the surface. Adlai's mouth gaped open. She hadn't called her shadow out. And this . . . her shadow was huge and physical. It threw Erikys from the hammock, slamming him to the ground. Another thump and the book careened past his head.

"No!" Adlai pulled on her shadow and willed it to come back. Ice burned through her chest. She gasped and her shadow slumped down. It drew away from Erikys, not fully returning, but lingering between them like a faint, cold breeze.

"Erikys!" Adlai ran over to him. "Are you all right?" She knelt by his side, hands shaking and clammy as she tried to think what to do. Was he hurt? Should she check him? Would he even want her near him?

"I'm fine," he said. But he didn't sound fine. Erikys stared up at her, squinting like she was the sun and he couldn't see straight. He frowned. "Was that . . . did your shadow just push me?"

"I'm so sorry," she said. "I don't know what happened. I didn't mean to do it, I swear."

He sat up, his expression closed from dumb, numb shock until he looked at her again. This time he smiled. "What, not even a little bit? You sounded pretty annoyed at me before. Are you sure classes aren't teaching you passive-aggressive attack moves?"

A laugh escaped her. Nervous and shaky. "All classes have taught me is that I have a lot more to learn about my shadow."

"It's still out, Adlai."

They both turned to the pit of blackness cast over the sands. It was still moving. Slowly her shadow reached to where the book had fallen. It swirled around the book, creating a false wind that blew the cover open. Pages rustled back and forth until, suddenly, the wind ceased. Everything stilled.

"No. Shadows. Near. The. Books!"

An old man hobbled from inside the storykeep, raising his arm at Adlai. He looked to be in his seventies and was easily the oldest person she'd seen on the island.

Adlai yanked her shadow back. The book remained open where it was.

"That's Caster Fecks," Erikys muttered to her. "He's a bit particular about his books."

Caster Fecks had thin white hair grown down past his shoulders and a slightly pinched face. He wore two black hoops on his left earlobe, which sagged as though it couldn't hold the weight of a third. But his eyes were sharp behind their spectacles as they looked at Adlai. It was a look she'd seen from others on the island. A cold, distrustful look that made her feel guilty of stealing something she hadn't.

"You must be Leena's girl," he said. "Yes, yes"—he confirmed it himself—"you have her look and her penchant for wayward shadow use."

Adlai wasn't quite sure what he meant, but it didn't sound like a good thing. She picked up the book, keeping the page it had opened out to. It was of a large illustration. One that was eerily similar to the window display in the classroom. A man, a woman, and a beast were depicted, but in this drawing the three of them came with titles. The man was called the Creator of Worlds, the woman was Taker of Lives, and the beast was Collector of Souls. They were all linked with a tree and the text "The Death Trio" floated above them.

"What's a Death Trio?" Adlai asked.

"The three gods of Death," Fecks answered matter-of-factly. "Manni, Kintesia, and Prisaant."

Adlai raised her brow. "There's only one god of Death." *I've seen him*, she thought, *I've heard him*. But the black beast was a detail of her death and revival she hadn't told anyone about.

Caster Fecks snatched the book up, his back creaking at the effort, and peered back at her. "Well, the kingdom might preach that there are six gods and six goddesses. The balanced twelve. But the truth is there are two more. Our powers wouldn't exist without them."

"Shadows come from gods?" Erikys asked.

"From Kintesia and Prisaant, yes."

Fecks shook his head and gestured for them to follow him closer to the storykeep, where outside there was a large rock. He sat down on it and carefully placed the book next to him.

"They were gods who fell in love with the mortal realm. With life," he said. "Unexpected for a god and goddess of Death, but there you are."

Adlai shook her head. "You're saying the gods came here? They can leave the shadow world?" If the black beast she'd seen was Manni, the god of Death, then the idea of him flying through these skies was terrifying.

"All gods can come to the mortal realm. How else to interfere with us? We don't see them bobbing around because what they do is subtle and of the spirit, not the flesh." Fecks tapped the book. "Ah, but it wasn't that way for Kintesia and Prisaant. Those two lived here. They fell in love with mortals, had children . . . did it over and over again because it's not in a god's nature to die. And yet with each new generation the gods began to age. Slowly, very slowly, they lost their powers as those powers were transferred down their bloodlines. It was a loss a generation at a time. With each child they had, and each child their children had, and so on and so on, because each child took from them a piece of their power. A piece of their godhood. It fell into their shadow, becoming what we have today."

Adlai shook her head. Caster Fecks spoke like he was reading a tale from one of his many books, but the story couldn't be true. "You really believe our shadows come from them? From forgotten gods?"

"Not forgotten by everyone. Your own shadow opened this book to the exact page that shows its own origin." Fecks looked up at her curiously. "We hold but a fraction of the power a god has, and yet I do believe some have a larger share than most. Your family, for one, has had many great displays of power."

"You mean my uncle?" She hadn't spent much time with her uncle; she'd seen him for meals, but not much in between. He hadn't lied when he'd told her he would be busy most of the time. But when she was around him she felt . . . well, she felt something unnatural about him. Power, maybe. Nadir had told her the earrings casters wore reflected their power, and her uncle wore five earrings, which was more than anyone else she'd seen, more than the four Caster Shani wore, and she was the instructor. It had to mean he was very powerful.

Caster Fecks shifted uncomfortably. "Luth is our leader because of his mastery. But it was your mother I was thinking of."

"You knew her when she was here?"

When Adlai had been part of a family.

"Well, your mother was never on this island. We lost Leena on the last settlement," he said.

Erikys drew away, but Adlai leaned in closer.

"Then you knew her there?" Her desperation was obvious and embarrassing, but she waited, hungry to know more about the woman who was nobody to Adlai and should have been everything.

"If you want to know about something, you don't read just one book," he said at last. "It's the same with people. Pick five different people here to tell you about your mother and you'll get five different stories."

"And what story would you tell?"

"The one that warns you to pay attention in class. Leena was gifted, but her shadow did things it had no right doing."

Sickness crawled in Adlai's stomach. Erikys had retreated further away, but she could feel the weight of his stare.

"What kinds of things?"

"Not the kind I like to talk about." He sighed. "Leena . . . she wasn't a bad person. As I said, you can ask around about her and you'll hear different accounts of the kind of woman she was. Many of them good ones. But it wasn't just that her shadow was powerful. Luth has a powerful shadow and we trust him." Caster Fecks sighed again. "If she'd been able to control it, she could have done great things for us all. Perhaps she could have learned. Perhaps she was close to her own kind of godhood."

<hr />

"ADLAI!"

Erikys was calling after her, but Adlai kept going. Caster Fecks hadn't told her of anything her mother had done, but it was through the way he talked about her that she understood her mother's powers weren't something to desire. That her powers might even be something to have feared.

Like her own shadow was becoming.

It made sense now.

The cautious looks from her uncle, from the woman with the stolen goods, and from Caster Fecks when he'd first seen her with her shadow out. They weren't sure if her shadow would turn out to be like her mother's. Was that why her father had taken her away? To quarantine her from their kind?

"Adlai, stop." Erikys caught up and grabbed her arm. She flinched and he held out his hands in a peace gesture. "It's okay."

"No, it isn't," she said. "Didn't you hear him? My mother didn't have control of her shadow, and mine just attacked you."

He raised a brow. "Do I look hurt?"

He didn't. His skin was smooth and eyes warm as he looked down at her. Her breathing hitched under his steady gaze, and she turned away.

Without intending to she'd led them to the beach. A sight so beautiful some of Adlai's tension rolled off her. The sun was setting and the sky had soft hues of blue and pink and orange that dripped down into the sea to make a wrinkled reflection that went on and on.

"No," she answered. A wave rolled over the sand. Lazy. It touched her toes and was gone again with a sigh. She stared down at the wet sand where the water had just been. The shells in the sand looked so clean, so perfect. "But I could have hurt you."

"If you think your shadow is dangerous, why keep using it?" he asked.

Adlai frowned. Her shadow wasn't something she could ignore. It was a constant presence, even more so lately.

"I have to learn to control it," she said.

"But if you never use it again. Say there was some way of getting rid of it. You could surely think of something else you'd want to do. A life without shadow or thieving. Something ordinary?"

"Oh." Adlai looked out to the ocean again. She couldn't believe how vast the water was. How did it not reach all the way to Libra? It shouldn't have taken her seventeen years to see something so huge.

"I guess I'd want . . . I'd want a stall of my own," she said finally. "Not in the desert market. My stall would overlook the sea. And I'd sell necklaces made of shells, scarves prettier than a picture book, and perfumes so sweet you'd want to eat them."

He laughed and bent down to pick up a tiny shell that fanned out around a golden blush. He placed it in her palm, fingers tracing over the shell's ridge.

"For your wares."

His fingers left hers and she closed her hand around the small shell.

"And you?" she asked. "What will you do?"

Erikys grinned. "The sea is nice. But I want to move around a bit. Maybe I've got a taste for traveling under the stars."

She scoffed. "You want to be a Cannie?" she said, thinking of the Cancen people that traveled all over the kingdom claiming the sky was their roof and no land could be owned.

"Well, maybe a better-dressed nomad. You never know who you might meet on an adventure."

His eyes found hers and she realized how glad she was that the boy in the cell opposite hers had been him.

All her life she'd prayed to Himlu for luck and even on her un-luckiest of days, the trickster god had thrown her in the path of an-other shadow caster. Someone who had saved her life as much as she'd saved his; who came by smiles so easily and who wanted to know her dreams.

Would he understand her nightmares? Would he listen if she told him she'd seen the god of Death and that his voice might be clinging to her shadow still?

"You don't like to use your shadow," she said. "Is it because you're afraid of it?"

"I'm not afraid of my shadow or yours." His words were soft, kissing the air in front of her. She swallowed as he leaned down a breath further. "Your family could have the powers of all the gods and I don't think I could ever be afraid of you, Adlai Bringer."

He pulled away and the sky darkened. She clutched at the shell in her hand, unsure if she wanted him close again or if she was glad of the space.

She didn't think she could be like Erikys, but she wanted to be. She wanted to be fearless. She wanted to forget what it had felt like to die, to go back to seeing Manni as the faceless god figure she could light a candle for and be done with. She wanted her shadow to be hers again.

And to never again hear the growl of Death's voice.

15

Dead Again

SINCE REUNITING SUBJECT 187 WITH his shadow, Dressla had resurrected him a number of times but the subject was proving difficult to work with. She was used to this, though she had hoped to be getting different results by now.

"You've already tried the door," she called out to the subject. He'd tried escaping through the window too, which was not a typical escape route; they were so high up the fall had killed him before he'd hit the ground. If he went through the door again it would be either Bosma or Corwyn who would deal with him.

Likely Corwyn, she thought, as the young boy seemed a little overeager with his knife and was certainly keen on impressing her. Either way, there was no escape.

The subject didn't answer. Instead he grabbed one of the containers, an expensive one made of crystal, and smashed it against a metal table. The container had at least been empty. The shards fell to the floor and he picked out the largest piece, an ugly splintered thing, and pointed it at her as he backed away to the door again. Corwyn had heard the noise and came rushing inside with his knife flashing. She shook her head at him.

"Let him pass," she said. It was important that the subject learn his limits.

The boy did as she asked and left the room. Dressla looked back at the subject; he was gripping his makeshift weapon so hard it cut into his palm. *Such a waste of blood.*

There was extra desperation in this escape attempt, she thought. He hadn't made himself a weapon before. But she wondered if escape wasn't his only goal. On his way to the door, he looked down at each of the other subjects he passed. They remained hidden under their covers, but their plaques identified them. Perhaps he was using this time to search for his wife or other friends of his. He might even be making a mental note of how many subjects were collected and the way they were stored.

She smiled at the idea that this man might be thinking of not just freeing himself, but freeing the hundreds of other subjects they had stored. A ridiculous notion, and yet he was the "Mystery Man"—the shadow wielder they'd captured without a shadow seven years ago.

Now she knew that shadow had been with his daughter all this time.

It was the kind of puzzle she enjoyed the most. First, because she alone had solved it. And second, because it meant that shadows didn't have to be forcibly taken; they could be freely given.

Her interesting subject passed the others and came to the exit again.

This time Bosma was the one who engaged him. Her old guard was still quick in his reflexes and remained efficient. He spun into the chest of the subject, grasping his arm and twisting the makeshift weapon out of his hand. Overpowered, the subject gasped in pain, staggering down to the ground.

"Enough," she commanded.

With a polite nod, Bosma let go of the subject and returned to his post, his breathing only a little haggard by the effort.

But the subject remained collapsed on the ground. He stared up at the ceiling with a blank look on his face. The cut on his hand was still bleeding slightly, though he showed no sign of noticing, no sign of emotion, not even one of defeat.

It was a ruse, she knew. After this many resurrections, she'd come to understand that this subject was never simply still. He was always anticipating his next move, and the most frustrating thing of all was the feeling that she never quite had his full attention. Even when it was her with the blade in her hand.

Dressla stared down at him.

"The doors and windows are fitted with suraci metal," she said. "Your shadow never crosses with you when you try to escape, so it is simply not in your interest to get past my guards. If I allowed Corwyn to use that knife—and believe me, he isn't shy about it—then you would die. Again. Perhaps permanently, as you seem to assume I will always return your shadow to you. Such generosity is not typical of me, I assure you."

The subject smiled. His waxy skin had been missing the sun's touch for too long and his smile sent a shiver down her spine.

But it was foolish to be afraid of these people. In the cold chamber, she was in control.

"You've seen me die a few times now," he said. "Do I look like I fear it?"

She scowled. "Death has had no consequences for you yet. But it can. Next time, I might decide to burn your body."

The subject paled even more. "You burn us?"

That was better. He might not care about himself, but he had a wife here, and he must know it was only a matter of time before his daughter was collected too.

"When a subject has no more use, then yes." She cocked her head and watched him squirm a while longer. "Do you have a use?"

The subject sat up and stared at her with such burning hatred that for a moment she thought he might spring up and attack. If he did, she had faith her guards would deal with him before he got too close. She was perfectly safe.

They are my *subjects.*

"I can't tell you things I don't know," he said.

Finally she had his full attention.

"Come," she commanded and forced herself to turn away, exposing her bare back to him as she walked further into the cold chambers.

He followed. Slowly. Glancing over her shoulder, she saw his gaze pass over the walls as though he could see the suraci metal through them. He did, however, find where his shadow was trapped. It was a faint casting, caught at the border of the door.

"I'd prefer you shadowless for the moment," she said, making no move to collect it. It would make him uncomfortable to be without it and she preferred him this way. "Will you sit?"

Dressla had prepared two chairs by a half wall that sectioned off the room from the tables of bodies. Her researchers used the space for lunch breaks; there were cupboards, a stack of chairs, a table and even a bench that could accommodate more researchers than she had on her team. In the days past, the teams had been large in numbers and small in accomplishments. Another thing she had changed.

She sat down first and crossed her legs; her long skirt shimmered in the pale light and she angled herself in a relaxed position. As though she had all the time in the world.

The subject didn't sit. He stared over the low wall and surveyed the many gray coverings running in seemingly endless lines. This time she was sure he was wondering which one contained his wife,

Subject 179. He wouldn't find her. Subject 179 was one of the danger-ous ones that she never resurrected without several equitors in the room with her.

"What do you want?" he asked. Already he was starting to trem-ble, a side effect of being without his shadow for the moment.

"I think you must be aware that it took us some time to locate your shadow," she said. "You've been a rather strange case. Subjects don't usually arrive here without their shadow."

The subject turned to her and said nothing. Watching him, she felt an excitement akin to that feeling she'd had when she'd first started working for Arbil. Back then she had thought she might change the world with the discoveries she made here.

"When I first started working for Arbil," she said slowly, "my predecessor, a very tiresome man, rotten inside and out, thought to play a joke on me. He led me into this room for a tour of the place. Me, that is, and another woman. I remember being surprised that they'd hired not just one woman but two of us. Truly astonishing!"

The subject didn't turn around, yet she could tell he was listen-ing. She had his attention still, and it was a little intoxicating after so many failed attempts.

She continued: "My predecessor was talking us through the equipment we could expect to use. Explaining how to collect the shadows, what materials worked best with what, the processes cur-rently being used . . . I'm thinking how amazingly dull he's making everything sound, when the work certainly is anything but. Then he gets one of the scalpels out of a drawer and demonstrates cutting through shadow."

Dressla uncrossed her legs and leaned forward, "You can't re-ally cut shadow, but it does respond. The woman next to me, she was young and attractive and had been trembling like a scared little rabbit the entire time. Now she cried out. I thought it was from the way the old man was staring at her, or from seeing the shadow move in such an unnatural way. How silly, I thought. Already I was feeling superior. Then the joke came."

The subject turned her way. She saw his body tense. The cut on his hand was no longer bleeding but had left a dark red smudge on the half wall where he'd gripped it. He wanted to hear the end of the story. She allowed the pause to lengthen.

"What was the joke?" he asked at last.

She waved a hand. "The other woman wasn't a colleague. She was a subject. He stabbed her with the scalpel. I watched her bleed out, only for the wound to heal before my very eyes. It was a thrilling sight. Of course, my old boss had been intending to frighten me away. To put me in my place. But it had the opposite effect."

Seeing the Mystery Man look down at her, his handsome face coiled in disgust, was novel in a way she hadn't felt in a long time. Here was someone who had done something she hadn't thought possible with his shadow. The more she unlocked from him, the closer she came to achieving the impossible.

"You kill us for entertainment," he said.

"Is that what you got from the story?" Dressla shrugged. "Well, I can't deny my predecessor may have done so on occasion. And since you don't stay dead, I suppose he didn't consider it killing."

She gestured around the room. The fabric of her dress was near reflective and the beading glistened as she moved. "I'm no longer taking orders from a cruel man. I want you to feel that this room is yours as much as it is mine. You just have to stay inside of its confines and understand that this research, it's my life's work. There is so much I wish to discover. Every subject is very dear to me, and the most puzzling ones, such as yourself, are even more precious."

"What was the woman's name? The one your boss killed?"

Dressla sat back. "She was Subject 84. The research conducted at the time was almost exclusively on young women."

"Her name?"

"She was born a hundred years before you were. You didn't know her," Dressla said. Of course she understood what he was really getting at and added, "But you won't hear me say her name in any case, just as you won't hear me say yours."

The subject moved closer and rested his shaking hands on the top of the empty chair. Without his shadow she could see the effort it was taking to stay standing. He kept glancing back at the border where it was held, and his breathing was becoming unsteady. *He really should sit.*

"What difference can it make to someone like you to call us by our names? You would still carry on with your experiments. We'll never be people to you. Not while we have what you don't."

She laughed. "You're probably right," she said. "It helps me though, to label you properly. Numbers, I find, work best. Of course that doesn't mean we can't be civil." She gestured again to the empty seat.

He didn't take it, and the silence stretched on.

"Very well. But if you're to be useful to my research," she said, "I will need to know how your shadow transferred from you to your daughter."

He withdrew his hands from the chair and stepped away, as though distance could protect his secret.

"Shadows are genetic," he said simply.

She arched her brow. "True, there is a genetic component to your gifts, but you must know genetics don't apply in this case. A father might pass down his genetic code for dark eyes, for example, but he doesn't literally hand over his own eyeballs. Your shadow is yours. It should have been found on you after you died. Why did your daughter have it?"

He dropped his head and kept his secret a moment longer. She could feel the promise of it in the air and watched his lips as though preparing for a kiss.

The lips parted. A breath like a weight rolled out before he spoke. "Because I gave it to her."

She leaned forward. "How?"

"I don't know exactly."

Dressla pulled back sharply and he tensed.

"I was afraid. The trappers." He shook his head and corrected the slang term: "the *equitors* said they were only coming for me, but if she was going to be left alone . . . I didn't want . . ." He closed his eyes. "She didn't have her shadow out, she wasn't even really looking at me, but I could feel her shadow. It's like her mother's. It was as if it knew my fear—sensed my weakness." He opened his eyes. "I let it take mine. I didn't fight it. I hoped . . . I hoped my shadow would mask hers."

"Her shadow stole yours?" She thought for a moment. "Does she have all her mother's powers?"

He hesitated, the sadness on his face surprising her. "She used to hear Manni's voice. Like her mother did." He looked back at his shadow. "I think the god knows the extent of our powers and speaks to the ones that can do what others can't."

Dressla frowned. These shadow wielders were so immune to illnesses, she'd never thought they could get mad. But hearing the voice of a god?

She decided to sidestep it. Perhaps she could make a study of it once she had the girl as a subject.

"Well," she said, "I suppose it was very fortunate she was using your shadow when our equitors took her. It could have been even more of a bloodbath otherwise."

The subject whipped back around to Dressla. "She would never use that power. Not intentionally." He lost the fight over the dizziness he had to be feeling and slumped down in the chair. "Our shadows can do nothing for you. Every experiment you do is a waste of your time. You will never have what we have."

Other shadow wielders had said similar things to her. Usually with some cursing, but always with the same arrogance. They thought themselves special. Chosen by a god. It was like thinking being born beautiful made you better than all the people who put time and effort into their appearance. Or being born intelligent meant that no one could ever outsmart you.

Well, Dressla was naturally beautiful but still styled her hair and darkened her eyes. She was intelligent but still studied to stay on top of new discoveries. And although she hadn't been chosen by a god to live forever, she was working on that too.

"Death might work differently for you," she said slowly, "but its effect is the same: *You don't exist anymore*. You died, and now you are a subject in my laboratory. One of many. There is no getting out, there is no reunion with family, you will never return to the life you had before. The only miracles here are of my creation."

16

Should Have Stolen a Sock

ANOTHER CLASS ENDED WITH ADLAI dizzy and deflated. The lesson had been in shadow stealing. Not stealing things, but actually stealing shadow. It was a practice that was strictly taboo outside of the classroom and something she felt uneasy about doing, given how eager her shadow seemed to be to do it. But it was necessary to learn because it was a technique trappers used. The point of the class had been to build up a resistance, but all Adlai had built up was frustration, having spent a lot of the time staring daggers at Kanwar as he pulled and twisted her shadow away from her. When it was her turn, her shadow had reached for the two youngest students instead, grabbing both of their shadows at once.

Nadir took pity on her, linking her arm through Adlai's as they came down the curving stairs.

"I'll ask Mama to pair us up next time," she said. "Kan really goes too hard on you."

"Thanks, but I'm not sure he's the problem."

Kanwar's arrogance and superior skill set wasn't helping her confidence, but it was the fear of what her shadow would do (who it would lash out at next) that was stunting her progress.

A body pushed into her on the stairs.

"Are you coming, Nads?" Farrin didn't sound like she was asking a question, and she didn't look at Adlai as she spoke, but rather past her as though it was just her and Nadir on the stairs.

"Where?" Nadir asked. Her arm was still laced through Adlai's, and she had to have felt the knock.

"Our place."

Nadir shook her head. "Adlai's had a bad class. Why don't we all go for something to eat?"

"She always has a bad class," Farrin said. This time she did look at Adlai, her green eyes flashing in the dim light. "Nadir has a soft heart for weak things."

"I'm not weak, or a thing," she said. Adlai hadn't been weak when at ten years old she'd had to walk through the doors of the orphanage. She hadn't been weak when she'd used her shadow to steal in the market. Or when she'd pulled herself back from death.

And yet she wasn't strong either. Mother Henson's words had taunted her, the trapper had overpowered her, and she was undoubtedly the worst student in the class.

Farrin reached the bottom of the stairs before they did. Nadir offered for her to come with them again, but she cast a scornful look back at Adlai and left the temple.

"Don't mind her," Nadir said. "Farrin has four siblings, and being the only girl, she's quick to feel a lack of attention. She was the same when Kanwar arrived."

"Did she try to push him down the stairs too?" Adlai might have liked to have seen that. Kanwar was huge in comparison to Farrin's light figure, and hardly one to be intimidated by a brat.

Nadir laughed. "No. But she was very jealous for a while."

They came outside and Adlai took in a steadying breath. The sun was so much less intense here than it was in Libra. The heat didn't burn; it danced across the sea and came out cooler and sweeter in the breeze.

"The classes will get easier, the more you practice," Nadir said. "How were you using your shadow before?"

They were alone on the steep, rocky path back to the houses. Adlai hesitated. The Shadow Game had always been a secret, and although she knew casters used their shadows to steal when they left to get supplies, she wasn't sure what Nadir would think of petty theft. "I used to steal from the desert market with it," she said at last.

Nadir nodded slowly. "Okay . . . well, Caster Mai could have been a lot nicer to you the other day. Did you see anything you liked in her stall?"

Adlai stopped in her tracks. "You're not serious?"

Her dark eyes glittered. "I'll even distract her if you like."

A wide grin swept across Adlai's face. Playing the Shadow Game had always filled her with excitement. It was the time when everything was in Adlai's reach. In her control.

Could she trick her shadow into stealing if she wanted it badly enough? Would it fall into old habits?

Nadir went to Caster Mai's stall by herself. Adlai hung back, hidden by the cluster of rocks that began the steep path back to the temple. It was a far distance away. Mai's bright orange tent shone like a beacon to her, but she could only see hints of a rail of clothing and a table with an odd assortment of shapes. She would never have let her shadow stretch that far in the desert market. She wasn't sure it would have been possible before, but now . . .

As she brought out her shadow, she felt the weight of its power roll down the hill. Her shadow was a part of her, but it was different since leaving the shadow world. Stronger. The power of a god, according to Caster Fecks.

She swallowed.

Her shadow had *the power of a god*. She would never be able to harness that kind of power. She'd been lucky to steal with it in the past.

No. She was playing the game today. She didn't even need to see into the stall to know what she wanted. She'd seen the item on that first day Nadir had shown her the stall. Behind Caster Mai on the railing had been a dress. The top had been the color of the sky with billowing sleeves that went from pale blue to white to completely sheer. The skirt was long and ruffled and melted from yellow into orange with the hint of red in its hem. It was day turning into a sunset, and she wanted it.

So she was going to get it.

She pushed her shadow out. It was a long stretch to reach the tent, but Adlai felt strangely calm. It was like being back at the desert market, where stealing had always been second nature, a simple flex of her shadow. As if her shadow was an extension of her arm. With it, she touched the cloth of the table, fingered a jewelry stand with earrings raining down, and glimpsed the shell necklace she'd also wanted.

But she moved her shadow away from these things.

The rail had an array of clothing. Heavy jackets, silk shirts, and finally, the soft breezy fabric of her dress slipped into her shadow.

She'd been quick. She'd been in control. And then ice shot through her shadow. Caster Mai was reaching into it, as the trapper in the marketplace had done. She felt the wrongness of her shadow being searched and yanked it back with a gasp.

Nadir was already running toward her. Adlai jumped out from her hiding spot and heard Caster Mai yelling something, but it was lost in the wind as they ran and ran and ran.

Further down the hill, they were laughing. Running, breathless and laughing. It was the magic of playing the game. They finally stopped by a brush of trees that opened out to more greenery. Everywhere was green and alive on the island: it was one big playground, and Adlai wished she could take a small patch of it back to the orphanage.

They sat on the grass. Nadir's face was sparkling. "Did you get it?" she asked.

Adlai brought her shadow out and pulled the dress from it. The colors dripped in the light and the fabric was as soft as sea foam in her hands.

"Beautiful," she said. Though Nadir was always wearing pretty dresses. Today was no exception. She had on a dark brown dress, just a shade darker than her own skin, that had orange beads forming flowers over her waist and fallen petals trailing down the skirt.

"Has my mother told you we used to play together as babies?" Nadir asked suddenly.

Adlai shook her head.

"I've been around enough of Farrin's siblings to know that probably meant we stared at each other and maybe pulled off the other's sock," she said. "But I know my mother was grateful to yours."

Adlai started. "To my mother?"

"It's hard being a single mother. At least that's what she's always telling me."

"Oh," Adlai said, understanding. "Did a trapper capture your father?"

Nadir's laugh was all the wrong notes, and her eyes were dead. "No, my father wasn't killed. He's probably still alive."

Adlai couldn't hide her surprise. Nadir saw it and explained: "He was a sunner."

"A sinner?"

Nadir shook her head. "Sunner. Sorry, it's a way of saying suncast. That's someone without shadow powers. You can't say shadowless because obviously they still have a shadow, it's just it only moves by the light." She shrugged. "He wouldn't have liked the person I grew up to be anyway. But he'll never know that, which means he'll always have regrets about it." She smiled. "I quite like the idea of him filled with regrets while I stop having them."

"He chose to leave you?"

It had been Adlai's fear for so long. That her father had decided to be free of her.

"He was afraid of our powers," Nadir said after a while. "And he didn't like some of my . . . choices." Her eyes flashed up to Adlai. "Farrin thinks I have a crush on you. I don't," she added quickly. "But she gets jealous."

Adlai pieced together what she was saying. Her eyes widened. "She's your girlfriend?"

Nadir nodded stiffly. Her soft, pretty features took on a hardness as if in preparation for something.

My reaction. She realized Nadir had opened up to her and she was just staring at her as if she'd never heard of such a thing. In truth she had seen a few same-sex couples in Libra, defying the lewd comments and the following stares. She'd always thought they were brave—and she'd always enjoyed stealing from the distracted, judging crowd.

"Well, she seems . . ." Adlai tried to think of something nice to say. Farrin hadn't exactly been friendly. And was apparently more than a little possessive. "Like a bit of a headache, honestly."

Nadir laughed. She lay back on the grass and Adlai could see the relief shining out from her.

"She is that. But she loves me, which is more than I can say of my father. He used to tell me I'd end up as one of the experiments in the Arbil pyramid. That I'd pay for my sins that way. Dead, but not dead."

"What?" Adlai went cold. "What are you talking about? What experiments?"

Nadir shot up and cursed herself. "Sorry. I shouldn't have said anything." She tugged at her braid. "Gods, I'm stupid. I should have stuck with staring at you and trying to steal a sock."

Adlai didn't hear her. Her mind ran over the words again.

Experiments. Arbil. Dead, but not dead.

"Why did you mention Arbil?"

That was a hospital. A shining, golden pyramid that people went to for healing.

Nadir shook her head, her gaze darting around for an escape. "You should talk to your uncle."

ADLAI SLAMMED OPEN her uncle's front door, her breathing heavy as she waited for him to appear.

But the house was dark and quiet. He wasn't home. Again.

He claimed he left for the protection of the island, or to help with supplies or some other noble thing. Now she wondered if any of that was true. What was her uncle really getting up to when he wasn't here?

She headed for his study, squinting suspiciously around every inch of it, but it was all so tidy and orderly. Handwritten notes contained day-to-day demands from other casters, scheduled meetings, and planned supply runs.

She crumpled one of the notes in frustration and moved on. Every room was more of the same nothingness.

Except there was one room she hadn't looked in.

Adlai spun around and went to the door that was next to her uncle's bedroom.

She bent down; the lock didn't seem too complex. A hairpin might do for it, she thought, and was moving away when she was startled by the noise of her uncle returning home.

"Adlai?" He called out. He hadn't seen where she was and she quickly rushed away from the door, out into the hallway.

Luth looked tired, his pale skin so much paler under layers of black clothing, as if he were wrapping himself in shadow. For a moment she felt pity for him, but then she remembered Nadir's words and it was a twist in the stomach. Her uncle was keeping secrets from her.

"Why didn't you tell me about Arbil?" she said sharply.

His eyes narrowed. Alert suddenly.

"Who have you been talking to?"

"Does it matter?" she asked. "Are my parents there? Is that where we're taken if a trapper gets us?" Her breathing was coming out in bursts and she clenched her hands into fists, afraid of the answers he might give.

Her uncle blinked at her questions. He sat on the edge of the woven sofa and his hands coiled around the wooden trellises. "It's where trappers train. And, yes, it's where our bodies are taken as well as our shadows."

"But why?" She drew toward him. Saw the lines on his face become more pronounced. "What do they need with our bodies?"

He shifted in his seat. His eyes flickered momentarily out to the hallway as if he was lost in some thought. When he spoke again, his voice was distant. "When you died, when any of us die, our bodies don't decay; they heal."

Her heart raced. She remembered having no wound on her neck after she'd come back to life. That was because of her shadow powers. And both her parents had shadows. Both of them had been taken by trappers.

"My parents . . . does that mean that they're not . . . that they can come back, like I did?"

"Their souls are in the shadow world, while their bodies and shadows are in Arbil. It is possible that they can return to the living."

He sighed. "My priority is to keep everyone here safe. But my hope is that we'll one day bring our loved ones home."

Bring them home. Adlai was speechless.

"I . . . you have a plan for us to get them out of there?"

"And this is why I didn't tell you before. I didn't want to give you false hope." He shook his head. "You couldn't handle one trapper, Adlai. You understand Arbil will be full of them?"

Shame burned over her skin like a rash. "I'll work harder," she said.

He looked at her sadly. "It's not always about working hard. Some people are just born stronger than others."

He wasn't counting on her being like him, she realized. She'd proven herself too weak in classes.

But even if she wasn't powerful, her uncle was. Caster Fecks had said he was more powerful than anyone had a right to be. So then he would bring her parents back. It was his sister, after all. And she'd met Yaxine in the shadow world. That had to mean his wife was in Arbil as well. His people.

"You said one trapper was as harmless as a bee's sting," she said.

He nodded.

"So Arbil is their hive. There must be a way to break it open."

Her uncle smiled at the thought. "There's nothing I want more than to tear down their walls, Adlai. If the gods are merciful, they'll show us the way."

17

A Golden Brick Giant

ADLAI DIDN'T WANT TO RELY on the gods; she wanted to get stronger, be a force to reckon with like her uncle. Only when she woke the next morning, the idea of class sent knots through her stomach. Kanwar would best her, Farrin would mock her, and she might hurt someone again.

She was a coward. And the house was too big and empty to stay in by herself. She needed to talk to someone.

Erikys was still living in the same house as Kanwar, the two of them barely speaking to each other, and the old couple who was supposed to take care of them was like many of the couples she'd seen coming to the orphanage. Kind, but better suited to adopting dogs than children.

Adlai knocked on the door and expected either Caster Tove or Caster Lossi to answer.

But Kanwar appeared and tilted his head at her. It was about time to be heading to class. She thought he would have already left but of course she had to be unlucky to catch him just as he was about to leave.

"Not going to class today?" He folded his arms across his chest, barely making it a question.

"Well I'm hardly here to buddy walk with you," she said.

It was enough that she kept getting partnered up with him during lessons.

Today she needed a break from it all.

She thought Kanwar might say something cruel back to her. But he looked behind him, presumably to where he knew Erikys was, and opened the door wider so that when he passed her they didn't so much as brush shoulders.

With a bit more light she saw Erikys eating breakfast in the kitchen and waved to him. He blinked at her in surprise and came over, still holding half a flatbread with yogurt spread on it.

"Don't you have class this morning?"

"It's as optional for me as it is for you," she said.

He smiled. A morning smile that was loose and easy. His curls were still ruffled from sleep and she realized, belatedly, that he was in his nightclothes, fabric that was a little too sheer in the morning light.

She stepped back.

"Why don't you finish breakfast, and other stuff, and I'll wait out here," she said.

He laughed. "Sure thing, little thief."

Erikys didn't make her wait long. He came out in the same green sleeveless top Penna had given him and black shorts. Adlai's mood had made her reach for a dreary gray wrap top and matching long skirt. All she had for comfort was the little shell Erikys had given her, tucked away in one of the pockets.

"So what's got you so eager for my company this morning?" he asked.

Instead of answering, Adlai started walking, setting a speed Erikys didn't attempt to match. With glances back she saw him following her with a bemused expression that only made her walk faster. She wanted to be free of the houses. Free of the community hall, the stalls, the storykeep. Free of the casters and their eyes.

When they reached a tangle of trees, Adlai slowed down and Erikys leaned against the bark of one.

"Are you going to tell me what's got you in this mood?" he asked.

She turned back. A flock of colorful birds swept into the sky.

"I found out yesterday that Arbil is not just a hospital." She was sweating from the walk and rubbed her hands against her skirt, finding they were trembling ever so slightly. Then she told him what Nadir had let slip, and what her uncle had confirmed.

"I'm sorry, Adlai," he said when she was finished. He came next to her and took her hand gently in his. "That's an awful thing to find out."

"Don't be sorry." She edged away from him. "Don't you see? My parents are in Arbil. They were so close all along." The number of times she had looked across the horizon and seen the golden pyramid staring back at her, never suspecting her family was there. "If we get them out, they can wake up, like I did."

"You want to break them out of Arbil?" Erikys took a step back, his face horrified. "It wouldn't be like that holding cell we were in. The building itself is the tallest one in all of Libra. A golden brick giant. It'd be like breaking into the palace."

"They're my parents."

Erikys held her gaze. They were an arm's length away from each other, but in that moment it felt as intimate as touching. Warmth, rather than pity, radiated from him, and she found herself closing the distance. As if it was the most natural thing in the world, she leaned her head against his chest. His arms, uncertain at first, wrapped around her.

"I can't leave them there. I have to save them." She sobbed. She hadn't intended to cry. She hadn't even known how many tears she'd been holding back, but once she started, she couldn't stop. They shook from her in wave after wave after wave.

Erikys held on to her, but inside she was falling, her mind racing through thoughts of what her uncle had meant. She had to become powerful.

Even when her tears dried up, she was still shaking. She sat down on the grass, leaning back against a tree and was glad that Erikys stayed close, coming down to sit by her. In silence they stayed that way; shoulder to shoulder, two weights keeping each other steady.

Her body finally calmed, and it wasn't until then that she trusted herself to speak. "In the desert, you mentioned a brother." She wiped at her cheeks with her palms. "Wouldn't you go to Arbil for him?"

Erikys shifted from her. As if he were uncomfortable with the thought.

"Of course I would," he said quietly. "But I'm supposed to protect him. He's my baby brother."

"What's he like?" She managed a grin. It stretched too wide on her face and she was sure she looked crazy. "Is he better-looking than you?"

Erikys laughed and she was glad, so glad she had someone to laugh with.

"Please. In what world is my baby brother going to be better-looking than me?" He cocked his head to the side, giving her his best angle. She could see the tiny stubble of a beard starting to grow and thought how ridiculous he would look with one. Like a man. But men were responsible and serious, and Erikys was as free as the wind, all boyish curls and charm.

"What's your brother's name?"

"Tian," he said. His gaze slipped through the trees, a softness curling through his voice. "He names all our livestock and makes us go through a day of mourning each time one of them has to be sacrificed. He somehow makes our mother's cooking edible. He can find new places to discover even though we've grown up around the same rocks and trees our whole lives. And he gets our father to smile, even on days the crops rot or the rains don't come as expected. He's the son they deserve."

Adlai frowned. "And you're not?"

"I'm . . . different."

"Because of your shadow? Your brother doesn't have one."

Erikys shook his head. "If he did, he wouldn't have been so sick."

Nadir had told her that not all of Farrin's siblings had shadows. That it didn't always pass down to every generation.

"But it isn't really a shadow thing," he said. "I just didn't want that life. I'm too restless. I even feel it here. Like wherever I go, I want to leave. Don't you ever get that feeling?"

Adlai nodded. "At the orphanage, every day." She hugged her knees. "But if my parents were here, I'd have a home."

He was silent for a moment. Palm leaves danced above them, flittering shadow back and forth. The sky was idyllic and calm.

"And what if you can't get them back?"

Adlai's face clouded over. "I don't know. As long as they're there, I have to believe it's possible."

Erikys brushed his hand against hers, and one of his fingers curled around hers. He smiled. "I've seen a lot of crazy things this last year. I even met a girl who came back from the dead. So I guess anything really is possible."

18

The Fifth Earring

ON ADLAI'S TENTH BIRTHDAY SHE rose early with excitement, not for presents or cake, but because she was going to play the Shadow Game on her own for the first time. She'd begged her father many times before, and now, finally, he thought she was grown enough.

So she chose to go to Second Skins, in the Low End of the desert market, where they sold precut clothes. Her own clothes were getting tighter and far too short in length.

A row of dresses in a rainbow of colors instantly grabbed her attention. As she looked them over, she saw a strawberry-red dress with yellow trim and a bow parceled around the neckline. It was a dress fit for a celebration.

Nervous and excited, she drew her shadow out. She was so sure of herself, already thinking of what to grab next. Maybe she would bring a gift for her father—a gold watch or a new cooking pot. But her shadow wouldn't move. A sudden dread filled her, and the busyness of the market seemed to hush to a whisper. She was cold. So very, very cold. Then a whisper took over.

What a fun game. Will you let me play, little child?

The voice didn't sound human.

She gasped as claws pressed into her shadow. Adlai's knees trembled and her resolve shook. She pulled her shadow back and ran.

She ran until she was home, and then she cried. She had nothing. Her skin itched as she told her father how her shadow had frozen and she'd heard the monster inside it.

"How do I get rid of it, Papa?" She looked up at him, hoping that now he would tell her she'd imagined it. Still just a child, he would think, and she wouldn't mind because nothing in her imagination could truly hurt her.

Instead, his face crumbled. So old, she thought. Her papa was getting so old.

"Your shadow is your own, Little Drizzle," he said, stroking her hair. "As much a part of you as your own arm, or your own mind. No one can take control of it. Not if you think of it like this and set your mind to what you want in front of you. Think of only that."

Her clothes stuck to her, dirtier than ever, and she thought back to the pretty dress and the ribbons she'd wanted to tie in her hair with bitterness.

"But I really *did* want that dress."

He smiled his crinkly smile and brought out her cake; a lemon egg, named for having as many eggs as lemons, and the one he'd picked was especially large. Too large for the two of them, but he cut her a big wedge.

"It's easy to get distracted," he said soothingly. "We can want many things. Sometimes our eyes are bigger than our appetites. Have you heard that saying?"

Slowly she shook her head.

"Well, it's true. Always focus on the thing in front of you. Too many desires can . . . be confusing for your shadow." He looked at her steadily, his brow arched. "Do you want this cake?"

The golden sponge with its bright yellow icing beckoned to her. She nodded.

"Then try again." Yet he held out a quick hand, covering the cake slice for a moment. "But, Little Drizzle, if you ever hear that voice again, do what you did this time and don't ever answer it."

With her father a few steps from her, Adlai brought out her shadow with ease. It swept over the slice and it was hers. When she picked it out again it was as cold and sharp as an icicle but delicious. It was her first taste of knowing what she wanted and getting it herself.

"WHAT WOULD YOU like to do for your birthday tomorrow?"

Her uncle was around for breakfast that morning which was a surprise in itself, but the mention of her birthday stopped Adlai in her tracks.

"I don't celebrate my birthday," she said and went for her normal bowl of oats, hoping he'd drop the subject.

"Eighteen isn't significant, perhaps," he said, "but I'd like for us to do something."

She looked at him from across the counter. The important birthdays were celebrated every five years of a person's life. With a pang she remembered her tenth birthday, and yet there was something muddled about her memory of that one. She'd lost her father a few weeks later; the whole year was a painful blur and she didn't wish to remember it. Pen had tried to make her fifteenth special, but Adlai had decided by that point that birthdays without family meant nothing.

"Well, even if you don't wish to celebrate, there must be something you want," he insisted.

"I'd like to not go to class," she offered.

Luth frowned at that. "Why would you want to risk falling further behind?"

Adlai shrank at his words. She was still the worst in the class. Her last impressive stunt had been stealing the dress from Caster Mai's stall.

"Perhaps this will improve your mood," he said, and took out a small black box with a white ribbon tied around it. "You were due this anyway, if you'd rather it not be a birthday gift. I had them made for you."

Adlai put down her spoon and reached for the non-birthday gift. She pulled away the ribbon slowly and opened the lid.

Inside were ten small, hooped earrings. The bottom ones were silver and the top an obsidian black. They were beautifully crafted with details on each of the hoops. Adlai looked up at her uncle, who wore all five black hoops along the top of his left ear. He was still the only one she'd seen wear five.

"What does each one mean?"

She knew they were related to skill level but these ones all looked so unique, each seeming to tell a story in their markings.

"This one," her uncle pointed to the first in the silver line, where a small hand grabbed around the hoop, "is yours to wear straight away. It means you can steal with your shadow."

The next one had a skull mounted in its center.

"You can also wear this one," he said. "It's for those who can use their shadow to bring themselves back from the dead. Not everyone will have one of these, because it's not a skill we like to test, for obvious reasons."

Adlai traced the skull, bumpy over her thumb, and she shivered. It seemed a dead thing in her hands somehow.

"Now this next one is a very useful skill," he said, pointing to the third hoop. It had an arrow pointing through it, which her uncle told her was for when she could travel. "And this one is a difficult one to master but useful if you come across a trapper."

The fourth earring was striped, like a snake was wrapped around it. Her uncle told her it was for when she could pull some-one's shadow to her, or resist her shadow being pulled from her.

The last one, the fifth, had a blade hanging from it.

"What's that one for?" she asked.

"That . . . is the least common one," he said.

He didn't elaborate. She wondered if it was a power her mother had had. If it was the reason some people seemed to have feared her shadow as much as they respected Luth's. "How many of these did my parents wear?"

"Your father, three. He was the most skilled with the first one," Luth said. Adlai felt disappointed. Three seemed to be the average and she didn't like to think of her father as average. Her uncle continued: "But Leena wore five. People said it was because we were twins that we were so equally matched." He smiled. "The truth was, your mother was not my match. She was far stronger."

SHE ENTERED THE classroom more miserable than when she'd woken up, and without any of the earrings her uncle had given her. The two powers she had seemed so insignificant. She was just a thief who'd cheated death. Her own mother had mastered all five powers and yet she'd died.

For all the power people seemed to think her mother had, it still hadn't saved her.

"Adlai!" Nadir came up to her immediately. "I'm so glad to see you here," she said breathlessly. "When you didn't turn up yesterday,

I thought it was because of me and what I said about . . . about Arbil. I really wasn't thinking."

"It's okay," Adlai said. Though Nadir wasn't wrong. She hadn't come to class yesterday precisely because of what she learned about Arbil. She'd been tempted to miss this class too and wasn't sure if she might have made a mistake coming back.

To make the class worse, Caster Shani partnered Adlai with Kanwar again and told them they'd be working on shadow resistance—the fourth earring, the skill that drained her the most.

She swallowed hard as Kanwar stood facing her. His face was unreadable and his eyes almost as dark as the trapper's had been in the desert market. Two black coals. The trapper had pulled her shadow toward him as though it had never been Adlai's shadow to begin with. Ripped it like the label was wrong on her.

Kanwar didn't bend down as the trapper had. If anything, he stood taller. Smoke from his shadow rolled over him and veiled his dark green tunic, embroidered as fine as any prince's.

"Have you been practicing?" he asked. His tone made it obvious that he knew she hadn't been. She gritted her teeth, recalling Caster Shani's teachings instead.

Caster Shani had told them to resist the pull by gripping tight on the connection with their shadow. To focus on it like it was a part of their body and let its weight fill the ground. *Weight. Heaviness.* Her shadow a rock, falling deep down into the ground.

Adlai thought these things, but she didn't feel them. Kanwar already had the fourth earring; the twisted silver glistened at the top of his right ear. Her shadow broke from her. It rushed to Kanwar. Like a rug pulled from under her feet, she was down on the ground, a wave of sickness crashing over her. Without her shadow she was disorientated. It was a shock like losing a limb, and the lack of power made the pain of the fall that much worse. She hurt from the inside out and didn't want to get up again.

Footsteps. A shadow loomed over her. She stared up at Kanwar's face; his mouth was curled down in disgust. Disgust for her, she realized. In one quick movement he returned her shadow, the way someone might throw coins down to a beggar.

"Do you even try?"

The pain and sickness left her. Power rushed back, like air filling her lungs again. Her body was sharp, on edge. She stood up and moved within inches of him. He didn't back away, but neither did she. They stood staring at each other for a beat longer.

"What exactly is your problem?" she said at last.

A secondary sense told her the attention of the class had shifted to them.

"My problem," he said, low and steady, "is that I have to share class with someone who only knows how to steal. If you bother to turn up to the class, that is." He was almost a head taller and looked down at her like she was the smallest thing in the world. "Your shadow will never burn. You and Erikys are no more than petty thieves hiding away from city guards. He's told me himself he's just waiting to go home."

Wherever I go, I want to leave. Adlai remembered Erikys's own words to her. She stepped back, a strange dizziness hitting her. There was ringing in her ears and a million thoughts chasing around her head, but her body seemed to slow. She blinked. The room had gone so quiet.

Erikys really was thinking of leaving. Would he go back to his family, or would he leave them behind as surely as he would leave her?

"I don't . . ." Her voice trailed off. Adlai didn't have a home anywhere.

All she had was Penna in Libra. And if Erikys left her here, then all she'd have was her new, still timid friendship with Nadir. Her uncle was so rarely around. She was alone.

He crossed his arms. "You know everyone talked about you coming. The daughter of Caster Leena. The niece of Caster Luth. Caster Shani even warned me I might not be the best in the class anymore. Your power would surely eclipse all of ours." He smiled, handsome and cruel in the same gesture. "I suppose you take from your father. He really was just a thief, wasn't he?"

Her attention was focused on Kanwar, but her vision blurred.

There was no smoke, no black fire. Her shadow moved as it always did: a stretch like her arm reaching out. Only the motion was stronger somehow. She had found muscles she didn't know she had. It felt *good* to move. All the fear and tension she'd felt with her shadow was gone.

This was freeing. This was right.

As though she was looking through a distorted lens, she saw Kanwar bend suddenly to his knees. How strange, she thought, but pushed the thought aside. She enjoyed the feeling of standing over him. She felt powerful. The air was light and charged with the same coolness that seeped through her. In that moment, she could do anything. Kanwar was the insignificant bug, and she was . . . she was magnificent. She was in control of not just herself, but of everything around her.

Thump, thump, thump. Her shadow pulsed with the rhythm. Quicker and quicker it raced, like there was a heartbeat knocking against her shadow. It felt like some wild bird caught in a trap, so small and afraid in the dark.

Kanwar clutched at the ground desperately. He was trying to pull her shadow from him but his grip was weak, and her shadow was large. She let the darkness swarm him.

"Adlai!" She heard someone shouting her name. There were flashes of movement around her, but it all seemed so unimportant.

Cold laughter ran through her shadow.

Very good, little girl. It's no more than he deserves.

Thump . . . thump . . . th-ump. The heartbeat weakened. Then stopped. The great wave of power she'd felt rise up inside her was calm and her mind slipped slowly into blackness.

19

Eighteen

ADLAI WAS COLD WHEN SHE woke up. She was lying on top of her bed, fully dressed, and she wasn't alone. Her uncle sat in the desk chair facing toward her. He was reading one of the books that had come like pretty decoration for her room. She saw the glitter of gold stars running up the book's spine as he snapped it shut.

"How are you feeling?" he asked.

"I'm not sick," she said.

Or was she?

Adlai couldn't remember what had happened, only that she'd been in class trying to use her shadow and, just like when she was a kid, she'd passed out from overdoing it.

Weak. She was always too weak for what she wanted to do.

"No, you're not sick, Adlai." Her uncle put the book away and came to sit on the end of her bed. "Drained and tired, perhaps? I fell into shivers the first time myself."

Adlai pushed herself up and looked across at him. "Did I travel?" Her heart quickened. Had her shadow brought her here, she wondered? She hadn't been thinking about her bedroom, but maybe for traveling the first time it was the easiest place to go.

"You didn't travel," Luth said, dampening that idea. "You did something far more interesting. Around here, I'm the only one with that power." He smiled. "*Was* the only one."

"What power? What are you talking about?"

"You were angry at Kanwar, so I hear," he said, not quite answering her. "I've spoken with him and he holds you no ill will of course. He's glad, as I am, that another of us has the gift." He saw her growing frustration and put his hand over hers. "If you think hard enough, you'll remember. It's a rather hard thing to forget."

But Adlai's mind was blank. Her heart was racing and when she tried to think back, cold sweat crept over her skin.

"I don't . . ." She stopped. She could see Kanwar kneeling on the floor, her shadow swarming around him—and this feeling . . . a feeling of power. *Dominance.* It had seemed as though she'd had his life beating in her hands.

Sickness curled in her stomach. His life *had* been in her shadow. She'd felt it, and she'd crushed it.

Her uncle squeezed her fingers. It was the most tender he'd been with her, but Adlai couldn't stop herself—she leaned away and vomited over the side of the bed onto the cream rug below.

I sent Kanwar to the shadow world. I killed him.

Even though he had a shadow and clearly had come back with it, she knew what that felt like. To die. To have to pull yourself back to the living.

Luth murmured something to her but she wasn't listening. All Adlai wanted was to crawl under the sheets and pretend she was back in the desert market. Back where her shadow was a thing of wonder, an extension of her father that could slip and steal anything she wanted. Now she wished she could rip her shadow out of existence. She never wanted to use it again. Not to steal. Not to travel. She didn't want to discover any other tricks, because now she understood why her father had told her she could only teach it one trick.

He hadn't wanted her to learn that her shadow could kill.

———

HER UNCLE HAD cleared away the rug and left her to sleep. When she woke again it was the middle of the night. Shakily, she decided to get out of her day clothes and into her nightdress. Her breath stank and she went to the bathroom to freshen up.

She was about to head back to bed but saw movement down the hall. Her uncle was still awake.

He smiled at seeing her.

"I got these out for you," he said.

On the coffee table was a box filled with scraps of paper, but instead of words, the papers were all filled with pictures.

She recognized her father in a pencil drawing that didn't flatter him at all. It was rough looking, and yet it captured something about him. Maybe it was in the crooked smile or the way his eyes seemed to be looking elsewhere.

"Those are your handprints," Luth said, pointing out a framed picture of several manic handprints smudging the paper. They were tiny and pink. "Except that one. The big one in the middle is Leena's."

Adlai took the frame and sank down on the sofa. Her mother had used the same pink paint, but her handprint was firmer, as though she'd pressed hard to ensure every part of her hand made it to the print. Adlai's own hands were scattered all over the place, but she couldn't stop staring at the ones that touched her mother's. They were half prints, and Adlai imagined her mother pressing down while Adlai's small hand ran riot over hers. They'd done this together.

She'd missed having a mother before. Usually the feeling came when she saw other people with theirs, but she had never missed the person that was her mother.

Her mother was abstract. A kindly figure she'd invented with no real life to her. But seeing her hand made Adlai ache for her in a way she hadn't before.

Her gaze snapped back to her uncle as she realized why he was showing her these things now: because Adlai had proved herself worthy by having a shadow that could kill.

"My mother's shadow . . . you said she was powerful. Did she have this power too? Was she a killer?"

Luth leaned back in his chair. His gaze drifted past her to the hallway beyond. "Your mother was a goofball. A very powerful goofball who couldn't paint or draw worth a damn, but she put her all into everything she did. She was a good person. In the end she risked her life to give others the time to escape."

He hadn't denied anything. How many people had her mother killed? How many had her uncle? She was part of a family of murderers and she wasn't sure she could call herself innocent either. If Kanwar didn't have a shadow, or if he hadn't been able to use it to come back, then she would have his blood on her hands.

"Will you really bring her back? My father too?" Adlai thought of the golden Arbil pyramid she'd once thought a beacon of her city and now knew was a glorified tomb. She needed to know if it was just hope that they would free her parents one day, or if there was a real chance she'd meet her mother and be able to find out for herself what kind of person she was.

"I'm going to try. Sometimes I think they might both still be alive if I'd shielded them better." His eyes caught hers, guilt behind them. "There's nothing I won't do to correct that mistake."

"But can it be done?"

Luth stared down at the drawings, his expression hard to read.

"The problem with Arbil is that there's so much we don't know about the place. It has secrets behind its walls, and to go in blind is to willingly sacrifice yourself." He raised himself up. "I don't plan on being a sacrifice. With your power and mine, I believe we won't have to be. But I don't have all the answers. Not yet." He smiled at Adlai. "This strength you've found has given me hope, though. I ask only that you hope alongside me."

THE MORNING CAME too quickly. Adlai lay in bed, determined not to get up, to just enjoy a moment of peace. Until a very insistent knocker started banging on the front door.

Her uncle couldn't be home or he would have stopped the banging. But Luth had slipped away again. She shouldn't be surprised. Why would today be any different?

Bleary-eyed, she came down the hall and along the way realized it wasn't morning. At least it wasn't early. The sun was high in the sky as she passed the living-room windows and the light glared through the glass at her. Another heavy knock. The door wasn't locked. It never was. She pulled it back and found Erikys, bright-eyed and smiling. He was wearing a smarter shirt than usual; it was cream white with green leaves embroidered over the shoulders. He'd even tamed his curls, slicking them back from his face with a product that smelled overwhelmingly of coconut.

"Sleeping on your birthday?"

Adlai stared at him blankly. How could he know...?

"Caster Fecks keeps a weirdly close eye on family lines," he said as explanation. "He wants to make a record of mine, even. Has everyone else's, he says. But I'm not so keen on parties myself."

"I'm not having a party."

"Good. Then we can just celebrate here."

He shut the door behind him. With it closed, she was suddenly very conscious that she was wearing only a long nightshirt; her legs and feet were bare and her hair was messy.

"I'm going to wash up," she said.

Erikys was already making himself comfy on the sofa, a difficult feat with only a rough-spun throw and a couple of cushions. It was the least comfy sofa she'd ever sat on, but Erikys made it look like it was a hammock built just for him. She washed her face and neck in the bathroom, pinned her hair up and put on the multicolored dress she'd stolen with blue billowy sleeves and a sunset-colored skirt.

Erikys wasn't on the sofa when she came back. He was peering into her uncle's study. When he heard her, he turned around with a mischievous glint in his eyes and ushered her over.

Her uncle, it turned out, kept the good booze in a glass cabinet in his study.

Erikys popped open a diamond-topped bottle with strong, clear liquid inside. He poured them each a glass but wouldn't let Adlai touch hers before he'd added a slice of lemon, a dusting of sugar around the rim of the glass and a dash of orange juice that turned the liquid a pale yellow.

Something gold. Her father had liked to steal shiny golden things any day of the week, but especially on her birthday. The bee pendant she'd given Gilly for luck hadn't been a birthday gift, but her father had a way of making every gift seem special, until the next one came along.

"Your birthday drink," Erikys said.

A warmth spread through her, their fingers brushing as she took the glass from him.

"Thank you," she said, the words coming out more emotional than she wanted. It was the memory of her father, she thought. Or perhaps it was the way Erikys was staring at her. Like he was waiting for her smile, or to see that the gesture mattered because *she* mattered.

They both took sips at the same time—and both gagged at the awful taste; Adlai's throat burned and her head flared like someone had smacked her. She'd never dared try any of Mother Henson's bottles, and this one had a far more intense smell. More like cleaning liquids than anything they should be drinking. She licked clean all the sugar and added much more than a dash of orange juice to hers. It was no longer golden but more a garish yellow when she drank from it again.

"When people say they're drinking to forget," she said, "I always imagined it being a nice, relaxing way to forget things. I didn't think it would feel like punching myself."

"Maybe we just have to get used to the taste," he said. His eyes lingered on her face and then his fingers reached up to brush her hair back behind her ear. "You go to the classes, but you don't wear the earrings the others do."

"Oh." Adlai's hands started to sweat and she put down her glass, turning her back to Erikys for a moment. "Well, I don't have the powers the others have."

"You haven't learned anything new?"

She kept her back facing him and shook her head. "Just stealing. Your shadow's as good as mine."

"I doubt that," he said, but he didn't push her.

He doesn't know, she thought with relief. With Kanwar living in the same house as Erikys, she wasn't sure if they would have talked. But no, if Erikys knew her shadow had killed Kanwar—even momentarily—he would have said something. He definitely wouldn't have looked at her so softly, mixing her a birthday drink and letting himself be alone with her. He would have treated her differently. He would have been afraid of her.

Erikys set his drink down on Luth's desk and eased himself into the chair behind it.

Adlai nervously glanced around. Luth's study was much like the rest of the house, modern and uncomfortably stylish. Everywhere she looked there were clean lines, pristine white furniture, and bland artwork. The two of them were like a set of mucky fingerprints and she was suddenly conscious of how obvious it would be that they'd been in here.

"We should tidy up," she said. It was probably already too late. They had spilled sugar on the floor and lemon juice over the cabinet shelves.

"Relax, Ads, your uncle isn't going to get mad at you today."

"He hasn't been my uncle long enough for me to test that."

But Erikys wasn't listening. He'd moved out of the chair and was looking around the desk.

"What are you doing?" she hissed.

"Looking. You say you don't know the man, well, here's a way to find out about him." Erikys pulled one of the drawers open.

She took a swig of her drink, knowing this was a mistake but curious all the same.

Inside were a lot of papers. Mostly maps. The first one was a large map of Piscet, the coastal province that was on the opposite end from Libra. Perhaps a place he was scouting if they had to relocate?

Erikys rifled through the papers dismissively. The maps weren't interesting enough for him and he went for the next drawer, but it was locked. He shook the handle violently.

"You'll break it," Adlai said. She was already scooping up the maps and trying to put them back into some kind of order when they both heard a loud thud.

Erikys had shaken something in the drawer. He opened the third and last one. It wasn't locked, but something had fallen from the middle one down into it. A false bottom had broken off, and the fallen thing was familiar.

A pocket watch. *The* pocket watch. The one she'd try to steal in the desert market. The one she'd been killed for taking—it was sitting in her uncle's desk drawer.

Her head spun. She clutched the maps to her chest and tried to steady herself, but black spots were creeping into her vision. She blinked them away and looked again at the watch, because it couldn't be the same one.

Erikys held it up to the light and something in Adlai relaxed. It wasn't the same one. The light bounced off it dully; the metal wasn't suraci. There wasn't that telltale gleam to the shine, where light not only danced over its surface but came alive inside it. Suraci had a fiery lick to it—this one was just copper.

But everything else was the same. The markings were the same ones she'd seen on the hooded stranger's watch. Looking closer, she saw what the markings were. Where numbers would normally be, there were letters and symbols, for each of the twelve cities and twelve gods. Instead of the number twelve, Libra was written and the symbol above it was of a black skull: the god of Death. On either side were Libra's two neighboring cities, Gem and Aquari, with the goddess of wisdom shown as a pair of eyes and the god of sky as a flock of birds. Piscet, the city her uncle had the maps for, was over by where the six would be on a normal watch. Instead the goddess of life, Amansi, was represented by a single water droplet.

"It's an equitor's watch," Erikys said, more to himself than to Adlai. She looked at him, puzzled, and he elaborated for her. "A trapper's watch is supposed to look just like this. Caster Fecks has books with drawings of them. The details are exactly right."

"But this is just a replica, isn't it?" Adlai said. "The real ones are made of suraci. I've seen one." Her voice shook. A book couldn't show how suraci looked; not even the best artist could do that.

"Of course you have." He put the watch down. "I'm sorry, Adlai. I shouldn't have been so nosy. I'm sure your uncle has his reasons for these things. I'll clean everything up, you sit down and finish your drink."

She stared at her sickly bright yellow drink and shook her head. She wouldn't mind forgetting the face of the hooded stranger, or the sensation of crawling on the sand, as helpless as an insect about to be stomped on. But the idea of sitting down and drinking to forget was a strangely depressing one.

They cleaned up in silence. Her uncle still wasn't home when they were done. Adlai thought about going to her room and resting before lunch, but Erikys didn't want to leave her alone.

"You were alone in Libra and now it's like you're living alone here." Erikys shook his head. "Even on your birthday. Whatever your uncle is getting up to, it must be pretty important to keep leaving you like this."

Adlai thought about the locked room and now the locked drawer in the desk; the maps to another city and a replica watch of those used by trappers. Was it all part of keeping them safe, or what was her uncle's plan for breaking into Arbil? Why did he have to keep it secret from her, when it was her parents they would be saving?

But Erikys was right; she didn't want to be alone.

20

Sandlicker

ADLAI WAITED OUTSIDE A LINE of houses. The sun grew warmer in the sky and she fiddled with the ruffles on her top. She was wearing the drab clothes her uncle had given her: a white top and gray skirt, but she didn't need to be in any pretty bright colors for the conversation she planned to have now.

She was shaded under a palm tree and could see well down the path. He would surely walk this way home. Adlai had a brief moment of worry that she'd made a mistake, that he would go to the food hall first, or somewhere else entirely. Then she spotted him. Even thinking himself unobserved, Kanwar walked straight-backed and quickly, as if every moment spent not at his destination was one wasted.

Perhaps he really wanted to get home, or perhaps walking felt too much like drifting, and he didn't want to be caught up in his thoughts, whatever those might be.

Adlai realized she knew very little about Kanwar. He was an orphan, like her, which meant he'd dealt with death before, even if he might not have actually died before. She didn't know how he'd come to the island.

But she'd sent him to the shadow world. An experience she wouldn't wish on anyone.

Were both his parents there? Had he been tempted to stay? Did the god of Death whisper to him now?

She stepped onto the path and he spun around, his body coiled like he expected—and was ready for—an attack.

Stupid. She should have known he'd be on edge. If she wasn't such a coward she would have waited outside of class to talk to him, not sneak up on him when he thought he was alone.

But when his eyes settled on her face, he relaxed. Dismissed her.

"Erikys won't be here," he said, turning away. "And you missed another class."

Her mouth was as dry as sand, but she cleared it and tried to say something. "Kanwar, when I . . . in class that day, I wasn't trying to . . . I didn't know what I . . ."

He waved her off. "Forget it," he said.

"No, really." She came forward; he had to hear her. "I'm sorry. I would never intentionally use my shadow like that."

Kanwar was handsome in a dark navy shirt with red beads running in straight lines down the front that matched the red headscarf he had tied over his forehead. His hair wasn't as closely cropped as it had been and stood, puffed, over the band. He swept his hand over it and sighed. "I know. You don't have to tell me you had no idea what you were doing. Your lack of control was very evident."

Her hands balled into fists. He wasn't hearing her. Or he was, but he wasn't letting her take ownership. She had nearly killed him and still he didn't see her as a threat.

"You know you don't always have to be putting people down," she said, "just because they aren't as amazing as you are at everything."

"That is not—" He stopped. He folded his arms across his chest. "I worked hard to gain the control I have."

Adlai mirrored him and crossed her arms. "I've barely arrived. This is all new to me. Surely you can understand that."

The sharp lines of his face froze more resolutely in place as he stared down at her. "No, I don't think I can," he said at last. "When I arrived, I had no powerful uncle waiting here for me. I didn't come with a friend. I had no one."

"So I should have come scared and alone, and then you would have been nice to me?"

He shook his head. "This is pointless. Next time you kill someone, just send them a letter to apologize afterwards."

He was walking away from her. Again.

"Have you died before?" she called out. He stopped. She thought he wouldn't turn back, but he did.

"I died with my parents in a random attack on the streets," he said, his voice low. Adlai drew nearer and watched as his expression shifted, no longer tense or guarded. He let out a breath. "The last time I saw my mother, she was forcing me down to the ground with more strength than I ever knew she had." He swallowed. "It didn't save me, but she died trying."

"Kanwar . . . that's . . . I'm so sorry."

He ignored her and continued: "My father had shadow powers, so he was waiting for me on the other side." His eyes cut into hers. "He begged me to go back, to try and save my mother, to save myself, and I had to leave him there in the shadow world because he couldn't do it. He couldn't find his shadow and pull himself back to life. His body was burning when I finally came back to the living. There was no saving my mother. I was alone.

"I didn't want to come here." His shoulders hunched. "I didn't want to have powers if it meant I would be alone. And I hated my father for his weakness."

Adlai was stunned. She wanted to reach out to him, but Kanwar didn't seem like the type of person you could just touch. He'd opened up and it wasn't for her pity.

"So you see," he said, "you don't have to worry that you upset me or hurt me. You can come back to class. I've been through far worse than anything you could do to me."

A light breeze tousled the palm trees above them. The sky was infinitely blue and calm. Everywhere Adlai looked she found beauty, as if the island had never known a storm.

"How did you find this place?" she asked.

"I didn't. Caster Luth found me. He knew I'd been in the shadow world, and he'd talked with my father."

Adlai frowned. Did her uncle routinely go to the shadow world? Or was Yaxine giving him information somehow?

"Nadir keeps telling me I should try being nice," he said suddenly. "She does it so easily."

"No, I think I understand," she said. "You hate weakness, and I've been acting weak from the start, needing rescuing in the desert, unable to keep up with the classes, afraid of my shadow."

"But you're not weak, Adlai."

"No, and you're capable of being nice." She looked him square in the eye. "You haven't told Erikys about my shadow, have you?"

"We share a roof, but we're not friends."

"Exactly," she said. "You could have easily told him out of spite. To make him afraid of me."

He shrugged. "He shows little interest in his own ability; I don't see what business it is of his to know of yours."

"Well, I appreciate it all the same."

Kanwar titled his head. "So you don't think I'm a—what's that phrase you Librans have? A sand eater?"

For a moment Adlai didn't understand what he was asking. Then she broke into a smile: he was joking with her. The relief of it spread through her like a hug. "Sandlicker," she said. "You were being a sandlicker."

"Exactly." Kanwar also smiled. It lit up his face, relaxing all the stiffness. "Yes. I was licking sand. An annoying habit."

"I could have tried harder in class," she said. "I will."

Kanwar nodded. She let him turn and head for home at last, but as she watched him leave, she wondered if, like her, he feared he'd always be alone.

***

LEAVING THE RESIDENTIAL area, Adlai headed for the food stores. Since her uncle was rarely around for meals, she didn't always bother with restocking the food at home, opting instead to eat in the community food hall. But word had spread of what she'd done to Kanwar. Stares followed her as she walked down the path. A pair of casters with three earrings each nodded to her as she passed them by. She was her mother's daughter. A killer. And while her uncle had told her that her mother had died protecting others, there wasn't warmth in the way they watched her, but fear.

She tried not to meet any more eyes. When at last she came to the food store, Caster Evena, the middle-aged woman who organized the stock, broke off gossiping to greet Adlai immediately.

"Caster Adlai! Keeping well, I hope? Shall I add a sweet loaf today? It's freshly baked."

The woman had a weekly basket already prepared for her, jam-packed with extras. Being Caster Luth's niece, she was used to receiving a basket better than the other ones she'd seen people taking, but this one was overflowing. When Evena addressed her as "Caster" again, Adlai felt her ears burn.

It shouldn't matter to her, the Caster nonsense. Adlai knew it was a term of respect and there was nothing bad meant by it. Only she'd earned the woman's respect, and everyone else's on the island who hid their whispers behind a mask of respect, from nearly killing a fellow student. She let the weight of the basket sag in her arms as she left the store.

They couldn't see it, or maybe they didn't want to, but she didn't have control of her shadow. She was a danger to everyone she passed. The more she thought back to that class, to the moment when Kanwar had been on his knees and her shadow swarmed him, the more she remembered how instinctive it had been. Like her shadow was made for pulling out the life force of another. All the trinkets she'd stolen were merely practice for what her shadow's true purpose was.

Stealing life.

Her head was cast downward so she didn't notice Erikys walking the path back from the storykeep until his hand dipped into her basket and stole one of the candied figs.

"Have my skills improved, or are you just very distracted?" he asked.

She glanced around them. A woman with a small child strapped to her back was carrying a pile of freshly washed clothes, but luckily it was only the child who stared at them as they passed by. Adlai felt exposed. Erikys had already mentioned his desire to leave the island. If he knew Adlai's shadow could kill, how much faster would he run?

He'll fear me, like the others do.

She pulled at him to walk faster, ignoring his offer to carry the basket for her.

"What's gotten into you, Ads?" he said, panting to keep up with her. They'd almost reached the homes. Her uncle's house loomed large on a hill separate from the other houses.

"Just hungry," she said, but her stomach dropped as she saw Caster Shani making her way toward them.

"I'll be in class tomorrow—" she started to say, but Shani held up her hand.

"No, it's Erikys I'm after, Adlai." She turned to him. Unease spread across his face. "Don't worry, classes are still optional. But I will require you to come see me sometime this week. I need to know the extent of your shadow powers. I won't teach you anything you don't want to know, but I have to be confident that you're in control of it."

"You have to?" Erikys asked. "What, are you worried my shadow will explode if you don't see it steal something?"

Adlai flinched. Caster Shani was seeking Erikys out because of Adlai's own failings. Her poor performances in classes, then missing them altogether after the Kanwar incident. She squeezed her eyes shut and begged the unnamed goddess of whispers that Caster Shani wasn't just about to reveal to Erikys that Adlai had accidentally killed with her shadow.

"It'll be best if you come early in the morning," Shani said, as if he hadn't spoken. "Before classes. Any day that suits."

She didn't ask for confirmation. They were on an island, after all, and Erikys couldn't avoid her forever. They watched her leave, and Adlai breathed a sigh of relief. She hadn't said anything about Adlai's shadow.

"Do you think she really means for me to go?" he asked.

"It's just a demonstration," she said lightly.

Erikys bent and fiddled with the chain around his ankle.

"Sure."

Several moments passed in silence. The sun began to soften and the island glowed a warm orange.

"I hate islands," he said suddenly. "There's nothing but time and ocean out here."

"What would you want instead?"

"Home."

Adlai was caught off guard by how much that word hurt.

"You mean Libra," she said. "It won't be safe for us there. The guards—"

Erikys waved a hand. "Hundreds of people come in and out of Libra every day. The desert market alone has crowds of strangers. And we got away. Libra's the last place any guards would expect us to be."

"You really want to go back?"

"Adlai, my family's there." He shook his head. "They're used to me being away some, but it's been long enough. If my parents aren't worried, then my brother most definitely will be. After his illness, I swore I wouldn't ever stay away too long without checking up on him."

Her heart lurched. Of course he needed to see his family. She'd been distracted with classes and her uncle, but Erikys had been alone so much of his time here. His choice, perhaps, but she could see how easy it would be for his mind to have fixated on these things; of what he wanted, of where he wanted to be, and what his family were doing without him.

And now he was decided.

Adlai had brought him to this point. It was her responsibility to bring him home.

21

Returning Thieves

I CAN'T DO THIS. ADLAI DREW Erikys further into the thicket of trees, away from Caster Shani or anyone else who might happen upon them. His brown curls were tousled in the low wind, and he looked down on her with an encouraging smile.

"You don't want to say goodbye to anyone?" she asked feebly.

He arched a brow. "No one's going to miss me here."

It was true enough. Erikys had separated himself from everyone except for Adlai, a grumpy old storykeeper, and an endless pile of books.

"You can do this," he said.

She stared down at the ground. So green and alien to Libra. Could she really bring them there with nothing more than her shadow?

Adlai had to try. She brought her shadow out; it blackened the ground and fear trembled through her.

Fear that her shadow would attack again.

Fear that it would listen and take them back to Libra.

This was a bad idea, that much Adlai knew.

She let her shadow drift over them both and closed her eyes, thinking of the desert and the city gate they'd left behind.

Take us there. Let me bring Erikys home.

She waited, and nothing happened. Adlai opened her eyes. Her shadow was still and silent, not even a wisp of smoke licking its surface.

"I'm sorry," she started to say, and then she felt something. A claw scraping between them.

She looked up in panic, but Erikys hadn't noticed anything.

I can take you, whispered Manni, the god of Death, in his beast-like voice through her shadow.

Her breathing hitched. The voice and the presence always filled her with dread, but this time something new prickled at her. A caress that was soft and gentle.

You can take us to Libra?

It would be child's play. Do you feel like playing?

Her heart drummed against her chest.

What would it cost me?

You have only to give me control of your shadow.

To travel? And . . . and then you'd give it back?

I did before, didn't I?

He had to mean when she'd been in the barrel, trying to escape Libra. She'd given her shadow over to the voice, and he'd saved her.

Adlai looked at Erikys. His body was no longer tense with anticipation; instead his shoulders were slumped and his eyes downcast. He knew she couldn't do this, and yet she saw so clearly how much he'd wanted it.

Her shadow was a weight at her feet. She pushed it toward the presence lurking in the dark and imagined herself without the weight. To be free of her shadow.

Smoke from her shadow rose up, blurring Erikys from her. She wanted to pull away but instead forced herself to be still as it wrapped around her like several claws sinking into her.

Then she fell through the air and into the dark.

THEY ARRIVED AT the edge of the desert. Adlai blinked and stared up at the wooden sign pointing toward the river. They were back home.

She looked ahead and splashes of color whipped about in the wind as the desert market loomed ahead of them. Evening was approaching. The sky was a hazy, pale gold, and soon stars would dust over the market.

"You . . . you did it," Erikys said. He patted himself as if not quite believing he was really there. And then he broke into a wide grin. "Incredible!" Suddenly his hands were wrapped around her waist and he was swinging her around. "You're amazing," he said, both of them breathless by the time he set her down again.

Adlai blushed. She didn't want to correct him that she'd had help.

"I got you into this mess," she said. "It's only right I bring you back."

And this was the perfect place to say goodbye. A month ago they'd stood here, chased by the city guards with the open desert in front of them. He'd thought she was mad to lead them that way. His adventure would have taken him down the dirt road leading to towns and cities and normalcy. Not trapped on an island with shadows that could kill.

Now he could redo that moment. She could give him that chance to take the adventure he wanted and travel all over the kingdom . . . or stay with his family and grow comfortable with a ordinary life. Nothing that involved her.

She shifted away from him. Now that the moment was here, she wasn't sure she could say goodbye. What would goodbye mean? Would he go back to his family and forget he even had a shadow? Forget her?

"Adlai." He said her name softly, but she quickly looked away.

"Try and spend at least a little bit of time with your family before you desert them for riches," she said. She kept her voice light, but her arms wrapped around her chest, protecting herself from this goodbye.

He stepped toward her. "Come with me," he said.

She frowned. "To see your family?"

"Everywhere." His hands pressed into her shoulders and his face, when she looked up at him, was beaming. "Come with me, little thief, and open up your stall by some faraway sea. Come with me, and let's explore the kingdom together."

She swallowed. He couldn't mean it, and she couldn't . . . "I can't just leave," she said.

"Why not?" His hands dropped from her, and she felt suddenly cold. "Your uncle's never around, you hate the classes and barely anyone's been nice to you since you arrived. You owe them nothing."

His words hit her like a slap. She felt the truth of them and wondered what it would mean to not go back. Could she live with herself, knowing her parents were in Arbil?

Would her uncle save them one day without her help, or was she fooling herself that their shadow powers could do anything against an enemy with suraci?

In her silence, he reached out again and this time took her hand in his, the grip so familiar that she didn't want him to ever let go.

But there was movement over Erikys's shoulder. A group of people were coming down the dirt road, headed for the desert market. They couldn't stay standing out in the open like this.

She swallowed and gently pried her hand away.

"Let's follow behind this group," she said. "I'll wait for you to see your family and then . . . and then we'll see."

He smiled wide. Going to the desert market was a bad idea—a terrible idea. She had to go back to where she was safe. Already her shadow tugged at her to do so. She could feel Manni's presence there, ready to take her shadow again and bring her back to the island.

But she didn't want to leave Erikys. She didn't want the goodbye; she thought she might even want the adventure.

———————

THEY ENTERED THROUGH the Unmade Stalls. Fear turned into thrill as she looked around the stalls that were so familiar to her. This had been home to her for so long, and she wasn't ready to let it go.

In this part of the market, products weren't quite ready for sale. They required personalization, or something particular from the buyer, but just about anything could be made. In one stall were rough, uncut gems. "Prices at seller's discretion," was written underneath. Another stall had blank canvases offering portraits.

Adlai became curious at a glittering table with crystal orbs and constellation charms. The woman who owned it smiled at her knowingly.

"Tell me the day and year of your birth and I'll tell you the man who will love you truest of all."

Adlai rolled her eyes. A heartgazer. She should have guessed. They pretended to have the knowledge of stargazers but focused only on matters of the heart, claiming the stars could be read on a far more personal level. But Adlai didn't believe everyone's fate was written up there. There were too many people that this life just didn't care about. She'd seen it often enough at the orphanage.

Erikys hovered next to her. "Curious what the stars will have to say?"

"Not in the least bit."

She pulled him away and he laughed, slipping his hand into hers.

"But you might miss your chance at true love."

"What about yours?" she asked.

"Mine?"

Her eyes darted to his long stride where the anklet he wore everyday was visible over his sandal.

"You never told me who gave you that," she said.

"And you think it was a girl?"

All this time he was still holding her hand. Like his hand had molded into hers. He was close to her, close enough that a layer of heat burned over her. For a moment they were both still. The air between them became thicker, her throat dry and her lips—she had never felt so self-conscious about her lips before. They seemed too large for her face and Erikys was staring at them as if he were thinking the same thing. She thought maybe she moved first. It didn't matter. They were so close together that any slight movement could have broken them apart or, as happened, brought his lips to hers.

The kiss was an intake of breath. Necessary and natural. His lips were warm against her, and she wondered how it had taken her this long to realize the heat of him.

His hands ran through her hair, grabbing piles of it as he kissed her harder. When he pulled away, his hands stayed on her neck and his thumbs brushed her cheeks.

He cupped her face. "I think I wanted to kiss you from the first moment you yelled thief at me," he said. "You looked so sure of yourself that day. Like you'd won some giant prize."

His smile was sad, as though it was a bittersweet memory for him too. But when she thought back to that moment, he wasn't there. She remembered only the bright, bubbling elation after stealing the suraci watch and the water from the fountain cooling her as she imagined how much she'd sell it for. She'd been reckless and stupid then.

She had known so little.

"I'll throw away the anklet." He pulled back and looked at her carefully. "My parents will give me some money and then you can buy me the cheapest, ugliest jewel you like and it'll be the only one I wear."

She smiled. "You want me to pay for something? Here? In the desert market?"

"No stealing, Ads." He cocked his head. "Will you promise not to take any risks while I'm gone?"

"Being here is a risk," she said. "But, yes, I promise to do nothing to attract any attention."

"Good." He kissed her forehead. "I'll meet you back at the stall where we first met before closing. Do you remember it?"

The fruit stall. The start of everything. She nodded. "I'll be there."

A STUPID SMILE was on her face as she walked over to the Stalls of a Thousand Suns, looking nostalgically over the shining stalls and bright tents. Why were things so much more tempting when they gleamed? Even cheap trinkets became desirable under the sun's touch.

"Ms. Adlai!"

Adlai beamed, drifting over to Izel's stalls with its tangled collection of necklaces and bracelets. She even spotted an anklet that reminded her of Erikys's. Like his, the chain was clearly not real gold and the jewel was red, not black, yet it caught the light in the same way his fake jewel did; dim and slow.

"You have been a stranger," he said, his accent as clipped as she remembered.

"And yet everything here is the same."

"It is so," he said. "Though Vima makes me wonder if business would be better with a pretty smile to greet the customers. You smile most beautifully."

"What are you talking about?" Vima wasn't ugly like Izel was, but she would hardly call his smile pretty.

"The orphan girl he has that is not my Ms. Adlai."

She frowned deeper. Izel often talked strangely but this was too strange to ignore. Vima's stall wasn't far from there, and her nerves scratched at her as she left Izel's stall. The market was beginning to crowd and that meant she had to walk slower,

Finally Vima's stall was visible. His tent was a deep purple, wind chimes itching in the slight breeze. He had no customers, only a girl who was looking at a set of candlesticks.

No—she wasn't looking, she was *cleaning* them.

"Pen?!"

A dark-skinned woman with Penna's curved figure was polishing a set of candlesticks. She looked up, and it really was Penna. Her eyes, her round face, and her childish, bright smile.

"Adlai!"

If she was shocked at seeing her friend, it was nothing to Penna's reaction. Pen ran to her, still holding a weighty silver-crested candlestick and it slammed into Adlai's back as she hugged her.

Adlai hugged her back. Warmth spread through her, the smell of Pen's lemon soap so achingly familiar that she held on a moment longer to soak it all in.

When Adlai finally pulled back, she saw Penna had changed in other ways. Her hair, usually tightly braided or covered by a scarf, was bursting out in frizzy curls that circled her face like a black sun. Her dress, too, looked like it was made of silk. It was lavender in color with silver beading and fine embroidery snaking over the hems and sleeves. She wouldn't be mopping the floors or bending over a sewing table in such a fine dress.

"But you never come to the desert market," Adlai said. That was perhaps the strangest thing of all. Penna had brushed off every offer to go with her over the years, preferring the places she knew and the people she knew. The desert market was a place of danger, existing outside the city walls, and home to thieves and murderers. She hadn't been wrong either.

"You're the one who told me specifically to come here!"

"Yes, well, that was to sell—" Adlai squinted at the stall Penna had left. "Are those the necklaces I had under my bed? And that gilded plate!"

"If you look closer, you'll find more of your leftovers." Vima's voice. He was as dark as Pen, older, and handsome in his way. A beard curled around his chin and his bald head was covered by a low-tipped hat instead of his usual headscarf.

"How much did you give for the goods?" she said, her eyes narrowed.

"A fair price."

She snorted. A fair price didn't exist in the desert market.

"It's true," Vima said. "Knowing you sent such a beauty to me made me stop cursing every miserly haggle you've caused me." He stretched his arm over Penna's shoulders. He took the heavy candlestick away in his other hand, leaving the free one touching her neck. It was like a man stroking a pretty pet.

"Dying gods, Pen," she said. "Vima?"

Penna still looked shy, but she was glowing too.

Adlai shook her head, hardly believing it possible that her friend could have fallen for one of the under-the-table vendors. That wasn't the fairy-tale ending Penna had dreamed of back in the orphanage. Vima was no prince. But if she could believe her friend was happy . . .

"How is it you're back, Adlai?" Penna asked, with those wide eyes she remembered so well.

"I came here with Erikys," she said. "He's seeing his family and then he'll meet me before closing."

"The boy you ran away with?" Penna asked. Adlai nodded.

"Let a runaway go, and they'll run off again," Vima said.

Vima had never given her a good price without making her sweat for it, and he'd never been funny.

"I don't know what Pen sees in you," she said. Penna, as she'd always done at the orphanage, pretended she didn't see an argument about to happen.

"Let's wait together," Penna said.

22

Tell Me How

"Y OU CAN'T TRUST VIMA, YOU know," Adlai said. They sat at a table in the food stalls with a couple of peach juices, sharing a platter of almond bread, cheese, yogurt, and rice balls. "I sold him leather gloves once for thirty turns, and then I find out from Izel that he sold them to a lady for three silvers. Plain lied to my face when I asked him about it."

Adlai sat with Penna on the bench, both of them turned to the fountain and scanning the crowd.

"Or Izel lied," Penna said breezily.

She fiddled with the delicate beads on her sleeve. "I quit the dressmakers last week. Vima knows people in the Unmade Stalls who pay me more for my work. I'll be able to settle my training debt faster doing odd jobs."

Adlai tore off some more bread and listened in wonder. How amazing it was to be sitting with Pen again. Penna had changed in the weeks she'd been away, and while Adlai didn't trust Vima, the sad thing was that most situations would be an improvement to an orphan from Mother Henson's.

"That's great, Pen," she said honestly. "You're not still doing Henson's work though, are you?"

Penna smiled. "I never minded helping," she said. "But no, I found a place. It's smaller than the attic and I have to share with two other women, but they're nice and it's cheap."

"You think everyone is nice."

"Most people are," she said. "Gilly's left as well. She got adopted. Mother said the couple had three sons and really wanted a daughter."

Adlai's brow rose. "And they were happy with Gilly being that girl?"

"I suppose. I see her playing along the river some days. She's the same as always, but now she has a home to go back to." Penna looked sideways at her. "And you? What happened, Adlai?"

She wasn't sure how to answer. A lot of things had happened, and most were things she couldn't tell Penna about. The fact that she had shadow powers for one, and that she could kill with them. Or the fact that she lived on an island hiding dozens of people that, if they used their powers out here, would be killed. As she had been. Or that she didn't know if it was better to go back and be with people like her, or whether she should live her life without a shadow.

"I found somewhere . . . safe. I have an uncle and I've been living with him."

Whatever Pen had been expecting Adlai to say, it wasn't that. "You have family? Where? Is that why you left?"

"It doesn't really matter," she said. Then, seeing Penna's face, corrected herself. "Okay, it does matter. It matters a lot. But I don't really know him." She scanned the crowd again. It was too early for Erikys to be coming back, and city guards were never in the market, but Adlai couldn't help being nervous every time she saw someone wearing a hood. Trappers could be anywhere. "I think he cares about me but I don't know. I don't know what I'm doing."

Penna's large eyes fixed on Adlai. "Are you okay?"

She swallowed. Adlai could answer yes or no and both times would be telling the truth.

Yes, she had a home and someone to call family, and she had more power than she ever thought possible.

No, she was stuck with a life she didn't choose, with powers she didn't want and the only person she'd come to really care about was leaving if she didn't go with him.

"I'm fine," she said instead. "It's you I should be worried about. Vima's a crook and a cheat."

Far from being embarrassed, Penna nodded. "He's a realist and an opportunist," she said. "He told me that stories only matter if they're books he can sell, and dreams are big ideas for making money.

"But when I brought all your things to him, he wasn't interested in haggling on prices. He hardly looked at them. All he wanted to talk about was me."

She nudged Adlai. "I didn't think he was my type either. And I thought he wasn't serious about me being his type. But if he hadn't asked, and we hadn't tried, I would still be where I was. Stuck. Alone. Fantasizing about when things would change. He made the change happen. I hadn't realized before him how far I was from ever rolling the dice for myself."

"Vima made you realize all this?"

She nodded. "And you leaving," she said quietly.

Adlai bit her lip. She wished she could tell Penna everything, but her friend had finally found a life for herself, one with silk dresses and a man she talked about as if he were the hero to her story.

Penna, Gilly, they had left the orphanage behind and were loved. She had a desire to play their old game. Tell me how, she would ask, How can I do the same?

As STARS CLUSTERED in a darkening sky, market stalls started to close up shop and Penna left to help Vima pack up. Adlai, with an unsettling feeling, headed for the fruit stall.

She still wasn't sure what she would tell Erikys. The island was beautiful but it wasn't her home. Maybe she could find one with Erikys. Her parents would want that for her, surely. And yet leaving felt like abandoning them. Giving up the idea that her parents would ever be a part of her life again. Her uncle had promised her that he was doing everything to make that a possibility. Running wouldn't help her parents.

Drinks were still being poured in a bar area but the crowd parted for her in happy stumbles and merry pats on the back. Finally, she came to the crates of fruit. Colors like wildflowers were all around the stall. She thought she recognized the vendor as the same man who had been there the last time.

Yes, he was the same and the stall was the same, but that was all she saw. There were no customers around. Erikys wasn't there.

The heat pressed on her, making her body and mind slow as she forced herself closer.

The vendor was busy sealing lids and taking down signs, ready to close shop. He swatted her away when she asked if he'd seen a boy matching Erikys's description.

"I see plenty of people today," he said. "Maybe for customers I be remembering."

She would have to buy something, she realized. The thief part of her protested, but she had a few coins on her. She needed to know how much time had passed since he'd been here. *If* he'd been here.

Adlai came away from the stall holding a bunch of grapes and a hollow in her chest.

The tents were closing and he wasn't back.

Something's happened.

She knew she was right. Even if she had missed him at the stall, he surely would have asked the stall owner when he hadn't seen her there. It was what she had done, and she didn't think the stall owner would have forgotten being pestered twice that same day.

Which meant he hadn't come back to the market. But why hadn't he? Had something happened with his family? Or had he been unlucky and met with a guard who'd recognized him?

Or worse: Had a trapper been around and somehow known he had a shadow?

It had happened to her. Erikys was as little prepared to meet a trapper as she had been. His shadow would be ripped from him. And that wouldn't even be the worst of it. Nothing could prepare you for the horror of having someone standing over you, blade in hand, as your life seeped out in blood and sweat on the sands.

Couples strolled past her, swaying to music Adlai couldn't hear. She couldn't see the market. It blurred and glistened behind tears she didn't want to shed. She wanted to scream instead because this place was cursed.

GOING TO THE desert market had been a bad idea. It had always been a bad idea, even before today. How, *why* had her father made the market seem so wondrous? She'd grown up viewing the tents and stalls as places to feast her eyes on, where gifts could be found on every table and shadow powers were just a game to play.

The game should have ended after her father disappeared, yet she'd kept going back. She'd kept playing, turning the game into a gamble every time she stole with the slip of her shadow. Until one day she lost. She'd lost and still she'd dared to go back one more time.

How much more did she have to lose?

"Erikys didn't meet you?" Penna asked.

Adlai came back to herself. Vima was packing away his goods. Colors were ripped from the sky as pink, blue, and orange tent hangings were pulled down around her.

"No," she said. Her answer sounded distant, like someone else was forming it.

"Do you want to stay with me tonight?"

The crowd was scattering. Dust clung to the air. Everything was falling apart.

"I'll be fine," Adlai said, mechanically. "How much longer will this take?"

Vima slammed the lid shut on a crate of goods.

"With such help as you give," he said, "expect to be leading the back of the line."

Adlai shot him a dark look, but Penna shushed him and ducked under the stall, emerging with a small wooden box. She handed it to Adlai. "You can carry this," she said. "It's yours anyway."

Adlai frowned. The box wasn't familiar. Yet when she opened it, her hands gripped the sides and she sank to the ground with it.

Inside was useless, worthless junk; fake gold bracelets, relics with cracked gold paint, a frayed sun-yellow scarf. It was a treasure trove of no value, except the beating it stirred in Adlai's heart.

"You kept these?"

Penna nodded. "They were from your father, weren't they?"

Adlai swallowed hard and brushed her fingers over each one, remembering.

She was wrapping her hair in the scarf when she noticed someone in the crowd that made her freeze. It wasn't fear, exactly. Her body turned rigid as if it didn't know how to process the man coming toward her. It seemed so unlikely that he was here. She'd died and he hadn't come to find her, and now, when she least wanted to

---

see him, here was her uncle wearing a look that told her he wasn't about to be helpful.

Dressed all in black, Luth stood out from the crowd the way a blot of ink muddled words on a page. His presence clouded the ones around him until he was all she could see.

"Dying gods." Penna never cursed, but the sight of Luth made her gasp and she looked from Adlai to him with wide eyes. "Is that . . .? He looks just like you, Adlai!"

"My uncle," she muttered.

Adlai snapped the wooden box shut and stood up as Luth approached the stall. The violet tent hanging Vima still had up shivered above him.

Her uncle looked down at her.

"I had to come," she said. "Erikys needed to see his family."

"You placed yourself in danger for that boy," he said. It wasn't a question. He didn't even use Erikys's name. That boy, he seemed to say, wasn't worth the risk.

"He's coming back," she said quickly. "But he's late. I'm worried something's happened."

A crowd of people shuffled past, wheeling crates and leading camels down the path to the city. Penna was pretending not to listen, trying in her gentle way to give them privacy, but the stall wasn't large, and Vima wasn't being subtle about being ready to leave. It was time.

She turned back to her uncle and caught the exact moment he pulled his shadow out. It seemed to happen in slow motion for her. He didn't move, he didn't blink. His black coat shivered in the breeze but his shadow was steady.

She could almost mistake it for a normal shadow; it was as still as he was, and like Caster Shani's, it didn't have a whisper of smoke. He was in total control of it.

"You can't," she said, her voice scraped with panic. "Not here."

Her uncle didn't seem to have heard her. "You could have been lost to a trapper," he said. "Again." He paused, letting the implication hang in the air.

The weight of his stare should have been enough to bow her head, but it didn't. Perhaps if her father had been saying the words, it would have, but she didn't think he would say them. He'd taught her to be safe, to play the game cautiously. He hadn't taught her to be a coward, and suddenly that was exactly what the island felt like: a coward's hideout.

"What's the point of gaining powers if we don't use them to help anyone?"

"You have no idea what you're talking about, and you've done enough today."

His shadow caught her, moving so fast she didn't have a chance to step back. Coldness seeped into her and it was like being submerged into icy water. She could drown in it. A part of her thought she was. She tried to call out, tried to pull out her own shadow and stop this, but it was too late.

Darkness and bitter cold dragged her down, and the market was ripped away.

23

Behind the Door

A DLAI STUMBLED AND DROPPED THE wooden box; it clattered to the tiled floor and pieces of gold spilled out.

"How could you do that?" Adlai looked around her uncle's living room, blinking but not really believing she was there. He'd taken her from the market. Had Penna still been watching them? How would she explain vanishing like that? "I never told my friend about my shadow!"

Her uncle regarded her. "It was my shadow that was seen. I told you I make false trails for trappers. My description is known to them. If anyone from the market says what they've seen, it will result in trappers combing the area for our hideout. There's nothing more to it than that."

"Nothing more?" She felt sick. If trappers thought there were shadow casters to hunt in Libra they would find . . .

Erikys. Where was he now? They had to go back; she couldn't be here.

Her shadow slipped out, feeling over the scattered treasures, all she had left of her father.

But they were hers. She didn't need to steal them. What she needed was her shadow to take her back to the market.

She closed her eyes and listened for the voice, but it wasn't there. She couldn't sense Manni and her shadow felt weak in comparison.

Yet she had to do it. Adlai forced the image of the desert market into her mind, bare of tents, with the city walls in sight and a crowd of people following the path toward them. She needed to be one of that crowd.

Heat rushed over her skin and she opened her eyes, thinking for a moment that she had done it.

There were faint wisps of smoke drifting from her shadow. So very faint and gone in the next moment.

No.

"Going to Libra wasn't just reckless, Adlai, it was stupid," her uncle said. "And stupidity is a weakness that no amount of power can save you from."

Her hands shook as she called her shadow back. Useless, unreliable thing that it was. It couldn't even take her out of this room, out of this house that was her uncles and not hers. Never hers.

SHE WAITED FOR her uncle to go to bed. The rooms were dark with dim moonlight slipping in through the windows, and when she stayed very still outside his door, she could hear his steady breathing.

He'd found her in the market. He'd known where she'd gone and with whom. The only way that was possible was if his shadow was like hers and the god of Death had whispered to him as he whispered to her. But her uncle wouldn't tell her this. Just as she hadn't told him that she heard Manni as well. They didn't trust each other. And they never would, not after today. Not only had her uncle revealed their shadow powers to Penna, but he'd flat out refused to listen to her about Erikys. He wouldn't help her, not freely, but maybe if she could understand what he was up to, she'd have some leverage over him.

She came to the locked door. Her body was heavy with tiredness, but Erikys could be hurt or worse right now. She couldn't be weak, and she couldn't waste another moment.

Adlai bent down. Using a couple of hairpins, she began fiddling with the door's lock. She hadn't picked a lock in a long while. Several minutes passed, each one swollen with her frustrated breaths and clumsier fingers. She couldn't get the concentration she needed. A hairpin slipped from her grip and dropped to the floor. She picked it up again and forced her breathing to calm. It helped when she stopped trying to listen for her uncle and focused instead on the little clicks from the keyhole and the scratching of her pins as she wiggled them just so.

Finally, the lock gave way. She grabbed the handle and pushed it open.

ADLAI EXPECTED THE room to be dark but it wasn't, not entirely. Blue, green, and yellow light came from tall crystals that had been smoothed out and placed in the sconces usually fit for torches. The light they cast softened the space, giving the blackness the feel of a warm night's sky. There were even twinkling stars. Adlai had come into the room to see what secrets her uncle had, but instead found her eyes drawn to the ceiling, where hundreds of small glass balls hung and bounced more light around the room. It was indoor starlight.

Whatever this room was, it was a beautiful space. A private space. Her stomach twisted at the thought that she was about to see something she would regret. She took a step back, hesitating, and then something made her freeze in place. An awareness of suddenly not being alone.

Her uncle was awake, was her immediate thought. And yet it wasn't a sound that had alerted her. The room was perfectly still and silent, only she wasn't alone.

She turned to a large armchair positioned near the window. The curtains were drawn and the armchair engulfed the figure so it wasn't at all obvious that anyone was sitting there. Only a quick glance of light had shown Adlai the shape of a person. A tingling sensation ran down her neck like cold sweat.

She swallowed and stepped closer. There was no point in hiding—this person, whoever they were, had surely noticed her. They had probably heard her fiddling with the lock and seen her the moment she came inside.

But the figure didn't move.

"H-hello?"

No answer.

Adlai's heart raced with a sudden feeling of dread. She wished the light was brighter, or that she'd chosen her sneaking for daytime, when everything would have been clearer.

A few feet away the crystal light caught on hair, turning it a shocking blue. The person was a woman. Familiar, even. Then Adlai saw that the blue wasn't a trick of the light, it was the woman's hair color. She recognized the sharp profile of the woman's face—regal and serene. It was Yaxine. Yaxine was slumped in the armchair and looking as though she was merely sleeping.

Only Adlai knew she was dead.

Her uncle had been keeping his dead wife's body in the room next to his.

A wave of nausea hit her and she turned away from that far too peaceful face. She gagged, wanting to throw up, but something was missing. Yaxine, she knew, had been dead for some time, and yet her corpse . . .

Although Adlai was sick to her stomach there wasn't a decaying-corpse smell to trigger her. She forced herself to look again—maybe it wasn't Yaxine, or maybe she wasn't dead anymore and really *was* sleeping. Adlai had come back from the dead; perhaps Yaxine had too.

She touched one of the woman's hands, noticing then that she was resting them over something soft in her lap. Her skin was cold and didn't respond. Adlai reached up and held shaking fingers to the woman's face: she wasn't breathing.

It was her. It was Yaxine, and she was dead.

She should go. Adlai should leave her uncle's place and go somewhere safe. Yaxine had been wrong to tell her to come here, but why, why had she lied?

She stood in the room for too long, questions spilling over her as interchangeable as the colored light. Why was her uncle keeping his wife in here? Why did she look like she'd died only moments ago? Was she frozen somehow? Between life and death? Was this how her parents would be?

She didn't hear her uncle get out of bed. She only heard him as he entered the hallway, and by then it was too late. He'd seen the door open, and then her standing inside.

Another question rolled over her as she met her uncle's eyes . . .

If trappers didn't take the body, how did his wife really die?

LUTH HAD BEEN mad at her before—furious, even. But now he wore a different expression. Shock passed over his face fleetingly and then settled on something colder. Fear. He walked the length of the hallway without meeting her gaze, and when he came into the room, he looked around it as though checking that everything was just where it should be.

He checked his dead wife last. His breathing calmed as his gaze settled on her, the panic and shock eased from his expression as if she'd woken up and smiled at him, telling him that all was well.

He was still looking at her lifeless face when he addressed Adlai. "This room, I believe, was locked."

"You're going to lecture me on invading your privacy when your wife's corpse is sitting there?" His voice might be calm but hers wasn't; she could hear the tremble of it and wished she could make it something fierce, something to cover up the fear she had standing in this eerily lit room.

"It isn't just my privacy you've invaded. I wouldn't mind it so much if it was just mine," he said, and now he did look at Adlai. The green crystal light flickered over his face and turned it deathly pale. She looked away quickly, hating herself for her cowardice.

She was afraid of her uncle, she realized. She thought she might have been afraid of him since the first moment she'd met him. Power radiated off him.

"Did you come in here because I called you weak? Stupid, even? Was it spite for that?" He didn't wait for her response, and she couldn't have answered him if she'd tried. Her throat was tight and trapped in all her words.

Luth closed the distance between them, and now there was no light on his face. Just darkness. "You thought to get back at me, did you? I must be a terrible disappointment to you, Adlai, for you to want to hurt me like this."

Hurt him? Adlai shook her head. "You pretend as though family is so important to you, but you're a liar. Trappers didn't murder your wife as you say. *You* killed her. You're not some victim." A wild idea came to her. "Who else have you killed and blamed on Arbil? Did my mother really die by their hands? Did my father?"

"Enough!" Luth's voice rose over hers. "Do you hear yourself, child?"

She flinched as he moved a hand up, but he covered his face with it and backed away from her. "I suppose I killed you in the market as well?" His breath shuddered out. "This is what you think of me? I should have spent more time with you. Yaxine told me to."

Adlai had plenty more to say but he held up his hand again. "I didn't kill my wife."

"I don't believe you," she said.

"Will you believe your eyes? Look at this room. Look at her!" His voice shook. "She's peaceful. She's . . . she's waiting."

It was the crack in his voice that made Adlai hesitate. She did as he asked and looked again at Yaxine.

She *was* peaceful, not like a person who'd just discovered her husband was about to kill her. And then she spotted something else. She'd thought Yaxine's hands held a pillow, but now she saw it was actually a toy. A soft gray rabbit with floppy ears.

Adlai took in the rest of the room, focusing on what the light glided past. There, against the wall and illuminated by the glow of the yellow crystal, she saw the unmistakable silhouette of a crib. There was other furniture as well, all small and child-sized. A box for toys, a little wardrobe . . . the rug at her feet was shaped as a cloud. It was a nursery. When she realized that, she felt sick again. She turned back to her uncle, the fear gone and a growing sadness filling its place.

"What do you mean, she's waiting?"

Luth stared around the room with dead eyes. He didn't touch anything and his voice was weary when he spoke.

"Yax was pregnant when the trappers came." He swallowed. "We were living in an even smaller community back then on the outskirts of Gem. Less than a dozen families, and we were careful, but still they found us." He sighed. "Some of us stayed to fight them off. I begged Yaxine to go. Your father had already left with you. All the children were gone. She had to think of herself and our . . . our baby. But she wouldn't leave without me.

"I should have just gone with her. Leena was fighting. Killing. She was so strong. We were outnumbered five to one and I remember seeing her cornered by eight of them and yet she seemed to be winning, she seemed to be in complete control of her power.

"Until she wasn't." He stopped. His breathing had become haggard. For a moment he looked entirely different. The cool, calm mask she was used to seeing was gone. Anger lit his face and warped his features. "Leena's shadow reached out and *pulled*. We all felt it. Everyone that had stayed behind to fight the trappers—she pulled on our shadows, and she *took* them. I saw Yaxine's ripped from her, while my sister's shadow grew larger and larger. Just holding on to my own shadow took all of my effort. I could only watch as hers weaved through our enemies and our friends, making no distinction between them."

For a long moment there was silence. Adlai felt as though she was standing in a grave she wanted desperately to climb out of, but she couldn't leave. The eerie light flickered over the three of them.

Then she found her voice. "My mother killed Yaxine?"

It couldn't be true. Adlai had met Yaxine. She hadn't seemed angry when she'd spoken of her mother.

"Leena didn't mean to do it," he said, soft as a whisper. "I know that. She lost control." His voice hardened: "But when I came to my senses, I didn't hesitate. I took Yaxine in my shadow and I left my sister to the trappers that remained. How they overpowered her, I don't know. Perhaps she was weakened by the effort. Or perhaps she realized what she'd done and let them take her."

Adlai shuddered. "My father, did he know what she did?"

He looked at Adlai. "It devastated him the most. I suppose I could have lied and told everyone that it was Arbil. That it was trappers who killed our people and stole our shadows. In a way it was. But I wasn't nearly so good at lying back then. When I came to this island I was grieving for my wife, my child, and my sister. For all the other lives we lost too." Luth leaned back, bathed in the glassy light from above. He seemed a million years old. So tired of the weight on his shoulders. "It feels like the grieving never ends. We're always losing someone."

Adlai had known grief, but watching her uncle she wondered what it would feel like to be responsible for so many lives. To be targeted over and over again for just existing.

"Did my father really think I'd be safer in Libra?" she asked.

"He feared what your shadow might become. I think he hoped keeping you away from other shadow casters could better help you tame it. The truth is that although we argued, I was relieved when he left with you. It was one less responsibility. You see, it's my job to protect the living and bring back the dead. Everyone in Arbil is waiting on me to find a miracle."

Her uncle stared down at Yaxine. His voice turned quiet. "I go to her sometimes. To the shadow world. I tell her I'll get her shadow back. I promise her the life we had before will come again. But I know our child is dead, and to go to Arbil will only lead to more death."

24

Without a Shadow

THEY CAME OUT OF THE ... nursery? Adlai wasn't sure what to call that room. Luth locked it behind them but he didn't need to. She was never going to set foot in that room again, and she hoped she could erase it from her mind. It was too sad, too lonely. Wordlessly, they fell into the living room, putting off sleep and where dreams might lead.

"You said you visit Yaxine," Adlai said. She drew her knees up to her chin on the sofa. Her uncle was sat a distance away. "Would she know if Erikys ..." She didn't finish her sentence. She didn't want to voice the thought that if Erikys had been caught, he might be in the shadow world right now.

Hope drained out of her as she thought of those black sands and the eerie silhouette of the city.

"Adlai." Her uncle's voice was sharp. "Don't think about that place. The shadow world is not somewhere to just go visiting. I do it because ... well, I shouldn't. There aren't exactly laws on this island, but when a loved one dies, we try to keep the family from doing what I'm admitting to."

"But why, when you can speak to them again? That's possible, isn't it? Yaxine wouldn't let me go through the gate, but that's where everyone is, isn't it?"

"Yes. But we don't go past the gate for many reasons," he said. "Not all our loved ones are at rest. Arbil conducts . . . experiments on our kind. The less information our people can provide Arbil about us, the better."

The word *experiments* echoed loudly in her mind. *Torture?* Were their loved ones being tortured for information?

"We have to find out if Erikys is safe," she said suddenly. "If he has been captured, he definitely has information to give Arbil. He's been in your study. He's seen those maps and the watch you have."

Luth sat up straight in his seat. "What are you talking about?"

But Adlai didn't care. He had to understand how important it was to get Erikys back. She quickly admitted to sneaking into his study with Erikys and prying through the drawers on her birthday.

When she was done, her uncle's face was a mask; she'd clearly worn out his anger.

"I'll send one of my men to check on him. If he wishes to come back, he'll be able to do so. Will that ease your mind?"

She wanted to argue again for herself to go, but her uncle had brought her back to keep her safe. It was the first time he'd shown that he cared what happened to her.

Could she trust him to do as he said? She'd seen him at his most vulnerable, and while that didn't mean he wouldn't lie to her again, she thought she could believe him on this. She had made him see it was in his interests, after all.

So she nodded instead. All her panic bled out of her, and she found that she was tired. More tired than her body and mind knew what to do with.

"Get some rest, Adlai," her uncle said, as though he could read her mind. "I'll let you know when I have news about your friend."

He led her out of the room, but as she went down the hall she turned back. He seemed somehow dimmer in the frame of the doorway, his golden hair diminished in the darkness, and she thought he must be feeling a similar way. Heavy and tired of all this. She had her parents and Erikys to be worried about. He had his wife and the hopes of everyone else on his shoulders.

"I want to help," she said. "With all of it."

His mouth twitched, a small smile.

"We'll talk more tomorrow," he said.

For a brief moment hope flared inside her. Tomorrow, Erikys would either be back, or she'd know he was safe with his family. She refused any other alternatives.

⁎

SHE FOUND ERIKYS in her dreams. He was running and wouldn't listen when she called out to him. So she reached for him, and her arm was her shadow, stretched out so long it grabbed him and forced him to stop. She watched him gasping for air before realizing her shadow was killing him.

In another dream she was the one running. The hooded stranger was chasing her, and she could hear a baby crying, but when she reached safety, she found herself in the nursery. Yaxine was there, only she wasn't resting peacefully; she was screaming for her baby.

⁎

ADLAI SKIPPED CLASS the next day and went to the storykeep. It was the place Erikys had always found so relaxing, and she wanted that peace. Inside, a chime called out her presence.

Caster Fecks looked at her from over his spectacles. In front of him was a tray of old leather-bound books that he was in the process of putting away.

He raised his brow. "If you're hoping to meet your sweetheart, he isn't around today. Haven't seen him all day, or yesterday as a matter of fact. I brought out some more books for him, but I suppose they've waited long enough to be read; a day or so more won't make a difference."

"Erikys isn't here," she said.

"I know that, child. That's what I'm telling you."

"No. I mean he won't be coming . . . he's . . ." Adlai shook, unsteady on her feet. She sat down in a chair by the window. It faced Erikys's spot. His hammock was outside with a mound of books weighing the middle part down.

"Lost interest, has he?" Caster Fecks peered at her more curiously than before. "I thought he was rather young to be spending so many hours reading."

She shook her head. "I don't know what happened." Suddenly she wanted to cry. To stop herself, she leaned forward and picked up one of the books he had in piles by the window sill. They were all within easy reach, as if he'd been worried of running out of them. The book she'd pulled was a medical one. It had diagrams of plants recommended for easing pain. She stared at the long, spined leaves, not really seeing them.

"Are you quite all right, child?"

"I didn't sleep well," she said.

Fecks nodded. "Well, take a nap if you like. My books won't disturb you."

Adlai didn't think she could risk falling asleep again. She didn't want to dream and her uncle could have news of Erikys any moment. But the lull of dusty bookshelves and lovers' lighting pulled Adlai into a peaceful doze.

When she woke, it was from the chime of the bell ringing again.

Kanwar, Nadir, and Farrin stormed into the storykeep. Or rather, Farrin did the storming. She marched straight up to Adlai, her features screwed up in rage.

"Did you know?" she spat.

Nadir put a hand on Farrin's shoulder. "Calm yourself, Rin. Adlai's one of us."

"Know what?" Adlai asked. She was groggy from sleep, but the tension between the three of them was hot in the air, like sparks buzzing toward her.

"Farrin's brother was sent to find Erikys," Kanwar said.

Adlai nodded. Her uncle had said he would send someone. But Kanwar was looking at her oddly. They all were.

"Is there news?" she asked.

"You could say that," Kanwar said slowly. "He's just now returned."

Adlai leaped from the chair. "With Erikys?" Her heart raced. Why hadn't her uncle come to find her?

"Oh, he's brought your lover back," Farrin said. The anger behind her words didn't make sense to Adlai. She ignored it, letting out a breath of relief that Erikys was back. He was safe. Farrin's petty jealousy didn't matter—though why she was angry about Erikys, Adlai couldn't begin to guess.

She made to move past them, but Kanwar blocked her way.

"You can't go to your uncle's, Adlai," he said.

Her jaw tightened. She thought Kanwar had wanted to be friends the last time she'd spoken with him, but here he was getting in her way for no reason other than spite.

"Watch me," she said.

"No shadows near the books!" Caster Fecks cried out. Adlai hadn't meant to bring her shadow out. All three moved away from her and she hastily pulled it back.

"I have to see Erikys," she said. "You can't stop me."

Kanwar eyed her warily. "You'd just get in the way."

"Of what?"

"The interrogation!" Farrin yelled, as if Adlai was stupid.

Nadir came over to Adlai and gently, like leading a child, guided her back to her chair. "Qwen discovered Erikys coming out of Arbil," she said softly. "They think he's a trapper."

THEY WERE WRONG. Adlai knew it in her heart that what they were saying about Erikys wasn't true. She knew it in her mind too, as she had *seen* him with a shadow. And he couldn't have lied to her. He wasn't even a good thief; it was impossible that he was some golden-tongued liar.

She didn't remember leaving the storykeep. She had a vague memory of the three of them shouting after her, of her arms fighting off someone. But the images were numb in her mind, and all she saw was her uncle's house getting closer.

At the door she heard voices. Her uncle's and someone else's. It didn't sound like Erikys.

But he was there. She opened the door and he was the first person she saw. Erikys was wearing fresh new clothes, whites brighter than the sand and leather bracelets trailing up his arms. If she didn't look at his face, she would say he seemed strong and healthy and definitely unharmed. These were all good things, but the expression on his face kept the unease pounding against her chest.

The man who had to be Farrin's brother, with lank brown hair and freckles, had his shadow out on the floor, snaking around Erikys like black ribbons moving in a continuous loop. Erikys's gaze was also on the ground, perhaps following the shadow's movements. He didn't look up—not when she opened the door, not when she walked toward them, and not when she called out for an explanation. Erikys had his shoulders bent and head low as if standing there caused him physical pain.

"What are you doing to him?"

"Adlai." Luth stepped towards her. "You shouldn't be here."

"I'm not going anywhere," she said. "What happened?"

"It isn't safe for you here right now," Luth said. "Not until I understand how he did it."

"Did what?"

He looked over to Erikys with none of his usual calm, instead fire fueled his gaze and he pulled out a flash of gold from his pocket. "Qwen found him with this."

It was Erikys's anklet. Only the chain was no longer painted a fake gold. Someone had cleaned it to reveal rich orange hues licking the metal like it was ablaze. Unmistakably, and impossibly, it was suraci.

"This is important, Adlai. I need you to think clearly for a minute," Luth said, his dark eyes intent. "Have you really seen his shadow? Seen him use it?" he pressed.

"I ... Yes."

Luth shook his head. "I don't understand how that's possible."

"Tell me what's going on," she said, really getting scared now.

What had happened to him? Erikys was a ghost of himself, refusing to look at her, refusing to say anything.

A coldness swept through the room as Luth drew his shadow out. One black line shot toward Adlai while two more moved to Qwen and Erikys.

It was a familiar feeling, but one she would never get used to. Her stomach lurched as the pull for her shadow became stronger. Her uncle was calm and entirely in control as he reached for all three of their shadows at once and tugged. Caster Shani had taught her how to resist such a pull, but this was something else. Her uncle was something else. It was all she could do to stay standing as she watched her shadow being dragged toward him.

A quick look at Qwen, and she saw he was losing the same battle. The shadow that had been circling around Erikys was now yanked straight and veered to her uncle.

Two shadows: hers and Qwen's, were at her uncle's feet like dutiful subjects. Only Erikys's remained, but when Adlai looked over to him, he was exactly as before. He was standing still, no sweat on his brow. His hands were unclenched and his expression steady. He wasn't reacting to anything, he was simply . . . standing there. His shadow wasn't being forced out.

He never went to class and yet he was fighting this pull. The first time she'd felt someone trying to take her shadow, she'd almost passed out in the desert market. The trapper had made her throw up on the sands.

"The boy's a suncast," her uncle said with a finality that she couldn't contradict. Not when she was looking straight at Erikys and there was no shadow there. He wasn't even denying it.

For the first time since she came into the room, his eyes caught hers and she found no warmth to them, only despair.

Her breathing slowed. One thought drowning out all others.

He lied. He lied, he lied, he lied.

25

Advantages

D RESSLA LOOKED ACROSS THE COLD chamber. Subject 187 was lying down in a reading nook surrounded by velvet cushions, with a blanket wrapped around him. A lamp flickered above several shelves of fat ledgers. From this distance he looked comfortable, but she knew that lying down was less a choice of his and more of a necessity these days. His energy levels were low, and he often complained of the cold.

He'd been almost a full month without a shadow now.

She rose from her seat, the billowing sleeves of her pale yellow dress slipping down over her hips as she walked leisurely toward 187. As was her custom when working, the only jewels she wore were the chained nose ring and ruby-red earring, but she made up for her lack of jewelry with the finery embroidered into her dress. Gold flowers and sunbeams shone over her body, highlighting her curves as she walked. Most men would drink her in and think themselves lucky to be in her company.

Most men would bloody notice her.

She cleared her throat when she was at arm's length from the subject, and still he ignored her.

And yet he was perfectly capable of giving her attention when he wanted something. In moments of regained energy, he'd make ridiculous requests. He wanted to see the hospital floors, or he wanted to go to the other side, where he might glimpse the desert market tents from the north windows. He wanted to see things, even if he couldn't do anything.

He wanted . . .

"Did you want something?" the subject asked, his gaze meeting hers with contempt. The standard white tunic and gray trousers he'd been put in were creased, his long dark hair ruffled and a beard was settling in.

"You were a thief, I believe," she said, "before you were captured."

He smiled as though his criminal life amused him. "I was."

"Thieves are known for being dangerous. Aren't they as likely to stab you as rob you if it was the difference between being caught or getting away?"

The subject sat up slowly. His face didn't betray any discernible change, but his shoulders, she noticed, tensed ever so slightly.

"Some have that opinion of thieves," he said. "Others understand it's a way to get by."

"You could have applied yourself to a legal trade."

He scoffed. "With what? I don't have a legal name. My parents were hunted, and their parents before them. You make us criminals because you won't ever let us just live."

Dressla ran her fingers on the back of the chair facing him. "If I'd been born with your advantages, there wouldn't be any limits to what I could do."

"My advantages?" His eyes flashed. "And what would those be? I've been hunted all my life. My wife was taken before our daughter could even remember her, just so you could run your sick failed experiments."

"Your wife has more blood on her hands than I do," she said calmly. "And yes, you had advantages. If I'd been born a man like you, I would have led armies. If I'd been born with a shadow like you, I would have done as the legendary shadow wielders of the past. They stole kingdoms, not trinkets from a market stall."

He leaned back, dismissing her as so many liked to do, and smiled. Her ideas amused him.

"You think I exaggerate? I've done more with shadows than in the entire history of Arbil. I understand how to extend life with them, cure diseases. Thanks to you, I'm close to—" She stopped herself. "But what's the point of telling you any of this? You have done nothing with your life."

"True," he said. He rearranged the cushion as if planning to resume his nap. "There's no point in talking to me at all."

She eyed him carefully. "Get up," she said. It was an order and her guards had trained him to obey her orders. Without looking at her, he stood up, and she knew he would follow her.

She made her way down the long lines of tables.

"You don't need me here," he said behind her. His voice was a soft murmur that seemed afraid of where she was taking him.

His fear was interesting. The experiments she'd conducted on him so far had been relatively painless. She'd taken his blood with and without his shadow attached. She'd taken partials from his shadow and examined different stimuli on it. Equitors, it was true, had been a little rough, pulling and testing his shadow's defenses. And he had been killed a dozen times, half of which had been his own stubborn fault. But he always healed, and would always heal. That was the gift of shadow. She let him stew a while longer as they walked, and then she called out for her new guard, Corwyn, to join them. His flame-red hair stood out among the gray lines.

Dressla stopped at the table where Subject 34 lay under the cloth. It was an old one, at least in the sense that the subject had been acquired some sixty years ago. Subject 187 wouldn't know this subject, but he stared down at the cloth as if he could see through it and the sight caused him pain.

He eyed Corwyn nervously and turned to Dressla.

"Whoever it is," he said, "let them rest."

She ignored him and picked up the subject's file. It read tragically enough. She quickly skipped over the notes of his last resurrection. Family—that was what she wanted to know. He was too young to have had a wife or children, but she saw that his mother and sister were both subjects here.

Mothers and sisters were important motivators.

"Experiments never work the first time you do them," she said, her voice faint as she closed the file. "But an experiment I did recently, it worked brilliantly the first time. Not perfectly. Not to its full potential, but more than I could have hoped for."

She removed the gray cloth, and a young boy lay as though peacefully asleep. He was the same age as Corwyn, but different in almost every way. This subject had dark brown skin and there was roughness over his lip and chin as though a beard had been attempting to come through. The white tunic he'd been put in had yellowed and his trousers were noticeably absent, his bare legs skinny as a small child's.

"You don't need me to help you with this," said 187.

"Technically, you're right. I don't need you," she said. She looked away from the boy on the table and stared across at her prize finding: The Mystery Man. It reminded her not to doubt herself.

"But I like you being around," she said. "I like what it means that you're awake. Every time your name is mentioned here, people say it knowing I was the one who figured out the puzzle. You help me every day by your mere presence." Her voice hardened. "The moment I let you become like this boy, that's the moment people begin to forget you were ever a mystery. You go back to being just another subject then. It might be decades before anyone bothers to revive you." She glanced down. "This subject hasn't been woken in over forty years."

"Does he have anything good to wake up to?"

"Perhaps not, but he'll wake up anyway because I require it."

Corwyn had been watching them, eyeing them back and forth like they were interesting subjects to him. She stepped toward him.

"Put this on." She held out a bracelet made of suraci metal with a clear gemstone hanging from it.

He shook his head. "I want to help with your research," Corwyn said, "not be the research. I'm not a subject."

Subject 187 turned sharply on Corwyn. "What do you mean, a subject? You don't have a shadow."

Dressla was no longer smiling. "Either do this, Corwyn, or go back down to the equitors department and find your assignments there. I have no use for you otherwise."

The boy's expression hardened. His face was still bruised, and his cuts were angry pink lines.

"I'll do it," he said. "But only if you keep me here. I'd be no good pretending to be one of them. I'm no spy."

Dressla clasped his arm. "If you were good at being a spy," she said, "you wouldn't have come to me all bruised and broken; you would have told your superiors what they wanted to hear. I don't want you to pretend. I want the shadow to be truly yours, with all of the power that entails."

She let go of his arm, and he took the bracelet.

"Your blade?"

Corwyn's dagger had a gilded handle and a crystalized red streak running down the middle. He handed it over, and she made a small incision in Subject 34's arm. Before it began healing, she collected the blood in a vial and gave it to Corwyn. He poured it on the ground, where his shadow lay gray and weak below him.

The blood turned his shadow black. When she gave the blood to Prince Thelan, it gave him back strength and some of his youth, but to an already young and strong man, it could give the power to steal shadow.

It was time for the resurrection to begin. Dressla opened the suraci watch chained to the boy's table.

A forced stillness and silence came over them as a wisp of black smoke drifted out from the watch. It clouded over the boy, pulsating above him until, suddenly, the subject let out a breath and the smoke around him vanished. Of course, Dressla knew it hadn't really disappeared. Instead it had become part of the subject again; it was his shadow, the source of his resurrection, the source of so many things that these people—these subjects—could do.

Subject 34 sat up with the alertness of someone remembering an attack. His eyes spun around the room, taking in the imposing figures of Subject 187 and Corwyn. He shrank from the sight of them.

Yes, Dressla thought, men would have been the last to have woken Subject 34 and she could well guess what experiments were done back then.

Subject 187 moved to shield the boy.

"Use me instead," he said.

"No," she said calmly. "And I'll have Corwyn put you down if you interfere."

She didn't quite know why it was important that this subject see what she was capable of. He'd shown himself to be ungrateful and entirely too arrogant. A man like all the others who believed she couldn't do what she knew she could.

Dressla was in control of this situation.

She sidestepped 187. Subject 34 was gripping the edges of the table and trying to make himself as small as possible. With just a tunic to cover himself, he kept his legs flat and bowed his head down, either in shame or fear.

"If this experiment is a success," she said softly, as though he were the only person in the room, "I can let you spend some time with your family. Your sister and mother are here, did you know that?" The boy's breathing picked up; his fingers turned white from gripping the table so hard. "Yes, I thought you probably did. They won't be harmed, but I can wake them. You can spend time with them. This man"—she gestured behind her—"he's been awake for several weeks."

The boy frowned and seemed to be processing the change of power in the scene. Dressla had offered to wake his family up. She had control over the resurrections.

Subject 187 moved away, a look of disgust on his face.

"You're one of us?" The boy spoke up, his question aimed at 187. For a moment he seemed to be expecting the other subject to come back to his side and help him somehow, but then the room did the work for Dressla. He looked around at the other tables, at the sheer number of subjects lying on them, and the reality of the situation sank in. He was trapped there. Corwyn seemed to sense the change too and relaxed, standing back behind her.

"What do I have to do?" Subject 34 asked. This time he spoke to Dressla, although his head was still lowered.

The sun was to Dressla's right, pouring in through a tinted glass window. The light cast her shadow, her very ordinary, slightly faded shadow off to the side.

She instructed Corwyn to stand where she was and his shadow became an unbroken form across the floor.

"Stand here," she said to the subject, and pointed at a spot where Corwyn's shadow lay.

The two boys were a similar height, though very different in looks and figure. One stood straight and strong in a dark uniform.

The other cowered in a frayed yellowed tunic and was cloaked in shadow.

"Don't do it," Subject 187's voice came in an urgent whisper. "Please, whatever you're about to do, just let this boy be."

She ignored him. The dagger flashed in her hand and she looked down on it with a moment's pause.

"I apologize that there isn't a more refined way of doing this," she said to the boy. "Shadows, unfortunately, seem to respond best to rituals. This ritual requires your death. Your family," she lied, "are uniquely useful for my purposes. If we aren't successful with you, we may have to try with your sister."

The boy turned sharply to Dressla. He'd reacted stronger to the mention of his sister than he had of his upcoming death. It was as she hoped.

"Why wouldn't it be successful? What do you need me to do?"

She put a reassuring hand on his arm. "It's all right. Just be very still. Imagine your sister is standing in front of you and all you desire is to protect her. Now, when you feel the tug on your shadow, don't resist. Let your shadow go. Do you think you can do that for me?"

The boy nodded slowly. He didn't look down at the dagger. Instead his eyes glazed over as though the deed was already done and he was a standing corpse.

Corwyn bent down and laid a hand on the ground, steadying himself, a calm, quiet focus drawn across his face. Subject 34 brought his shadow out. Dark as Corwyn's own shadow had turned, the subject's was stronger. A pit of black that circled around his feet.

Then the tug came. The subject's shadow was pulled toward Corwyn's fingertips. But instead of being twisted and dragged across the ground, as Dressla had seen with her other experiments, this time the shadow ran as smooth as a river called in by the sea.

When the shadow was in Corwyn's grip, Dressla plunged the dagger through the subject's chest. The stained tunic blossomed in red. She dragged the blade further down, losing her footing as the subject's legs gave out. They both stumbled, blood coating her hands and pouring down to the ground.

It has to fall in his shadow.

Her arm trembled as she pulled the dagger out and watched the subject die.

The first part was over. She hated how this experiment looked. It was more like a blood ritual than science. Yet it didn't look like blood, but like their two shadows had expanded and were inked out over the ground.

Corwyn winced slightly from the effort as he pulled the shadow in his grasp into the suraci bracelet. It flashed and then the clear charm hanging from it started to darken, turning black.

Dressla smiled weakly. The shadow was Corwyn's. It had worked again, but it wasn't enough.

"Test it," she said. It took a while before Corwyn heard her. He got to his feet and moved away from the body. Sunlight poured over his face and he drew the shadow out from the charm.

Subject 187 was several tables away from them. He'd fallen to his knees the moment Dressla had used the dagger, as though she'd stabbed him instead of the boy. His horror-struck face turned to one of disbelief as he watched Corwyn move the shadow around the room.

"Take something," Dressla said.

Corwyn smiled. He was enjoying the feeling, she thought, and was glad for him. Then his shadow whipped over her and a quick sense of cold—of fear—spiked in her. The boy was reckless, he was a killer and she—

She let out a breath as Corwyn bent down and retrieved a flash of gold from his shadow. Her nose ring. She felt her face for where it had been.

"You look prettier without it," he said.

Dressla laughed.

Foolish boy. Foolish men.

She came toward him and grasped his arm as she had done before. Her other hand still held the dagger.

"You're strong. The shadow will obey you," she said to him. "Use it and live."

Dressla didn't plunge the dagger in as she had done with 34. She didn't want to risk Corwyn striking back at her. She drew the blade over his throat instead. Quick—a slash that tore his artery.

"Die and come back," she was saying to him, but she wasn't sure he was hearing her. Blood was draining from his neck, and his hands, his strong hands were cutting into her, pulling her down with him.

Bosma appeared as if he'd been waiting in the shadows, watching. He was between them in an instant and yanked Corwyn away from her. The boy hit the floor, and still he wasn't dead.

If she'd explained this part of the experiment to him, would he have still done it for her? Looking at his betrayed face, she thought not. But she had to know if it was possible. If possessing a shadow meant the ability to resurrect.

Her body was strangely steady. Looking down, she saw that her beautiful yellow dress with the exquisite beading was ruined, but she found she could look around the rest of the room with some level-headedness. Subject 34's wound had already healed. He lay dead and peaceful. She would watch and wait for Corwyn—Subject 198—to do the same.

26

In a Murderous Way

ADLAI FELT ALONG THE RIDGES of the shell Erikys had given her. She wanted to hurl it into the ocean. It was right there. Moonlight teased off waves and shone down on the tiny shell as she held it in the palm of her hand. One flick and this lie at least could be gone. Footsteps came gently over the rocky path. She closed her fist around the shell.

Nadir sat down in the sand next to her. She tugged on her braid. "You have the most right to be angry," she said.

Adlai grimaced. Anger didn't quite cover it. She was deadened to the rage. She felt a puncture in her chest, and she wanted Erikys to feel it too. She wanted to hurt him back, or at least show him how much he'd hurt her.

"Are you angry in a murderous way, or angry as in talking might help?" Nadir asked.

"I don't need to talk about anything."

Nadir shook her head. "Not with me," she said. "With Erikys."

Adlai's head snapped in Nadir's direction. "I can't talk to him."

"Not if you're going to kill him," Nadir said. "But if you just want to talk, he's being held in the Sun Room. My mother's guarding him."

Adlai's breath quickened. Briefly, she thought how ironic it was that Erikys had finally been forced to go to class, and then she pushed the idea out of her mind.

"She isn't going to let me speak with him."

"Ma's stubborn, but she isn't heartless," Nadir said. "She'll let you through."

THE TEMPLE WAS empty of prayers, the ground floor vacant though incense still hung in the air, and the soft rainfall sound of sand could be heard as Adlai climbed the stairs. Outside the door to the Sun Room, Caster Shani was stationed alone. She was a guard with no visible weapons, sitting on a wiry chair with a small flame flickering above her and a book opened on her knees.

"You shouldn't be up here," Shani said. Adlai recognized the chair she was sitting on from class—it had the ugly cover with the eye on it. Shani leaned forward, and the larger-than-life eye stared at Adlai from behind her teacher's back.

"I need to speak with Erikys."

Shani closed her book. "Go home, Adlai. The situation is being handled."

"By who? You and my uncle? Qwen with his shadow wrapped around Erikys?" Adlai took two steps forward. "I brought him here. Let me . . . let me understand this."

Shani let out a deep breath. She shook her head. "Luth really wouldn't want you in there," she said. Then, more softly: "The boy's lied to you. You understand that, don't you?"

"Yes, and if I go in there, he'll lie to me some more." Adlai swallowed. She closed her eyes. "But I need to see him do it," she said. "It didn't look like lies before."

Adlai wasn't aware of Caster Shani putting the book on the floor or of her walking the few steps toward her, but suddenly there were arms around her. Her eyes blurred when she opened them. Shani's tattoos looked like ink stains spotting her arms.

"You really should go home and get some rest," Shani said. "This isn't your problem anymore."

Adlai looked over Shani's shoulder to the door. Erikys would be able to hear them. Perhaps he was hoping Shani's arguments would win out and she wouldn't be allowed in.

But hope was an easily crushed thing.

THE CLASSROOM WAS lit by a muted darkness. Starlight glinted through the stained-glass windows, but unlike the dazzling effect this had during the day, the colors on the floor were soft whispers instead of shouts.

Erikys sat with his back up against the windowpane. Behind him the black beast glittered against a blue background. Dribs of these dark and cold colors reflected off him and it gave him a pale, eerie look.

"Adlai?" He said her name like a breath of relief then glanced behind her, perhaps expecting Shani or her uncle to be standing there. But she had come alone.

She walked into the classroom until she was a few steps away from him. For a moment she remembered the heat of him, out in the desert market. How his touch had molded into her in a way that had made her want more, to be as greedy as a vendor catching sight of a heavy coin purse.

Now it was as though they were standing in separate layers of air. Erikys was huddled with his knees up and arms wrapped around himself. She looked down at him.

"Why were you in the cell opposite mine that day?" she asked, and was pleased at how steady and empty her voice sounded. Someone else was asking him the question, a stranger.

Erikys let out a long sigh and gripped his hands tighter together. "I almost wasn't there in time," he said. "You woke up barely half an hour after I was locked in. That day . . . a lot of things happened that day."

"I remember. I died. Did you see that happen?"

Erikys looked away. She took that as a yes and hated him some more. "Do you know the person who killed me?"

He cringed at the question. "He's not a bad person."

"You're friends with him?" For a moment Adlai was too genuinely shocked to say anything. Then she laughed, feeling a hysterical sob at the back of her throat. "Of course you are."

"You don't understand," Erikys said. His hands broke apart. "I was the one that was supposed to . . . you were supposed to be taken to Arbil by me. Corwyn, he saved me. He was meant to be the distraction, but then he took over. He knew what it meant if I didn't do this assignment." Erikys's lips twitched. "My first assignment was you."

"You weren't trying to rob me."

He shook his head slowly.

"You were trying to kill me?"

"Adlai, I didn't know you."

She laughed again. "Right. Because once you got to know me, you decided to lie and lie and lie until you got all the information you needed to run back to Arbil."

"It wasn't like that," he said, his voice sharp. She'd offended him. "I joined Arbil because—"

"I don't care!" Adlai stood straighter.

She hadn't meant to raise her voice. As she calmed herself, a coldness swept over her and she realized her shadow was itching for release. That wasn't good.

She would control herself.

"It doesn't matter to me why you joined," she said, a degree calmer. "I just want to understand how you came to be in my life." *So I can pull you right out.*

Erikys nodded as though he understood. He clasped his hands together again and looked down as he spoke.

"Arbil has a list of known shadow wielders. I was given your name for my first assignment. Madam Dressla, the woman who runs the research there, she requested you." He cleared his throat. "We don't call it killing. You don't really die, at least that's what we're taught. Your shadow can resurrect you, so the death part is only needed to trap your shadow . . . I—I realize now that it is a death, the lives of all those people have stopped, they've been taken from their family and friends. It is death."

Adlai gritted her teeth and had to concentrate very hard to keep her shadow away. "I told you I'm only interested in what happened that day."

He sighed. "You had to die that day, Adlai. Arbil doesn't accept failure, and for my family's sake I couldn't lose that job. Corwyn did what I couldn't. He saved the assignment. He saved me."

It should have been Erikys who looked away first, but a wave of heat, of nausea passed over her, and she had to focus on the floor.

The hooded stranger of her nightmares, the one Erikys had comforted her about, was a friend of his. Without his smiles and little nicknames, Adlai didn't recognize this boy in front of her. *I never knew him.*

"It all went wrong when he tried to take your shadow," Erikys said. She forced herself to turn back to him.

"I felt him take it," she said. "I *saw* him hold my shadow in his hands. Why didn't he trap it?"

"He did. It's just a little complicated." Erikys spread his hands out. "Obviously you still have your shadow. When you died in the market, we went back to Arbil, me and Corwyn. I thought the assignment was done, but—" He stopped. "When I heard you'd woken up, I felt relieved. I thought it meant Corwyn hadn't really done it, that I hadn't just made my friend a killer."

Adlai paced away from him. "But he did kill me, and you say he did trap my shadow. Are you deliberately not making sense? You think the more you talk, the better chance you have of getting out of here?"

"No, Adlai." He said her name softly. "I'm just telling you what happened."

"You're telling me how you felt. Which means you're lying again."

Erikys leaned back and dropped his head against the glass. "All right. The bare facts then. You woke up because you still had your shadow. The shadow Corwyn had taken wasn't yours, which didn't make sense to anyone at the time, least of all us. We were both brought before Madam Dressla to answer her questions. She seemed more curious than angry. She was interested to know if you'd seen me in the market and if you'd remember me. I told her you might but that you thought I was a thief. She liked that. Told me to think up a backstory and, if I was religious, to pray."

"Are you religious?"

It was another thing she didn't know. He'd talked of his father being religious and scorned it, but perhaps it was religious mania that had led him here.

"No," he answered. "But I did pray after."

"After what?"

"Madam Dressla was running an experiment. It had been failing, but she had a new idea that she thought could work. She made me her test subject along with another boy. He had a shadow. He was my age. Her idea worked, and I . . . I was given his shadow."

Adlai froze in place. "How were you given his shadow?"

"I've told your uncle how she does it. Don't make me tell you," he said quietly. "Madam Dressla told me I could clear Corwyn if I discovered what had happened—whose shadow he had taken and why you still had yours. But really she wanted you to trust me so you'd bring me here and I could find out where the hideout was and how many of you there were."

She smiled at him, her heart twisting in her chest to hear how stupid she had been.

"You did very well then."

He shook his head.

"From the moment I saw you I haven't wanted to do what Arbil asked."

Adlai laughed. "Stop, Erikys. Just stop."

"You don't believe me."

"I think I trust my uncle more than you right now."

"You shouldn't. He wants Arbil destroyed, all of it, and he doesn't care who he sacrifices to do it."

"You were spying on my uncle. That day you wanted to search his study—it was for Arbil, wasn't it?"

Erikys sighed and closed his eyes. "Arbil isn't evil, you know. Its methods are, I understand that now, but it's right in its ideas. Researching shadow and shadow wielders has opened up so many pathways to cures. Your powers aren't what you think they are. Stealing or traveling. Killing. Shadows are meant for healing. You have a thousand cures in your shadow. It should be shared. Madam Dressla might be wrong in how she discovers those cures, but . . ." Erikys opened his eyes and looked up at Adlai. "I told you my brother had been sick, didn't I?"

"Another lie, I suppose," she said.

"No. He's perfectly healthy now because of Arbil, because of Madam Dressla's research. He would have died without shadow research."

"Is that supposed to make me feel sorry for you? Or be glad that my parents were taken from me *for research*? Would you give your parents up so some strangers can live?"

He shook his head. "I'm sorry," he said. "I didn't mean it that way. I just wish everyone here understood what their powers could do. I've read your books on healing, and there's so much left out. If shadow wielders were to do the research themselves . . ."

"I'm sure that'll be our first priority once we stop getting murdered."

"I didn't want it to be this way, Adlai. I asked you to take me back because I wanted it to be just us. I really was planning on leaving Libra and Arbil, all of it. When I asked you to come with me, I meant it. That's all I wanted."

"You were using me."

Erikys flushed. "I was falling in love with you!"

She scoffed, turning away from him. "You just wanted information for Arbil. That's why you didn't meet me back at the market. You were there."

"I had to end things on good terms with them," he said, his words sounding desperate to Adlai. "If my brother ever got sick again, I couldn't risk them not helping him."

"So you did give them information."

"About your uncle. Not you. He isn't a good person, Adlai."

Adlai turned to go; she'd heard enough. He'd been sent as a spy and he'd done his job well, so well that he was a stranger to her now.

"The complicated thing," Erikys said, getting to his feet in a rush. "The reason why Corwyn took your shadow but didn't have your shadow—it's because the shadow he took from you wasn't yours."

She kept walking to the door, determined not to look back. It was just more nonsense meant to keep her there.

"The shadow was your father's."

She touched the handle but didn't turn it. Her breath caught in her chest. It shouldn't be possible that another lie from him could hurt her, but this one punched right through.

"I saw him, Adlai. Madam Dressla must have some interest in him because he's not like the other subjects. He's awake. He's being kept awake."

27

Bait

"YOU SHOULDN'T HAVE GONE TO see him," her uncle said. He paced the living room dressed in shades of gray with his feet bare. She didn't think he planned on sleeping tonight.

"But is it possible? What Erikys said about my father?"

Luth shook his head. "I can't imagine why Dendray would have given you his shadow. Or why Arbil would let him stay awake. The whole story is ludicrous."

And yet Adlai felt her shadow had been different since the trapper attacked her. She'd thought it was from coming back from the shadow world, but what if for the last seven years she'd been using her father's shadow? What if all that time she'd felt her shadow as a comfort, it was because she'd still had some part of her father with her? And now he had his shadow back. The trappers had resurrected him. If Erikys was speaking the truth, her father was alive, waiting for her in the Arbil pyramid.

"We can't wait anymore," she said. "If he's awake we have to get him out somehow."

Luth stared down at Adlai, considering her for a moment. "If we go to Arbil, it will be for everyone," he said. "Are you serious in wanting to risk your life for the chance to save them all?"

He asked the question as though there was a real chance that they could do this.

"You have a way into Arbil," she said.

"I have, for the first time, a trapper."

"Erikys?" She blanched. "You can't trust him."

"I don't need to trust him," he said. "I need to trust the prisoner he'll take with him to Arbil."

Her uncle began to explain his plan. One of the secrets to Arbil was the suraci hidden in the entranceways. Setting foot inside the hospital meant losing your shadow to the metal. But Erikys's anklet could store a person's shadow inside it. Without their shadow, a person could walk into Arbil. They could pretend to be captured by Erikys and let themselves be led through Arbil's defenses. And then when they were far enough inside, Erikys would release their shadow back and they could clear the way for reinforcements.

Adlai stared at him. She wasn't sure where to start on such an obviously flawed plan. "Has Erikys agreed to this?" she asked. "Because you know he lies. He won't give the shadow back."

"Erikys will do as I ask because he believes in stories," Luth said. "The Arbil pyramid has many stories of me. They know my shadow can kill, and I may have . . . warned him that his family won't be safe if mine isn't."

Adlai paled. "You threatened his family?"

Her uncle brushed a hand in the air. "I'm not really going to hurt them. But stories are powerful, and he believes I will."

Adlai's stomach turned. She shouldn't care that Erikys was being threatened—he was a trapper, his job was to threaten her life.

And yet his family members were innocent.

"Even if he did get someone into Arbil and gave them back their shadow, there'd be trappers everywhere," she said. "What could one shadow do?"

Luth reached into his pocket and placed the copper watch she'd seen in his study on the coffee table.

"It really was a trapper's watch," he said. "My shadow destroyed it."

"It destroyed suraci?" She frowned. The metal she'd seen in the market was fire, it was power—it was the trappers' greatest strength. "How?"

"How do we kill with our shadows? Yours and mine, Adlai, we can overpower things others can't. We can destroy suraci." He took a breath, but his eyes held a manic look. "One of us simply needs to get inside the heart of Arbil."

"One of us?" She laughed. "There won't just be one watch to destroy. Or one trapper to get past. One person can't do it."

I can't do it.

"One person can start it," he said. "You have the power to destroy the way in." He knelt down in front of her, their faces level and his voice a whisper. "You hear him too, don't you? Manni will make sure nothing happens to you. His power will guide yours and wherever you go, I'll be able to find you."

Adlai drew back, afraid that talking about him would bring the god of Death into the room. "That's how you found me in the market," she murmured.

"Yes. It doesn't matter where they take you, I'll come for you, and then we'll release all our people trapped up there. Think how many there are. Our numbers will be greater than theirs, and we'll destroy all their suraci. Every last piece."

"I can't control my shadow," she said. "Not like you. It should be you that goes with Erikys."

"It can't be me. Arbil knows of my power. They won't believe one boy was able to capture me."

Luth came to her and cupped her face.

"You will give the appearance of weakness," he said. "They will never suspect your strength."

ADLAI HAD TO talk to someone who wouldn't lie to her. Who would tell her, honestly, if she could execute this mad plan or not.

It was late but she didn't even have to knock on Kanwar's door. He must have seen her coming, as he was waiting outside when she came up the path.

"Did you speak with Erikys?" he asked. He had a long navy jacket on that was open, and it rustled in the night's breeze. She tightened her own jacket, the camel one Penna had given her what seemed like a lifetime ago.

She nodded. They should go inside to talk, and yet Kanwar seemed to know that she wasn't going to step inside the house Erikys had stayed in.

Cold as the night was becoming and with no destination in mind, they began walking. Kanwar's strides were slower than usual. He turned to her after a beat of silence. "And is he really . . ."

"A trapper," she finished for him. "My uncle thinks he can use him to get into Arbil."

Kanwar frowned. "Use him in what way?"

Adlai told him. Her voice shook as she repeated the plan, and she wasn't sure if it was from fear or excitement. She wanted to be the hero, she realized, but she was afraid.

"And does your uncle intend to bring many casters with him?"

"I don't think he's bringing any. He said he'd free the ones in Arbil."

Kanwar stopped walking. "But if the plan works, and you're able to free them, they'll all be newly resurrected. Some will have been stuck in the shadow world for many decades. They won't be able to just get up and fight."

Adlai hadn't considered that. Had her uncle overlooked that point, or was there more to his plan than he was telling her?

"What would you do?" she asked.

Kanwar cocked his head to the side and considered her. "Your shadow's powerful," he said. "I've felt it myself. If, as you say, you have the extra power of Manni helping you, then I'd believe a few trappers and some suraci might be no match for you. But we're talking about the Arbil pyramid. You and your uncle can't do this alone, and if you do, then you'd be putting your life in the hands of the god of Death."

Adlai wrung her hands. "You make it sound like we're dead either way."

"I've met Manni, in the shadow world when I first died," Kanwar said. "And he wanted me to stay dead."

She swallowed. "You wouldn't go to Arbil then? You think this plan won't work."

Kanwar looked away from her. The darkness of the night coated him in shadow and she couldn't read his expression.

"I don't think you should go," he said. "Not alone. Not just with your uncle and the hope that a god will help you. You need something better to rely on." He sighed, his eyes bright. "But if my parents were in Arbil, I would go regardless."

* * *

ERIKYS WAS STILL being kept in the temple, but his appearance had changed. His clothes looked new; he wore a fresh tanned shirt, a collection of leather bands around his wrists, and dark trousers with gold thread marking the hems. It was a much finer outfit than she'd seen him in before, and she wondered if he'd chosen these clothes himself—if the farm boy fool she'd met had never existed.

Erikys flinched when he saw her. His eyes darted to her uncle. "Her? You want me to take Adlai?"

"You're not the only one who can pretend," she said.

He shook his head. "Someone else. You have to bring someone else," he said.

"I don't have to do anything," Luth said. "You've made your choices, and she's made hers."

Her choice. Was it her choice? Talking with Kanwar had made her realize how foolish it would be to go to Arbil—and how impossible it was not to. She couldn't leave her parents there. Not if there was a chance that she could bring them back. Going wasn't a choice. Doing nothing wasn't an option.

Her uncle brought the suraci anklet out and Adlai's heart ached upon seeing it. The black gemstone was no longer black. She could see now that it was clear and hollow. Erikys had kept his shadow that she supposed was never really his inside the orb, and now it was empty.

But not for long.

"Are you ready, Adlai?" her uncle asked.

She took in a breath. Giving up her shadow would be temporary, but she remembered how it had felt to have the trapper in the market rip her shadow from her. How it felt in every class they practiced stealing shadow.

Her eyes found Erikys's. His bulged in panic. Her uncle was making him part of the plan—Erikys's choice was as much guided by family as hers was. Which meant she would surely get her shadow back. He wouldn't risk his family.

They're not at risk. Her uncle wouldn't really hurt them. His threat was a bluff. And yet she hated everything about this situation.

Erikys didn't want it to be her going, and she didn't want it to be him she had to go with.

She stood opposite him, feeling like a fool as their true roles fell into place. Erikys with the suraci chain—and Adlai with her shadow out toward him.

But it was her uncle who guided her shadow into the orb. It was less brutal than the desert market and still Adlai was shaking when it was done. She was so cold. And weak.

I can't do this.

"It's all right, Adlai." Luth's voice was calm. Soothing. He didn't sound like someone about to lead her into a death trap, where he'd promised that he'd follow. "Take a minute."

She'd fallen on her knees. Sickness curled in her stomach, but she forced in steady breaths.

She was vaguely aware of Erikys crouched down next to her. "Don't do this, Ads. Let it be someone else. You never have to see me ever again, just stay here and be safe."

Another breath in and out. The sickness was passing. She found her voice.

"You promised me an adventure, didn't you? Just you and me."

"Arbil isn't an adventure. It'll be your death if you go."

She shook her head. The colored lights from the temple windows were blurred and muddled together. "If you care about my life, you'll give me my shadow back when I need it."

She wanted it back now. She was weak without it, but she looked up at her uncle. "I'm ready," she said.

Her uncle smiled. His shadow was as smooth as a black river rushing over the floor. It turned the air to ice. The power of it took over the entire room, flooding it in darkness, and she felt herself soaring into nothingness.

28

Arbil

ADLAI WAS SURE THE ARBIL pyramid had grown since she was last here. Had it always been so massive? The desert sun burned across the golden brick. It eclipsed all other buildings and dwarfed the city walls so that it seemed as if the city was merely a series of shrines gathered around it.

And if the city was so easily swallowed by it, what chance did she stand? The pyramid had been around for hundreds of years. It would stay for hundreds more.

She thought over her uncle's plan and it fell apart in her head. Like collapsed tent poles, the covering blew off in the wind. Her uncle wouldn't be able to find her; she'd be left alone in there, and the hooded stranger . . . *he* would find her, and this time he wouldn't fail; she would die in that building.

A city guard at the gate called them over. Adlai's heart raced. The fear wasn't of the guard recognizing her or denying her entry; it stuttered like a panicked mouse over the moment they'd be let through and she would have nothing stopping her from going into Arbil.

A selfish, cowardly thought. Her parents were in there, that should be more than enough of a pull forward. And it was; she kept her feet moving, but she couldn't deny the other pull, a stronger one, telling her not to go through with this.

While Erikys talked to the guard, Adlai looked over her shoulder, past the queueing crowd and out to the desert market they'd left behind. She couldn't see her uncle, but she knew he was there somewhere. He would be following them on his own—her second shadow. A much stronger one. She didn't doubt he was itching to leave the colorful tents and head through the city gate himself. Her uncle wouldn't be hesitating like she was.

The guard let them pass. They made for an unremarkable couple coming into the city. Erikys in his tanned shirt and leather wristbands, and Adlai in a long skirt the color of dust tracks and a sleeveless black top. Plain and dark. Nothing like how she'd dress for stealing in the market, but she was playing by her uncle's rules this time. It was his plan, and she'd volunteered to be a part of it.

"You don't have to do this," Erikys said. She glared at him, angry that he could seem to read her mind. He'd turned into a stranger for her, and she wished she could do the same, to transform into a girl he didn't know. Preferably a girl he hadn't kissed and made a fool of.

"You aren't like your uncle," he continued. "Arbil's a hospital. Whatever you plan on doing, you'll be putting people's lives at risk. Sick, vulnerable lives."

"As if you care about innocent lives," she hissed.

He grabbed her hand. She tried to yank it away but his grip was strong and hers was trembling.

"We can still go. Leave everything behind like we planned. I don't . . . I can't watch you die again."

Finally she pulled her hand away.

"We're barely ten paces from the gate and already you're going back on your word," she said. "I'm not like you. My words mean something."

"It shouldn't be you going in there!" Erikys dragged his fingers through his hair. "I'd take anyone else." He flushed. "You should be helping us. Your people have all these books and knowledge on shadow. We could be allies in making cures."

She laughed. It was calming. "You're naive if you think we'll ever work with Arbil," she said. It was pure naivety and she started to walk again, her steps more determined.

"If you saw the cures being made," he said. He hadn't moved but his voice carried over the wind. "Cures like the one that saved my brother, you'd want to be part of that. I know you would, Ads."

Her smile was stiff and frozen across her face as she turned back to him. "Probably you're right. You know everything about me. And I know nothing about you."

<hr />

ADLAI HAD NEVER been inside the Arbil pyramid before. Her father had said it would be inviting illness and death, which had of course been another lie, like the one about suraci metal being cursed, or her shadow only having one trick. All to keep her from the truth. So many lies.

She'd never been inside, but she had admired the outside from a distance. Arbil had seemed to be in the corner of her eye at all times, as much a part of the landscape as the sun in the sky.

But as beautiful as the exterior was, for some reason Adlai hadn't expected to find it just as beautiful, even more so, inside.

It was a dark kind of beauty. Dozens and dozens of torches were fitted along the walls, making for pinpricks of starlight inside the golden brick, but the space was just too large to illuminate fully. It gave a softness to the air and drew her eyes to what things the light did pass over. Large arches and stone staircases curved playfully from one corner to the next. There was a garden in the center with water trickling down and seating arranged under the shade, miniature trees acting as privacy curtains in some areas. White stone columns were stamped from ceiling to floor with carvings that had constellations swirling around them. Bed frames had silk curtains and the marbled floor had rolls and rolls of beautifully embroidered rugs. She couldn't believe half of what she was seeing as everything was so ostentatiously rich. Were patients sick on those rugs? Did they bleed on silk beds? The idea seemed ridiculous. This wasn't a place for the sick; this was a palace for kings.

No, Adlai reminded herself, *this isn't a palace—it's a prison.*

Erikys led her to a staircase, this one straight instead of curved but equally daunting to climb. She was so tired. Without her shadow, her body just wanted to sleep. She blinked away the thought. But then Erikys went around the staircase and examined one of the columns it was attached to. She recognized the hero Menko's constellation worked into the stone. He pressed on one of the stars and in the wall behind the stair a concealed door shuddered open.

Through it was a dark passageway with a fiery gleam at the end of it. *Suraci.* They reached a large copper cage, big enough to fit several people inside, and the lick of suraci coated the top and bottom bar.

A young boy, perhaps fourteen or fifteen years old, sat inside, bored. He glanced up at Erikys, recognition lighting his eyes before they turned quizzically to Adlai.

"Who's she?" the boy asked.

"Madam Dressla has some questions for her," Erikys said.

The boy didn't lose his frown but he opened the cage for them to step inside. Given how much suraci was wrapped around the cage, he must have felt secure letting anyone inside.

With the door closed, the boy began spinning a wheel and the cage lifted from the ground. It was a slow ascension. Nerves ripped through Adlai, the only thing keeping her alert when every part of her body wanted to lie down where she was.

Great idea to do in a cage.

She focused away from the bars. Erikys was standing a touch too close. Close enough that she could see a strand of his hair loose on his collar. The kind of closeness that would have had her pulse racing just a few days ago.

It was still racing, but she put that down to being inside a cage in enemy territory without any power.

Finally the cage stopped moving, and they were locked on a new floor. One that had to be very high up on the pyramid because the darkness below her seemed to stretch on forever.

The boy opened the door and Erikys and Adlai stepped out into another dark passageway. Fire sconces lit the path ahead. Adlai looked behind her as the cage began its slow descent and felt her stomach drop with it. They had to be getting close to the gate, the one her uncle wanted her to pass through before having her shadow returned to her. Would her uncle really be able to follow her up here? She hadn't known about the cage. Would he be able to destroy that much suraci?

Erikys slowed his pace as they reached a corner they needed to turn. His face glowed in the torchlight.

"Adlai, whatever your uncle has planned, if it doesn't work out and you end up . . . a subject," he said the word carefully. "I want you to know that I'll find a way to get you out. You can believe I don't care about you, that I was just using you, but I won't let them keep you here."

She looked away from him and his burning gaze. "If you're okay with all the other people like me being stuck here, I don't see why I should be any different."

He was about to say something else, but she was no longer listening. She turned the corner and gasped.

The corridor was black from the walls to the ceiling to the floor. But there was light. Glowing paint along the walls showed constellations, with planets paving their path on the floor. Mercury was in the right position to give strength to the Thinker constellation. Venus was overseeing justice by the Gallows. It didn't look like an accurate star chart, being more of a decorative one that showed a simplified version of how the stars and planets could be read. She thought it was beautiful, until she approached the end of the corridor.

Here there was a gate with a larger-than-life dagger shot through the bars. Menko's dagger. The one from the storybook that killed shadow wielders. Like the story, the blade was covered in flame.

Adlai shivered. The fire was a trick of the light, as the dagger's blade was made entirely of suraci. Erikys caught her up and they walked in silence toward it. This was the gate she had to destroy.

She swallowed. She wished she was back in the desert market. Choosing marks there had been so easy. Stretching her shadow out had been second nature. What she had to do here seemed impossible, even with a god's help.

"Back again?" There were two guards behind the gate, and one of them smiled at Erikys like they were old friends. "Can't seem to get rid of you these days. The peace we had when you were away playing make-believe with your shadow."

Erikys smiled, but there was a falseness to it that she could see now. "Apologies for making you get off your ass and have to lift a key to a lock. You have such demanding work, watching a gate."

The guard, who was far from fat but rather bulked up with pure muscle, laughed as he swung a set of keys around. The other guard rolled his eyes and nodded to Adlai.

"This isn't a bring-your-girl-to-work kind of place," he said. "And we've had no mention of any visitors due."

Erikys pointed down to his anklet. "She doesn't bite," he said. "Trust me, Madam Dressla will want her to be let through."

The two guards shared a look. The muscular one shrugged and slipped a key into the lock.

A wave of heat passed over Adlai as she came through the gate.

THE COLD CHAMBER had been cleaned and Corwyn had been put to rest, not on a metal table, but on the sofa by the research tomes. He had a number, but he wasn't quite a subject. Not in the sense Subject 187 was. Subject 187 would never have his shadow returned to him for his own, but Corwyn . . . if he would only wake, Subject 198 would be the start of a whole new era.

Why won't he resurrect?

Dressla brushed her fingers over his bare neck. It was pale as milk and made the red slash across it look more violent—like a scream coming from his throat. His bruises and cuts also remained, and this wasn't right. This wasn't one of the beautiful deaths her subjects were supposed to have.

The experiment should have worked. For the previous equitor she'd had to forcibly take a shadow and connect it with him. But Corwyn had been *given* his freely. The ground shook suddenly and the nose ring Corwyn had stolen from her fell from his limp fingers. She turned and found Bosma hovering nearby.

"Find out what that was," she ordered.

As her guard left, she looked across the room.

Subject 187 was as far from her as the cold chamber allowed. Corwyn's corpse had taken over 187's usual corner, and so the subject had taken a corner of the room that had no seating, no books—nothing but a window. She pulled her beaded shawl around her and made her way to him.

"What is it like when your shadow is returned to you?" she asked.

Subject 187 had his forehead pressed against the glass and hadn't moved at her approach. His voice, when he spoke, sounded weary.

"It feels like you've been walking around naked and cold and now finally a path opens that blazes warm in front of you. You follow it."

"Then why doesn't he? Why are his wounds not healing? Why does he stay like that?"

The subject peeled his head away from the window. "That boy is dead. You killed him. The shadow world is for my kind. The god of Death barely tolerates us being there. He won't accept a boy born without a shadow."

Dressla frowned at him in puzzlement. He hadn't struck her as the religious type.

"Do you claim a god gave you your shadow?" she said. She smiled. "If so, what does that make me?"

She wasn't expecting an answer, but the subject shared her smile. It was the kind she hated though. A small, sad smile she'd seen so many men give her when they thought she wasn't seeing the full picture. As though her female eyes could see only so far.

"It makes you destined for disappointment," he said. "Eternal disappointment."

FEAR FLOODED THROUGH Adlai as the gates locked behind her. One of the guards caught her panicked look and shook his head at Erikys.

"You should have let the healers bring her up here. The usual way."

Dead. They meant dead. She shivered and glanced at Erikys. If he was going to betray her, it would be now, trapped as she was in enemy territory.

"I don't like doing things the usual way," Erikys said. He had his back to the two guards, his hand on Adlai's arm, and he guided her further down the hall. There were stairs at the end of it, but if she walked up there without her shadow, she might never walk down them again.

Without her shadow, she was trapped.

She stumbled and tried to pull away from him. She needed to think. If she could just get her shadow she could be strong again. His grip tightened, holding her in place and his eyes darted to find hers.

"When I release your shadow," he said quietly, "run up those stairs and leave the guards out of it. This is just a job to them."

She relaxed in his grip. He wasn't trapping her here. He was keeping his word. But why was he worried for the guards?

"I'm not here to harm anyone," she said, angry that he thought she would. "I'm here to free my people and break suraci."

She shouldn't have said anything. The guards might not have been able to make out her words, but she wasn't supposed to talk back to her captor.

"Is she giving you problems, Erikys?" the larger of the guards called out to him. The other guard had sat back down at his post, but he also looked over at them.

"No more than I can handle," Erikys said back. He should have pushed her forward, made a show of his authority, but instead he let her go. With a smile just for her, his next words were a whisper. "Then go steal freedom."

He bent down. For a bizarre moment it looked as if he was bowing to her. She heard the confusion of the guards, the shuffling of feet moving toward them. Then it was drowned out by the rush of power that swept over her as her shadow was released.

They'll take your shadow again if you don't act fast, the beast whispered. *Give it to me.*

Manni tugged inside her shadow, his claws pressing down through it with impatience. She hesitated. Her uncle had promised her that Manni would keep her safe and destroy suraci. But giving the god her shadow would make her powerless again.

A yell brought her back to the moment. The big guard had drawn out his sword. Erikys pulled her behind him. She had to act now. Adlai closed her eyes and let her power slip into those claws.

Her shadow became a wave of darkness. It roared up from the ground and pushed toward the gate.

Thump. Thump. Thump.

Adlai snapped open her eyes. Heartbeats throbbed in her shadow. The two guards were lifted into the air and she watched with horror as they slammed into the gate.

Thump. Thump. Thump.

The heartbeats slowed. The ground shook—and then, silence. The guards hit the floor.

Adlai ran forward but it was too late to help them. She saw it in their glazed, stupefied eyes. They were dead, and the gate . . . the gate was broken through as if a giant fist had punched its center. The gleam from the fire-licking metal was gone. Dead.

Her shadow was a blaze of power, devouring the light. The corridor sank into darkness. She wanted to pull it back, to reign in her shadow and control what was happening. But she couldn't. Her shadow was as oppressive as Libra's sun, only she felt no heat, just a thick relentless weight to the air that seemed to scorch her flesh when she tried to pull her shadow back. She flinched and looked up at Erikys. He was crouched beside her and still had the suraci anklet open.

"Take my shadow back!" she cried.

He blinked slowly. He'd known those guards, and her shadow had just killed them. Adlai tried again to pull her shadow in. This time the darkness rolled toward her. Only her shadow wasn't coming back to her as she'd thought. It lunged instead for Erikys.

"NO!" The scream came as a guttural call from deep inside her. A denial so strong that she thought it must change what was happening. She reached out and her fingers clawed at her shadow, desperate to drag it away from him.

Thump. Thump. Thump.

No. No. NO!

Darkness wrapped around Erikys like black velvet. A sickening silence filled the air. Finally her shadow calmed and she pulled it back, feeling the familiar power seep into her. Only she was still shaking.

Erikys lay on the ground, his curly hair mussed around his face, which was still and silent. She bent over him, pushing his hair away. His skin was cold to the touch. That was impossible though. She remembered the heat of him next to her and how he radiated warmth in his smile, in his eyes . . .

They stared at her blankly. Unseeing. But he couldn't be dead. She wouldn't let him be.

29

Untethered

FOR TOO MANY YEARS THE Arbil pyramid had taunted Luth. Brighter than the sun, taller than any building, it was rooted in the sands like a mountain he could never climb. The surface was too slippery. Arbil was a place of healing for the sick and vulnerable, but its walls were crafted to be a tomb for people like him. How many shadow casters had it ensnared over the centuries of its evil practice?

But no longer. Incredibly, and more so for not being of his making, he at last had the perfect way in. His sister's child was the key. A naive and rash key, but she wasn't only these things. The girl had raw power, just like Leena, and though she didn't know how to use it all yet, she was brave enough to try.

Try. He hated that word. Adlai must not *try*, she must *do*. Do the impossible. Destroy Arbil from the inside.

He stood by the entrance and cast his shadow out barely a handspan in front of him. He just needed to know when to begin.

Manni's presence filled his shadow. Eager, as he was, for the beginning of the end. As he waited, Luth looked for city guards or trappers that he could use when the moment came. But there were just sick and ordinary people wandering around with no sense of urgency, no sense that change was in the air.

It's time.

Luth hesitated. Yaxine wouldn't like what he was about to do, but he saw no other way. Her shadow had been out of his reach for so long, and now he had a chance to get it back. No matter the cost.

It's time, Manni repeated. Luth wished he could destroy suraci another way. One preferably without the god of Death's help. But it was unavoidable—he knew that, and so he let his power sink into the clawing darkness.

Manni showed no hesitation. Using Luth's shadow, the god leaped into action and grabbed a passerby at random. From his size and bulk, Luth thought it was a grown man, but when he felt the heartbeat inside his shadow, it was young and fast and healthy.

Too late to change his fate. The man—boy—was thrown against the entranceway. The heartbeat stilled. The boy's death leaked down and coated the walls and floor.

It was regrettable. But so was much of Luth's life. He stepped over the body and his shadow, large and menacing, stayed with him as he entered Arbil for the first time.

<hr />

KANWAR SUCKED IN a breath. They'd been watching Caster Luth for some time wondering when, or if, he would enter Arbil. Farrin fidgeted next to Nadir.

"I told you it wasn't safe. We should go back," she hissed. He knew she'd only come to keep Nadir out of danger, but seeing Caster Luth kill a stranger at random like that made Kanwar feel the same way.

This really is dangerous. More people will die.

But Adlai was inside Arbil already, as well as countless other shadow casters. This was supposed to be a rescue plan, not a massacre.

He started moving forward. Nadir tugged on his arm.

"Kan . . . what good can we do?"

"Nothing if we stay out here," he said simply.

LUTH WANTED TO laugh. Manni's voice had guided him to just the place the trapper had told him about—a secret entrance behind a straight set of stairs. Only the trapper had failed to mention that the hidden door would have no handle or any clear way to open it. Perhaps the boy had hoped staring at the wall would make Luth think twice about coming up. Perhaps he'd hoped Luth wouldn't even have been able to make it past the entrance with his shadow.

He pushed his power out over the wall and focused on the shape of the door. Black smoke trailed the ridges of it and he let the entire door sink into his shadow. Luth was getting Yaxine's shadow back today. He was bringing her home. He was bringing them all home, even if he had to rip out every damn door to do it.

ERIKYS'S EYES WERE still open. Wide and afraid. Wide and screaming at Adlai to do something.

The boy who had lied to her, the boy from the cell who had made her laugh and kissed her as though he needed her was lying still and staring, staring, staring.

What had been the last real conversation she'd had with Erikys? She couldn't remember, but it would have been cold. She'd treated him like he was a stranger because that was how he'd felt to her. Not now. The boy lying on the ground wasn't a stranger. His laugh had been real. His kiss had been.

Moments she had doubted before appeared razor sharp in her mind, and she didn't doubt them now. He hadn't wanted her to come to Arbil because he'd feared she would end up lying cold on the ground, as he was. He had cared about her, and she had walked him to his death.

Her shadow had killed him.

In desperation, she moved her shadow over him. Bathed him in the darkness and tried to look through it. Did it contain his last breath? His soul? She couldn't have stolen something so precious. She didn't want it.

Take it back! She willed her shadow to bring him back to life. Her father had told her once that she had to *want* a thing for her shadow to do it. That was all.

Trembling, she closed his eyes, wanting more than anything for those lashes to flutter, for this to be a mistake, because Adlai didn't just want Erikys to come back, she *needed* him to.

And yet nothing happened. Her shadow held no miracle. Erikys stayed dead.

Time passed, each moment worse than the one before because there was no change, only a heavier silence. As if she were staring down a void, and it was staring back telling her there was nothing, nothing, nothing.

Then she heard movement. She looked up as her uncle stepped through the broken gate, and hope burst through her.

"My shadow," she said, stammering, "it attacked Erikys."

Luth came over, but it seemed to her that he did so in slow motion. He tried to lift her up, away from Erikys, but she shook him off.

"No, you have to help him," she said. "What did it do? Do you know what it did to him?"

Her uncle knelt beside Erikys. She thought he was examining him, until she saw him look down at the suraci anklet. Like the one in his study, it was now just copper.

You can't trust your uncle. Erikys had told her that. She heard him say it with such clarity, it was as if he was saying the words to her right now. Her shadow had destroyed suraci, just as her uncle said it would. But he hadn't told her it would kill to do so, and that anyone wearing suraci would be a target. That was why her shadow had gone for Erikys. Because of his anklet.

"Help him!" she yelled and dragged her uncle's hands over Erikys's chest. "Use your shadow, do something!"

Erikys had said their shadows could heal, and her uncle was the most powerful caster of them all. He could do it. He could save him.

Finally he moved. He checked Erikys's pulse, then he looked at Adlai and spoke, but the words were meaningless.

It was only when he left her there and moved toward the stairs leading up that the words hit her.

You'll thank me, Adlai, when you meet your parents again.

⌁ ——— ⌁ ——— ⌁

BOSMA HADN'T RETURNED. That wasn't like Dressla's old guard at all. It wasn't in his nature to keep her waiting.

She paced around the cold chamber. Death seemed to cling to the air more than usual. Her eyes kept falling back to Corwyn, drawn to his shock of red hair like blood and the stiffness of his body, reeking of failure.

Subject 187 was the only living person in the room besides herself, and he would kill her if it meant escape. She held tight to the dagger.

Truthfully, 187 looked too weak to move. He was slumped far away from her and had his eyes closed. When was the last time he'd eaten? Perhaps it would be best if she put him down like the other subjects. His information hadn't even helped her with her experiment. Yes, the shadow had attached, but so had it before. She wanted more. She wanted the shadows to give their new hosts resurrection ability. *Power over death.*

A scream ripped through her pacing. She stopped short and 187's eyes flashed open. The scream had come from the floor below, where the ground had shook moments ago. But there were dozens of equitors down there, many of them seasoned fighters. They wouldn't be screaming in terror—there was no danger on those floors.

And yet there was another scream from below, louder this time. Uncertainty flooded her. Dressla gripped the dagger's handle so tightly she thought she'd bruise her palm.

She was too exposed in the cold chamber; it was too full of potential enemies, she thought, as she side-eyed 187.

The logical thing to do would be to kill him and lock herself in her office. But, she realized with distaste, she was afraid. Fear drew her to his secluded corner of the room, so well hidden from the entrance, and she crouched down beside him. It felt better to be hidden, to be next to someone, and to be the one holding the dagger.

If 187 noticed her fear or her sudden closeness, he showed no signs of acknowledgment. His eyes stayed closed, his breathing slow and weak. It could be all an act though. Dressla kept the dagger steady in her grip.

From this low position, she watched the door open. But it wasn't Bosma. It was a face she recognized, though she'd never met him before, because he was the mirror of his sister, Subject 179. Like his sister's, his power loomed large, and even from this distance she felt the air change as though his shadow came with a wind of its own. She shivered.

Luth Blacksun had entered the cold chamber room.

The leader of the shadow wielders had been sighted all over Zodian for decades. A phantom that could appear on the beaches of Piscet one morning, then across farmlands in Virgo the next. He was everywhere and nowhere. Arbil had hunted him throughout the kingdom, never catching more than a sighting, a mere whisper to add to his legend. Now he was here. Dressla shrank further into her hiding place. It was impossible. He couldn't have escaped so many equitors. One man could not have done this.

Footsteps rushed toward Adlai. She tensed, expecting enemies to come through the broken gate, but when she looked up, she saw three familiar figures.

Through the gloom she made out their faces. Kanwar. Nadir. Farrin. They'd followed somehow. Perhaps Kanwar had been worried after their last conversation. Or Nadir's mother, maybe even Farrin's brother, had known more than Adlai about what would happen here.

She gripped Erikys harder. Protective. Tense. Afraid of what they would say.

They came cautiously. She saw their eyes take in the two dead guards, the broken gate, and Adlai crouched over Erikys, holding on to him as though he would slip away otherwise.

Nadir bent down on the other side of Erikys. The concern wrinkling her face made Adlai want to vomit.

"Did . . . did Caster Luth . . ." she began. That was worse. Adlai couldn't keep listening. She couldn't tell them that it was her shadow that had done this.

She turned away and caught Kanwar's gaze. His eyes were lit with an intensity as if he already knew what she was going to ask of him.

"Save him," she said, her voice hoarse. "Bring him back."

He was the top student of the class; every task Caster Shani gave him, he completed without struggling for a moment. He never failed at anything.

But Kanwar shook his head. Slowly. Sadly.

"He doesn't have a shadow," he said. "He can't come back without one."

"He can have mine."

"It doesn't work like that," Nadir said. Her voice was soft but final.

But it did work like that. Erikys had *had* a shadow. He had taken it somehow to trick them all. Arbil had found a way to give people shadows, and Erikys had told her uncle how they did it.

She relaxed her grip on Erikys and slowly pulled away from him. It all came back to her uncle. His plan. His secrets. She would force him to help her this time.

Farrin was whispering urgently to Nadir, the two arguing about something. Adlai drew away from them and headed for the stairs her uncle had gone up.

Only Kanwar stepped in front of her.

"This isn't the place for us," he said. "We came to take you home."

She flinched at the word *home*. "I chose to come," she said, moving around him. "You can make your own choices."

"The girl has a death wish," Farrin said. Adlai ignored her. Already Nadir and Kanwar were following her up the stairs, and then even Farrin, with some more grumbling, joined them.

Each step got heavier. She was leaving Erikys behind, and she prayed, as she'd never prayed before, that it wouldn't be the last time she saw him.

The doors on the fourth floor were as tall as three men, heavy, sturdy things that had been flung wide open. The rooms inside were large and entirely destroyed. Bodies, weapons, books—they were muddled as though a giant toddler had gone on a rampage and tossed their toys in every direction, breaking them.

"Did your uncle . . .?" Nadir started. "How did he do this?"

Kanwar answered for her. "He couldn't have caused this destruction. This is a god's power."

Manni. The god of Death. Her uncle was using the god's power, as she had, and this was all it knew how to do: to destroy.

The hallway on the fifth floor was less chaotic than the one below. Only a handful of guards lay dead. Adlai heard something clatter to the ground behind one of the doors and headed in its direction.

Inside was a huge, gray room with neatly lined metal tables surrounding the space. Goosebumps prickled over her arms. The air was deathly cold, and in the center of the room was her uncle, his shadow impossibly large as it spread across the many tables, his back to the door as he focused on his task.

The four of them stood transfixed. Farrin with a protective stance in front of Nadir, and Kanwar looked at Adlai warily. She moved away from them. Whatever her uncle was doing, no good could come of it.

Clang.

Suraci watches broke from their chains and clattered to the floor as she walked the path to her uncle. Each one opened as it fell and black smoke trailed upwards, darkening the ceiling like a night sky.

Her steps faltered. She was awed by her uncle's power, too scared to move forward and feeling more than ever that Kanwar was right: she shouldn't be here.

Then she saw a figure rise from the corner of the room. She wouldn't have noticed him if he hadn't moved; that end was blocked by a half wall and too much clutter.

Unsteady on his feet, the figure of a man came toward her, swaying like he was drunk. But the face . . . the face . . .

Adlai had struggled to remember her father's face all these years, but now she thought it hadn't changed, not one bit. He had looked exactly like this. Dark, messy hair, a thin, scratchy beard and bright, bright eyes as he smiled.

Her feet could move again and she ran to him. Burying her face in his chest, she started shaking and sobbing as she clung to his familiar smell. He was real. She had been lied to over and over again, but this was true. Her father was alive, he was here.

"Little Drizzle." His voice rumbled by her ear. The same voice, the same nickname. Adlai wanted this moment to stretch on, to be as endless as shadow and frozen in place. She had her father now, and he would know what to do.

"You have to help," she said, though her voice was muffled and she didn't think he heard her. She lifted her face up but her arms were still hugging him and she became aware of how baggy his clothes seemed to be. He was so skinny, paper-thin flesh wrapped around awkward bones, and his whole body trembled.

She'd never seen her father ill before. She'd never seen him weakened by anything.

"What have they done to you?"

He didn't get a chance to answer. The room brightened around them and they both turned to see that Luth's shadow had lessened. He stared across at them over the mounds on the tables, bewilderment written over his face as if seeing a ghost, but the wrong ghost.

THE WORK IS *not complete. There's still more suraci.*

Luth ignored the growl in his shadow. He stared at Dendray hugging his daughter and something twisted in his stomach. Why, of all the shadow casters here, would he be the only one to resurrect? His power had never been anything special.

"Where's Leena?" he asked.

"Brother," Dendray said, smiling still. It wasn't a true smile though, just as they weren't truly brothers. Dendray looked over his shoulder and Luth took in a breath, thinking for a moment that Leena would be there and all would be right. But although Luth registered a woman slowly rising as if out of a dream, it wasn't his sister.

He didn't know this woman. She was undoubtedly beautiful though in a rich blue dress, and a gold band like a crown was laced through her dark, puffed hair. And she was holding a dagger.

"What number did you give my wife?" Dendray asked the woman.

"Number?" Luth scowled. She wasn't a shadow caster. She wasn't one of them. The claws in his shadow itched and he let them extend the twenty paces out toward the woman. "Who are you?"

"I'm Dressla. Head of Research in Arbil." She said the words as if they were an achievement, a light she'd pulled up in front of her and not a death sentence.

"And where," he said through gritted teeth, "do you keep my sister, Leena Bringer?"

"We don't resurrect 179," she said.

His shadow lost its patience and ripped the dagger from her hand. She stumbled backward, marveling at her empty palm as if something interesting was written in its lines.

"Today is a special day," he said. "Perhaps your last if you want to make things difficult."

The woman—Dressla—looked at him carefully. Assessing an opponent, he thought, which was ridiculous because this woman merely studied power; she had no power herself.

"She's over there," Dressla said finally, pointing to a line of tables a few rows behind them.

Luth moved quickly to the line of tables. Leena had taken many shadows that day; it was time for them to be released.

THE CEILING ABOVE them rumbled. The black smoke Adlai had seen leaving the watches had gathered like clouds building toward a storm. Power she didn't understand was shifting above them.

Adlai drew her father to the door. She wanted to leave. To be safe somewhere with him.

"Can we go now, princess?" Farrin called out to her. The three of them hadn't moved further into the room. Their shadows were out, smoke trailing upward as if they were ready and waiting to leave.

But something was strange about their faces. The strain written across them.

"Adlai," Nadir said. "Our shadows are being pulled. I can't . . ."

Adlai looked again at the smoke. It was trailing upward, as she'd seen so many times in class, but there were wisps coming down from the ceiling. As if coaxing her three friends' shadows to join them.

Nadir fell to her knees. Adlai rushed to her but not before Farrin took charge. Her shadow swirled around Nadir and the two of them vanished.

Kanwar blinked in surprise. His own shadow was trembling. He looked at Adlai and her father.

"I can't take both of you."

Suddenly there was a cry behind them. They all turned to see Luth bent over a body. It was a woman. Adlai saw a glimpse of golden hair, the mirror of Luth's. The mirror of Adlai's.

You'll thank me when you meet your parents again.

Her uncle's words repeated in her head. He had done all of this for this moment. Her father was here and soon her mother would be too.

She stayed rooted to the spot. She couldn't picture her mother being here. She was someone Adlai wasn't supposed to see because then she would be real, and then Adlai would need her.

They should go. Kanwar could take her father away, and Adlai . . . she would find a way out of here, somehow.

But her father looked down at her, a soft expression on his face.

"She'd want you to be there," her father was saying to her. "She won't want to miss another moment."

It was a mistake. Kanwar's eyes bore into her as her father took her hand and led her through the tables, like he was bringing her through the desert market and she was that little girl again. Safe because her father held her hand.

"I don't understand." Luth's golden hair covered his face as his fingers gripped tight on the watch still chained to the table. It had turned to plain copper like Erikys's anklet. Like most of the watches in the room. Which meant that her mother's shadow had been released.

And yet her mother was lying still on her metal bed. She didn't look like Yaxine had—it was harder to mistake her for sleeping because her skin looked deathly pale, her lips had a bluish tinge, and the stillness was too absolute. Too final.

Everyone had told her she looked like her mother, but Adlai couldn't recognize herself because this wasn't a person: this was a corpse.

Luth threw down the watch. He stared wildly around until he found what he was looking for. *Who.*

His shadow twisted out and wrapped around Dressla, the self-proclaimed head of research, and dragged her toward them.

"Where is her shadow?" he demanded. "Explain what you've done to her."

The woman caught her breath. She steadied herself, watching Luth's shadow retreating with something akin to hunger, Adlai thought. That shadow could as easily kill her as it had dragged her across the room, but still the woman looked at it like it was something she could reach out and take for her own.

"They aren't resurrecting," Dressla said, quietly as though to herself. She picked up the broken watch Luth had discarded. "The shadows are released, but they don't attach themselves . . ." Again, it was like she was making notes to herself. She looked up at the black smoke pulsing above them. The released shadows had grouped together and were drifting untethered. Raw power just waiting to fall down on them.

"What does that mean?" Luth said. "You're here." He pointed to Adlai's father. "Why would you be the only one to resurrect?"

Her father opened his mouth to answer, but Adlai answered for him.

"It's you," she said to her uncle. "Your shadow killed them."

Luth shook his head. "No. I—there were others downstairs. I killed trappers on the floor below. It's their deaths that are destroying the suraci now."

But he didn't sound convinced, looking around the room with new eyes. There were still some bodies his shadow hadn't reached. Adlai could see the suraci metal gleaming in the distance.

"They're dead," Dressla said, astonished. "My subjects are really dead."

30

The God of Death

THE SHADOWS ABOVE THEM SHIFTED. Like a curtain being drawn, the huge black cloud split into two and then fell. Each half spilled onto the floor and reformed. Smoke swirling and flickering, switching to fire and back again. Two raging black fires were before them, and through the smoke, shapes appeared. Figures. A figure that looked like a woman formed in one, while a man formed in the other. They were faceless, flickering eerily between body and smoke.

The room had been cold before; now it was freezing. The black flames radiated ice. Adlai's father hugged her but she couldn't stop shaking. Then a third flame came, and from it emerged a single shape: a huge black beast. It didn't flicker; this shape was solid, a physical and alive presence that she recognized from the shadow world. Manni. The god of Death was in Arbil. All the light in the room suddenly dimmed and even the shape of the beast seemed to sink into the darkness until Adlai could see only the eyes.

Cold blue eyes.

Life should really hold more value.

The voice came from the beast, though not from its mouth. The words bled out from somewhere inside those eyes.

Then the darkness moved. Adlai was aware of the two black flames still blazing behind the beast as it moved toward them.

"You have to go." Her father's voice. He was pulling her back, but it was hopeless. The darkness took over the whole room, it froze her in place.

"I—I can't."

Adlai's father spun her toward him. His eyes were frantic.

"Go with that boy," he said. Kanwar had run over to them as soon as the beast had materialized. His shadow flickered in panicked waves.

She shook her head at her father. "What about you? Do you know the hideout?"

"I know it. I'll be right behind you."

He wasn't looking at her, and his fingers pressed too deep into her arms.

"You're lying." She pulled out of his grasp. But why would he lie? Why wouldn't he leave with them?

"Your shadow," she said. "Bring it out."

Her father paled. He looked so sick. So lost.

He doesn't have his shadow.

"It's time we go," Kanwar said.

"No." She moved away from them. Luth was fixated on Manni, pleading with him about something, and the research woman looked like she was about to faint.

Adlai couldn't leave here without her father. And then there was Erikys. She closed her eyes and saw Erikys lying on the floor. Warm, brown eyes that looked so wrong in death.

Death. Death was everywhere.

Her mother was supposed to have resurrected; all the shadow casters were supposed to be saved, and yet nothing had gone as planned.

Adlai stumbled through the maze of tables. A corpse lay on every surface. She wanted to be sick. Her uncle had pushed several out of the way to kneel in front of Manni. Adlai stopped still at the sight. He'd looked so powerful before, but now darkness loomed over her uncle and he seemed a tiny, flickering candle, desperate for the wind to be kind.

"Leena's watch is destroyed, but her shadow is gone," Luth said.

"*Her* shadow?" There was unmistakable anger in the beast's voice. The entire room was blackening. Shadow seeped over the walls, the floor, the tables. It was as though the room had become part of the shadow world and the beast's shape was getting lost in the darkness. But the voice, the voice pierced straight through her. "It was never her shadow. You can't know how insulting it is to see a human wearing shadow. And what you do with it, performing your little tricks . . . it is a gross misuse of the power. Today, at last, is the beginning of the end."

"The end of Arbil," her uncle said, rising. He spoke as though trying to find his footing on loose soil. "The end of trappers."

Manni didn't answer. He came from the shadow world; it seemed impossible that he could be here with them now. Not hidden in her shadow but a physical form looming down on them.

"Luth, brother," her father said, "remember Leena. Remember what this thing did to her. What her shadow became because of him! You can't trust a word he says."

"You promised me her shadow," Luth said. It was hard to see his face in the darkness but she knew he wasn't talking to them. Perhaps he hadn't even heard her father.

"I promised you that I would help you destroy suraci," Manni said. "You are the one that stopped me from completing that task."

"But the shadows—"

"They are released, also as promised." A sharp frost entered his voice. "I never said I would return the shadows to your kind."

His voice was a low, rough growl. He paced the room as suddenly as a shift in the air. "It's selfish of you really. You have power you've no right to. Power that is needed to restore balance in this life and the next. I have done my best and I have waited for your lines to die out naturally, but you keep breeding, diluting the power more and more until I begin to think my siblings will never return. The trio must be reformed. The world of the dead is mere shadow without my brother's power, and the world of the living grows too fat without my sister's."

Adlai didn't understand. The shadows were supposed to resurrect the shadow casters, but Manni was talking as if he planned to resurrect his siblings—*resurrect gods.*

"Please," her uncle said, desperate. "Give me her shadow."

"And which would that be? Your sister's? Your wife's?"

Luth fell to his knees. He was silent. As though he couldn't say the word.

But Manni, Adlai knew, could speak to him through his shadow.

What deal are you making with him? she asked into the depths of her shadow.

Cold laughter filled it. And then the god's voice rippled through. *He's choosing his wife. He's giving up his shadow for hers.*

Adlai didn't believe the voice. But as she watched her uncle, she saw his shadow stretch toward Manni. A black wave that became consumed by one of the flames. Then, out of the other flame a small, faint shadow fluttered over to Luth. He wept as it wrapped around him. In his hands he made it smoke.

"Luth!" her father yelled. He understood what her uncle was going to do before Adlai did. But again her uncle didn't seem to hear. The smoke turned into flames and her uncle was gone.

"Damn him," her father said.

What will your choice be?

Adlai froze. Her pulse seemed to throb through her ears as she listened again to Manni's voice in her shadow.

Your mother or that boy you loved? Give me your shadow and one of them will live again.

Her chest tightened. She understood her uncle falling on his knees. She understood his desperation, and she thought . . . she thought she might even have understood his choice. But it wasn't one she could make.

Pinpricks of light came from the scant few suraci watches left. They glowed like dying stars in the dark; there were still some shadows trapped inside them.

Shadows were what Manni wanted, and if there was one thing Adlai knew how to do, it was stealing what others wanted.

She stretched her shadow out. Sweat poured off her even in this cold room. Her skin felt like fire, like it was about to explode.

"No!" Manni saw what she was doing. Her own eyes were blacking out and yet she felt each of the watches as they dropped into her shadow like pebbles into water. Each one was a person who could be woken. Those were the lives she could save.

You think you can keep them? he growled. *Very well.* In the next moment he pulled the research woman and her father toward him like strings through the air. The only two people in the room without shadows.

The only two people who couldn't defend themselves.

Adlai grabbed her father. Not with her hands, but with her shadow. He was suspended in the air. Tugged on one side by a god of Death, and on the other side by his daughter.

Dressla was thrown into one of the two black fires burning behind Manni. Adlai yanked harder. She wasn't going to lose her father. Not again.

Her father fell to the ground. Manni's shadow retreated, but only for a moment, and then whipped out again. This time it took Kanwar in its grip.

Adlai crouched over her father, exhausted. She watched with horror as Kanwar struggled in Manni's grip, his own shadow swallowed up by the god, before being tossed into the other open flame.

"Stop!" Adlai yelled.

"Your kind called us the Death Trio," Manni said. "But it isn't a trio if only one god is left to do the work. I have more need of these shadows. The old powers of my siblings must be reawakened. I tried to do it once before with your mother. There weren't enough shadows then."

Adlai shuddered. There were plenty of shadows now. She looked up and saw the research woman writhing in the air, black flames licking through her and so many shadows snaking around her, into her.

Adlai's father was whispering to her, urging her to use her shadow and go. She shook her head. The flames were getting colder and colder.

Deep in the other flame Kanwar's eyes shot open. The whites of them were full black. He was drenched in shadow, and yet Adlai sensed he was looking straight at her. As if a void had opened up in the space between them and was pulling her toward him.

Hot tears ran down her cheeks, but her skin was so cold. She was shaking. She didn't think what was happening to Kanwar could be stopped, but she was afraid to leave him, afraid to leave Erikys, afraid to leave her mother. Leaving meant accepting they were gone.

"Run!" Kanwar yelled.

Manni laughed. It was the least animal his voice had sounded, and yet it didn't sound human either.

"You can't run from me," the beast said. "Everywhere you go, I'll be waiting in your shadow."

Even now Adlai felt Manni in her shadow. A cold, clawing presence. And yet he didn't comprise all of her shadow. Her power was her own—only his when she'd given it to him.

She needed that power now. It was hers, and she would use it to save her father. Ignoring the beast, she focused only on her power. Her shadow started to smoke. Power burned through her and it was more than she could handle. She'd already stretched herself so much, she could feel her hold slipping as the enormity of her shadow crashed over her.

It was the power of death. It was a changing force. A shift in time and space. It wanted to take everything it touched. It wanted so much.

But its wants were tied to Adlai's. It was a part of her.

She reached for her father, the same way she had a thousand times before in the desert market. Her shadow grabbed him, and his weight sank into it.

Her shadow was fire as it raced back to her, ready to take them out of this place of death.

When she closed her eyes, it wasn't cold, endless black that greeted her. Instead she was surrounded by warmth and color. The bright tents of the desert market blazed in her mind and she heard the raindrops of tiny hammers, felt the ridge of a shell and her father's arms wrap around her as she thought of home.

Epilogue

ADLAI STOOD ON THE ISLAND'S beach. Her shadow trailed smoke as it left her father and came back to her.

She'd done it. She'd brought herself and her father home. Or not quite home. The ocean was vast and nothing like Libra and the little shopkeeper's apartment they'd once lived above. But it was full of memories and glittered like its possibilities tipped the waves.

Her fingers reached inside her skirt's pocket, where the tiny shell Erikys had given her was tucked away. She hadn't been able to throw it away, and now it was all she had of him. His life had been in her shadow. It was as much her fault as her uncle's or Manni's, because she hadn't been able to take back control. She'd failed him.

Her father shivered and eased himself down on the white sand. He looked ready to fall into a deep sleep. He seemed to have aged in the last seven years, though Adlai knew his body had been suspended in an ageless state for most of it. His exhaustion came from the strain of being without his shadow. Being without power.

She knelt down beside him. His hand reached for hers, and he smiled.

"Little Drizzle," he said. "I didn't think I would ever leave that place."

"We can't stay here," she said. "Manni will come for us."

For me. He'd want the suraci watches and the shadows inside them. He'd want all their shadows. He wouldn't stop until his siblings, the Death Trio, were fully restored. Adlai didn't know what that would mean for Kanwar, but she knew the people on this island wouldn't be safe with her tainted shadow around, one Manni could whisper into at any moment.

And yet she'd seen her uncle take his wife's shadow, and she'd used her father's shadow for all those years, hadn't she?

Adlai drew out the suraci watches from her shadow. Clumped together they looked like a small fire pit on the beach. She took one and handed it to her father.

"Take the shadow in there," she said.

He hesitated, perhaps feeling the wrongness, as she did, of taking someone else's lifeline.

Adlai picked up another of the watches. Wisps of black smoke drifted up as she opened it. She let them drift a moment, drawing out her own shadow.

I'll still find you.

Manni's voice rumbled through her shadow, an edge of desperation making it louder than before.

You might not like me when you do.

To protect the others, she would have to trap her shadow, which could kill, in the suraci watch for now. Manni had used her shadow to kill. He'd taken Erikys, her mother, and so many others. Even now he had Kanwar at his mercy.

Adlai didn't care how long it took: she was going to send the god of Death back to the shadow world and make sure he never had the ability to kill again. She was done losing people. She was done running. And she was done fearing her power.

It had just been a game at the start, but the rules had changed; her shadow could do so much more than she'd believed herself capable of. She was no longer playing the Shadow Game her father had taught her. She'd been tricked into playing her uncle's version, and Manni had tricked them all. *Now*, she thought, *it's time to play mine.*

About the Author

H. J. Reynolds is a british writer. She was born in Reading and studied Film Studies at the University of Exeter. She then went on to complete her Masters in Creative Writing at the University of Lincoln. She now lives in Lincoln with her husband, two little ones, and her even more needy cat. You can follow her on her blog where she posts reviews of books, dabbles in writing advice, and features bonus content of short stories, usually of the surreal/supernatural variety; because fiction is magical, so why not add zombies or pirates with wings? *Without a Shadow* is her debut novel.

$$\cdot\!\cdot$$

Acknowledgments

 M I REALLY AT THE acknowledgment stage? I love reading this section in books—it's always so crazy to read how much work goes into every one of the books you find on the shelf.

My first thanks have to go to my parents. You can be the biggest dreamer in this life, but it's important to have people who believe in your dream as much, or maybe more, than you do. My parents imagined my work being published long before I thought it possible. They not only took my writing seriously, but I have my mum to thank for my book-nerdiness, and my dad to thank for my movie-geekery. Both forms of storytelling shape every idea I've ever had. Thank you for being the kind of parents that cheerlead and inspire.

Thank you also to my husband, who was my very first reader— at least of the first page, which I wrote in Spain, the country that inspired me to write about shadow magic. For all the adventures we go on, for all the love and support you give, I know this book would not have been possible without you. That and the crazy pregnancy hormones, which I also have you to thank for.

Without a Shadow was an abstract idea back in 2016 that I tried to develop for my master's degree, then dropped and didn't come back to until 2020, when I merged it with another story idea. Many, many drafts later it started to take shape but couldn't have become the story it is today without my incredible, insightful, truth-telling editor, Elana Gibson. Thank you, Elana, for pushing me on the world-building, for all your cool ideas for the characters and for pointing out what wasn't working while somehow making me genuinely excited to do the necessary changes. I love the transformation the novel made in your hands. Thank you also to Abby Conlon for your comments in the first read through—everything you pointed out was spot on and your enthusiasm was hugely appreciated.

Without a shadow of a doubt, this book would not have been possible without my amazing publisher: CamCat! Thank you in particular to Sue Arroyo for making that call and the whole team for getting behind my story. The draft I sent was certainly not the finished product, so I thank my stars that you could all see its potential.

Of course a book has to have beta readers, and I was incredibly lucky with the ones I had. Thank you to Oisin Herron—the writing journey is always better with a friend, and I look forward to more drafting, scraping, and swapping in the future. To E. M. Leander (author of *Wren and the Tarnished Tiger*): it was such a joy to read your work; thank you for all your comments. Thank you also to Suzan Phoenix (writer of sci-fi/fantasy); your perspective was very helpful, and I'm truly amazed by your creativity and the love and fun you put into your characters. To Nori Shoreline (author of *The Steam Witch*): thank you for beta reading the messiest of drafts and encouraging me despite the chaos on the page! My thanks as well to Lizzy McIlwaine from White Willow Editing: your comments were almost too accurate and really helped me move on to the next stage. Honestly, all of your stories were so cool and motivating to read. Thank you so much for being kind to this story in those early stages.

To my friends and family, who cheered me on with the edits, gave me feedback when I needed it, and in general have been so supportive: thank you to Anne, Christina, Csenge, Ellie, Graham, Jayne, Jessie, Laura, Natalie, Pippa, Rachael, and Simreen. I always feel like I get honest advice from you guys, and so much love.

Last—but not least!—my thanks to you, the reader. Thank you for delving into this world. Every book has a bit of magic in the pages, but it's the reader who can wield it into something far beyond the author's imagination. I hope *Without a Shadow* inspires you to create your own kind of magic, in whatever form it takes.

If you enjoyed
H. J. Reynolds' *Without a Shadow,*
please consider leaving a review
to help our authors.

And check out another great read
from CamCat,
Andrea Lynn's *Dust Spells.*

CHAPTER

1

STELLA WOULD HAVE THOUGHT THE sky was a harbinger of the apocalypse if her world hadn't already ended. The early-morning light was sickly yellow and filthy as always. The clear blue skies and lush green fields of five years ago seemed a dream. It was hard to imagine her home had ever been anything but diseased and covered in dust, though she knew it had. She knew a lot of things she didn't want to know, like how the entire world could be upended overnight, forever changing not only her life but also the lives of millions—and none of them had the power to change it back again, not ever.

She pulled her family's Chevrolet pickup into Jane's driveway and put it in park. When she cut the ignition, the engine sighed as if as tired as she was.

Don't you die on me now, she thought. *You're the last luxury we have.*

A harsh, discordant clanging met her ears when she stepped outside. Jane's neighbor, a widow named Mrs. Woodrow, had an ungodly number of wind chimes on her already cluttered porch. Stella cursed her silently as she hurried up Jane's drive. Why have even *one* wind chime in a place where the grimy, choking wind never let up? Where dust storms called black blizzards rose up and blotted out the sky, raining debris on cars and buildings, tearing through the cracks in the most well sealed homes, and mutilating the Great Plains as thoroughly as they had mutilated Stella's life forever?

Stella opened Jane's back door and let herself in. She closed it behind her, muting the chimes, but then heard the equally irritating sound of a baby's cry.

"Morning, Stella," Jane called, rushing into the kitchen with Jasper in her arms. She sat down at the table and opened her blouse, baring her right breast. "Sorry. I meant to feed him before you got here, but he wasn't hungry."

"Not a problem," Stella replied, grateful no writhing parasite depended on her for its sustenance. She had too many people dependent on her as it was. "Is everything ready?"

"Yes," Jane said as Jasper found her nipple and quieted. "I filled the jars last night."

Grateful that part was already done, Stella turned and crept down the rickety stairs to Jane's basement. When she passed the large copper still, she fought the urge to blow it a kiss.

When Jane's parents died, they left her two blessings: a house with a paid-off mortgage and her father's old moonshine still. President Roosevelt had repealed prohibition the previous year, but that didn't matter in Kansas, which had been dry since the last century, and Stella—who almost never prayed—prayed it would stay that way. With liquor outlawed, she and Jane could make fifty cents a pint.

The idea had been Stella's. Though Jane was four years older, the two of them had been friends since childhood. Jane married right out of high school, but her dirtbag husband abandoned her and Jasper after losing his job last winter. Jane made ends meet by taking in laundry, and when Stella remembered Jane's father's old still, she suggested they go into business. Jane brewed the moonshine, and Stella delivered it, hidden among the freshly washed sheets and towels.

Her heart thumped as she crouched down and picked up the crate. Sixteen beautiful jars. She held the equivalent of eight dollars in her hands. After three months, she and Jane had twelve consistent clients. And the demand was growing. Their only competition was the local drug store, where the owner sold malt whiskey smuggled in from Colorado, but most people couldn't afford it. Jane's moonshine wasn't cheap, but it wasn't so expensive it would break the average person's budget. If they had a bigger still, or more people to help, Stella knew they could make their little sideline a real business.

But they didn't.

And Stella knew enough to be grateful for what she did have. She started up the stairs, holding the crate that would bring her the only thing in the world that was hers alone. The thing that, once a week, brought her closer to her dreams.

Jane had finished feeding Jasper by the time Stella was done loading the crate and laundry into her truck. When she walked back inside, Jane was burping him over her shoulder.

"Do you ever want to murder Mrs. Woodrow?" Stella asked, closing the door behind her.

Jane laughed. "I hardly notice those wind chimes anymore."

"How? They're maddening."

"She thinks they ward off evil spirits."

"They're about to ward off my sanity."

Jane laughed again, and Stella wiped her brow.

"How are you on ingredients?"

"I have plenty of corn and yeast, but I'm running low on sugar."

"I'll pick some up."

She smoothed her hair and checked to make sure the patches she'd sewn beneath the worn spots on her dress were well concealed. "How do I look?"

Jane smiled, her dimples showing. "Like a sweet eighteen-year-old girl."

"Wash your mouth out with soap. There is nothing sweet about me."

The last thing Stella wanted to be was sweet. Greta Garbo and Jean Harlow weren't sweet. They were vixens wrapped in diamonds and furs who consumed men like champagne. Jane was a sweet girl.

Sweet girls ended up alone with a baby.

"But sweet girls aren't bootleggers," Jane countered. "They'll never suspect."

"True," Stella agreed. "I'll be back with some sweet, sweet dough."

THE SUN HAD barely risen, but the inside of the truck already felt like an oven by the time Stella reached her first stop. She dabbed at her forehead with a handkerchief and checked her lipstick in the rear view. Just because she lived in a dusty prairie town didn't mean she had to look like it.

The money she would earn today could buy powder, blush, mascara, and maybe even a new dress, but it was going straight into her Folger's can in the attic, so lipstick alone had to do. The crimson stain was perfect, so she stepped out of the truck.

Her first client was a man named Lewis Johnston, who lived with his mother and preferred to take his deliveries at work. Stella always made his stop first, because he worked at the train station, and the train-hopping bums who loitered around the place were mostly asleep in the morning. They camped in the hobo "jungle" in the nearby woods, and some of them liked to whistle and yell at the women who walked by.

That morning, the coast seemed clear as Stella clipped up the drive to the station, holding Lewis's shirts, with the mason jar between the folds. But then she heard shouts, and two men tumbled out from between the trees. The first one fell onto his back, and the second leaped on top of him and punched him square in the face. Stella shrieked and jumped back.

With a savage groan, the first man shoved the other man off and scrambled to his feet. Then, he gripped the man's shoulder and swung his fist deep into his stomach. The man doubled over, and the first seized his head and drove it down into his knee. Blood burst from his nose and splattered the pavement as well as the man's pants. He crumpled to the ground, and the other man spat on him.

"You bastards always make the same mistake," he sneered. "You go for the face."

"What's going on here?"

Both men looked in Stella's direction. She blinked and spun around. A police officer was jogging up the drive. She heard a scuffle and turned back around to see both men bolting toward the trees, the first moving like lightning and the second stumbling and clutching his stomach.

"That's right, get out of here," the cop yelled, and Stella turned back to face him. He nodded and tipped his hat. "You okay, miss?"

Stella stared at him, suddenly very aware of the mason jar in her arms. "Oh, yes. They didn't hurt me. They were fighting with each other."

"Dirty bums," the cop grumbled. "Why can't they kill each other out in that jungle, away from decent folks?"

Stella nodded and started back toward the station.

"What's a young lady like you doing here so early anyway?"

She stopped. After closing her eyes and taking a deep breath, she turned back around.

"I'm delivering laundry. To a man who works at the station."

The cop stepped closer, glancing down at the shirts. "He doesn't want it delivered to his house?"

He looked back up, but before he met her gaze, his eyes lingered a few other places. Her crimson lips, her dark curls, the swell of her breasts beneath her dress.

Men.

"I guess not," Stella said with a laugh. She stepped closer, glad she'd taken the time to dab on a bit of her dwindling reserve of perfume. "You men can be so silly sometimes. I never know what you're thinking."

He smiled sheepishly and blushed. "I suppose we can be. Well, go ahead. I'll make sure no more of these hobos get in your way."

"Thank you so much," Stella said, flashing a smile. Then she turned and walked up the drive, thinking Jean Harlow couldn't have done any better.

OVER THE NEXT hour, Stella made the rest of her deliveries. Not all were for moonshine; some were just laundry. When she finished, however, she cursed herself. She needed to get more sugar for Jane, but the general store was all the way back by the train station. She should have gotten it after her first delivery. Now she would have to go all the way back and risk arriving home late, running behind on her chores, and disappointing her Aunt Elsa.

She sped to the store, went in, and used two of the of the eight dollars she'd made to buy twenty pounds of sugar. Then, she hoisted the two ten-pound sacks over each of her shoulders and trudged out into the heat.

"That's a mighty amount of sugar."

She turned around and stifled a gasp. The man who'd beaten up and spat on the other man at the train station was leaning against the wall. He was more of a boy than a man, she now saw, just a year or two older than she was. His lower lip had been split by the blow he'd taken to the face, and he was picking small chunks from a stale loaf of bread, eating carefully. There was a bakery next door, and Stella guessed the loaf had been thrown out with last night's trash. Her stomach turned, and she flopped the sacks onto the bed of her truck.

"What's it to you?"

"Just wondering if you might have the same amount of yeast and corn somewhere."

She froze, and then spun back to face him. He read the guilty look on her face and grinned.

"That's what I thought."

She stared at him. Besides the split lip, he had a yellowing bruise beneath one eye and a scar through his other eyebrow. His skin and clothes were filthy, and his hair was a rumpled mess beneath his flat cap. Her gaze slid down to the knee of his pants, stained with the other man's blood. He followed her gaze, popped a piece of bread in his mouth, and looked back up.

"Don't worry," he said as he chewed. "I'd never hit a woman. You could come at me with a knife, and I'd just let you stab me, sugar."

She flushed, determined not to let him know she'd been afraid. "How thoughtful. If you'll excuse me."

"Hold on." He stood up from the wall and stepped into the sunlight. "I'm interested in becoming a customer."

He had a backwoods Southern accent. Maybe Texas or Oklahoma. Some desolate, nothing place even dustier than Kansas.

"I don't know what you're talking about."

"Come on, now. No girl in worn-out out heels is gonna spend that much money on sugar unless she expects some kind of return. And I watched you work that lawman this morning. Saw the fear on your face when he looked at those shirts. Saw the way you turned on the charm to fool him. Pretty impressive."

Stella's lips parted. Even the man who'd sold her the sugar hadn't questioned why she'd bought it. He was just happy to make the sale. This boy talked like a hick, but he was smart. She studied his face. It was pleasant. Beneath the dirt and scars anyway.

But then she remembered his rude remark about her shoes.

"You couldn't afford it."

She purposefully raked her eyes over his filthy clothes as she said it. But his grin only curled, and he stepped closer.

"Ain't you heard, sugar? We got a depression on. People trade and barter for things all the time."

"Stop calling me that. And you have nothing I want."

He placed another chunk of bread in his mouth and looked her over. "We've only just met." He lifted his gaze. "You don't know what I got to offer."

She flushed again. "You're disgusting."

"Disgusting?" He cocked his head to the side. "My, what dirty thoughts you've got in that pretty head of yours."

Feeling a sudden kinship with the man who'd punched him in the face, she spat, "Don't flatter yourself," and turned away, tossing her curls.

"I see those patches in your skirt, sugar," he called. "Don't pretend you're better than me."

"At least I've taken a bath this century."

She didn't look back when she said it, but she caught sight of his face when she opened the door to the truck. His smile was gone. Guilt rose in her throat, but she swallowed it, got in her truck, and drove away.

She sped toward Jane's house, now certain she would be facing Aunt Elsa's wrath when she arrived home. There were six dollars in her pocket, three of which were hers, but she found herself too shaken to enjoy their comforting presence.

Because the boy had been right. Her family was barely hanging on by a thread, and though they weren't sleeping in hobo jungles and fishing stale bread out of the garbage, that could change at any moment.

Nothing was certain. No one was safe.

CHAPTER

2

TELLA PARKED OUTSIDE HER FAMILY'S three-story, Victorian house, its formerly cheerful robin's egg blue exterior now gray and peeling. She'd taken its luxury for granted until four years ago, because—while she still lived there—it wasn't her house anymore.

For the first few months following the stock market crash, Stella's family remained one of the most comfortable in Dodge City. But as fewer and fewer people could afford cars, her father's dealership suffered, especially when the dust storms arrived to terrorize the farmland. It was 1930 when Stella's world imploded, when the dealership went bankrupt, her mother died, her father left to search for work in Wichita, her Aunt Elsa turned their home into a boarding house to make ends meet, and Stella and her sisters moved into the attic to help her run it. The creaking of the old walls against the wind was the only sound Stella heard when she crept inside, which told her the boarders had already left for work.

Dammit.

She trudged to the kitchen. When she stepped inside, her older sister, Lavinia, spoke without looking up from the dishes.

"Aunt Elsa's stripping the beds. And yes, she's mad."

Stella groaned, pulled an apron from one of the pegs near the door, and joined her at the sink.

"I would have made it back in time, but I was accosted by a vagrant."

Lavinia's head shot up, her coffee-brown eyes bulging. "What?"

"Well, not exactly accosted," Stella clarified. "He tried to get me to sell him some moonshine. I did see him beat up another bum by the station earlier, though."

Lavinia let out a breath and returned to the dishes. "You shouldn't go down there alone. It isn't safe."

"Don't worry. There was a cop who put a stop to it before anyone got killed."

Lavinia's head shot up again, which, this time, had been Stella's intention.

"It was fine," she assured her, laughing as she took the dripping bowl from her hands and dried it off with a towel. "He didn't suspect a thing."

"You take too many risks," Lavinia scolded her, picking up the next bowl.

And you don't take enough, Stella thought as she watched her scrape the oatmeal out from inside. Lavinia's hair was as curly as Stella's, but instead of a black so black it was almost blue, her hair was a vibrant, apple red. She wore it the same way as Stella, but for a different reason. Stella cut her curls in a chin-length bob because that's how Myrna Loy wore her hair in Penthouse, but Lavinia did it so she could hide her face more easily.

Over the last three years, Stella had grown used to the jagged scars that covered the left side of Lavinia's face, a patchwork of puckered, white gashes that clawed their way from beneath her left eye to the hinge of her jaw, as if she were a porcelain doll whose left side had been smashed and pasted back together by a hasty, trembling hand.

Lavinia had always been the most reserved of the Fischer girls, but since receiving the scars she'd withdrawn even more, rarely leaving the house or looking strangers in the eye.

Stella wasn't sure how she would have reacted if it had happened to her, which it could have just as easily. Perhaps, she would have withdrawn as well, but she still wished her sister wouldn't act as if her life was over at twenty-two, resigned to working at the Fischer boarding house the rest of her life, the husband and children she desperately longed for forever out of reach. To Stella, Lavinia was still beautiful, as well as good, loyal, and hardworking. She was nearly as bright as their younger sister, Mattie, and as nurturing and resilient as their mother had been. Not what Stella sometimes suspected she thought she was.

Which was worthless.

"Jane says, 'hello,'" Stella said as Lavinia handed her the next bowl. Jane hadn't, but she would have if they'd had more time to talk. She and Lavinia were the same age and had been good friends in school. "You should visit her sometime."

Lavinia looked away. "I know. It's just hard to find the time. Things being the way they are . . ." She paused, glanced up from the sink, and lowered her voice. "And I think things are even worse than Aunt Elsa is letting on. I saw the water bill in her room this morning. It's due tomorrow, and I don't think we have enough. Daddy hasn't sent money in over a month. And I know Aunt Elsa paid for Mrs. Kelly's last doctor visit."

Stella gaped at her. Mrs. Kelly, one of their boarders, was an older woman with lung trouble exacerbated by the dust. Dust pneumonia, they called it. Mrs. Kelly slept in a gas mask at night, and her room, which used to be Stella's, always smelled of Vick's VapoRub. Stella pitied the woman, but still wished Aunt Elsa would control her damn bleeding heart.

"You don't think they'll turn off our water?" Stella whispered. "The boarders—they'd leave, and we'd—"

"Stella Marie Fischer."

Stella looked up to see Aunt Elsa hurrying in with a basket of sheets. She plopped it on the floor and slammed her hands on her hips.

"Aunt Elsa, I'm sorry—"

"When I said you could help Jane with her laundry business, you promised it wouldn't interfere with your duties here. Mattie had to help Lavinia and I make breakfast this morning, and now she's behind on weeding the garden and I'm behind on the laundry."

"I know. I'm sorry."

"I don't understand why Jane needs the laundry delivered anyway," Aunt Elsa went on. "Why can't her clients come to her place and pick it up themselves?"

Lavinia met Stella's gaze and then turned to the sink to hide her face. At least she was aware of how bad she was at concealing things.

"She can charge more money if she delivers," Stella replied calmly. "But of course, she can't do it herself. Not with Jasper."

As she'd expected, mentioning the baby deflated Aunt Elsa's anger. Her face lit up and she pressed her hand to her heart. She looked more like her brother, Stella's father, when she smiled, her emerald green eyes crinkling at the corners.

"How is Jasper? He must be getting so big."

"He's got more hair," Stella said with a smile. "Silvery blonde, like Jane's. Not dirty blonde like that low-life Jacob Ryan's."

The three of them instantly spat at the mention of Jane's husband, a habit they'd picked up from Stella's late grandmother, Aunt Elsa's mother.

"Well, don't be late again," Aunt Elsa said, retrieving the basket of sheets. "Lavinia can finish the dishes. You do the dusting, then beat out the front rug. Oh, and feed the chickens. I don't think Mattie has done that yet."

Stella dried her hands on her apron and hung it back up on the wall. Then, she walked out, climbed the stairs to the third floor, wrenched down the attic ladder, and climbed it as well.

The stuffy, cramped space was hers and her sisters' bedroom now. They shared a single mattress in the middle, but each of them had a section along the wall that was their own. In one corner, Mattie stored her books, their father's Kodak camera, and a framed picture of their late grandmother. Lavinia's romance novels, old porcelain doll, and empty jewelry box sat nearby. Stella walked to her corner, which contained her lipstick, magazine cut-outs of her favorite movie stars, and her precious Folger's can. She took the three dollars from her pocket and slid them reverently inside, gazing up at Greta Garbo like she was the Virgin Mary.

One day, soon, she would have enough money to get her to Hollywood and out of this dusty town. Her sisters knew of her plan, as well as the sideline she'd created to make it happen, but not her father or Aunt Elsa. It would break their hearts, she knew, but she had no choice. Lavinia had no desire to leave, and Mattie was smart enough to get a scholarship to Kansas University or Kansas State, which both accepted women, but there was nothing for Stella in Kansas.

All she had was her looks, and they would get her nothing in Dodge but marriage, children, and an endless cycle of hard work and misery. Here, she would always remain as she was—a poor, powerless girl who could be blown away and forgotten. But in a big city, or up on the silver screen, she could be someone. Someone high above the chaotic struggle of poverty. Someone respected, admired, and in control of her destiny. Money could make her matter, could make people see her as someone worth something, and every dollar she made brought her closer to that dream.

She slid off her dress and put on a white, cotton shirt and overalls, trading her heels for a pair of old, leather boots. Running a boarding house was just like running a hotel. Everything had to be cleaned while the tenants were out, and the constant filth in the air made dusting a daily activity. Stella ran wet rags over the banisters, stairs, and floors. Then, she made her way through the boarders' rooms, dusting their shelves. First, her parents' former room, where Aunt Elsa now slept, then Lavinia's, where an old nurse and a young hairdresser now lived, Stella's, where Mrs. Kelly and a railroad telegrapher resided, and Mattie's, which now housed a hardware store clerk and a musician.

Once Stella finished dusting, she grabbed the bucket of chicken feed and trudged to the back yard. After feeding the squawking creatures, she started back inside the house, but then she caught sight of Mattie, kneeling in the vegetable garden. She was picking tomatoes, but as she plucked them, she bent down over the vines and bowed her head, murmuring something.

"Are you kidding me?" Stella asked, approaching her younger sister. "Please, tell me you didn't take that bunk seriously."

Mattie barely spared her a glance. "You know what puri daj would say if she heard you call it bunk."

"How does someone who reads the books you read and gets the grades you get still believe in her grandmother's fairy tales?"

"Stories aren't just stories," Mattie replied. "They contain wisdom gleaned by our ancestors over the ages. That's why they endure." She looked up at Stella, smirking and tossing her braid back over her shoulder. "If you read a book every now and then, you'd know that."

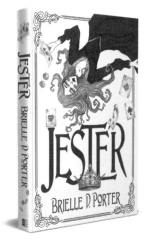
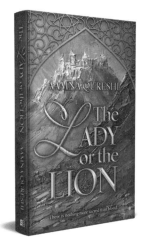
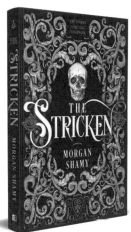

CamCat
Books

VISIT US ONLINE FOR MORE BOOKS TO LIVE IN:
CAMCATBOOKS.COM

SIGN UP FOR CAMCAT'S FICTION NEWSLETTER FOR
COVER REVEALS, EBOOK DEALS, AND MORE EXCLUSIVE CONTENT.

CamCatBooks   @CamCatBooks   @CamCat_Books   @CamCatBooks